Suzanne Rylee Ridolfi

Molly, Mistletoe & Mr. Right

Suzanne Rylee Ridolfi

Molly, Mistletoe & Mr. Right

Nantucket Press

Cover art: Josefina Fernandez

Printed in the United States

Published by Nantucket Press
212 Regency Road
Edgewater Park, N.J. 08010.

For information regarding permission, write to: Rights and Permissions Department,
Nantucket Press Publishing,
212 Regency Road
Edgewater Park, N.J. 08010 USA.
Or contact@nantucketpress.com

Library of Congress Cataloging-in-Publication Data

Ridolfi, Suzanne Rylee
Molly, Mistletoe & Mr. Right

Paperback: ISBN 978-0-692-57466-9
Ebook

1. Novel: Romance 2. Christmas
I. Ridolfi, Suzanne Rylee II. Title.

20 19 18 17 2016
5 4 3 2 1

Printed on acid-free paper. ∞

This book is dedicated to my amazing family. First my three beautiful children: Ashley, for her valuable insight and continued help every step of the way, Nicholas, who taught me to go for my dream and Ryan, who shares my love of writing and encouraged me to never give up.

To my mother Lee and my sister Karen, for their unwavering support and faith in me.

And lastly to my wonderful husband, Joe. Without his belief in me and an incredible amount of patience, this would not be possible.

Also, a special thanks to Josefina Fernandez, my illustrator, whose talented vision is responsible for creating the cover.

And lastly, a huge debt of gratitude to my editor, Judy Roth. Thank you for teaching me so much about the writing process.

Dear Reader,

The holidays are simply my favorite time of the year. Truth be told my family is convinced I'm part elf. Our family celebrates Christmas with a number of traditions. One of my favorites takes place every Christmas Eve. My entire family, aunts, uncles, cousins, and grandparents attend Christmas Eve mass together. Then we return to my house for a big Christmas Eve dinner. When the extended family leaves for the night, my husband and I, along with our three children, Ashley, Nicholas and Ryan unwrap our new Christmas PJs and read the Twas the Night Before Christmas by the fireplace. (And yes all family members are required to partake even though my children are all grown up.) It is one of the few times where the world seems to slow down, even if only for one night, and the peace and joy of the season is upon us.

Wishing you a very Merry Christmas

With love,
Suzanne Rylee Ridolfi

Knowing what you want out of life is the key to achieving it; unless, of course, what you think you want is not actually what you want at all.
Sometimes you find the things you desire most are right under your own mistletoe.

Prologue

Molly McKenna had never been referred to as the beautiful sister. Rather, the youngest McKenna had accepted her title as the smart one, but for this one night everything would be different.

Reaching over to the desk, she slid on her red cat eye glasses. "One last look," she said as she observed her reflection in the full length window. A slight smile crept across her face. She barely recognized the woman staring back at her. Her once milky white skin now glowed in Jamaican Summer Nights spray tan. Her fiery red cork screw hair lay smooth like strands of silk on her bare shoulders. And the dress in emerald green, sparkled in sequins from the halter on her delicate neckline down to her shoes. Oh, and those shoes. She marveled at the way they sparkled with each beam of light. Diamond encrusted stilettos with the thinnest of ankle straps. She was certain they cost more than her whole wardrobe. Steadying herself in those skyscrapers would prove to be a real challenge, but not nearly as challenging as foregoing her glasses.

Startled by a thunderous boom that shook the walls, sending paperweights, staplers and mugs vibrating in tandem across the desks, she lost her balance and nearly fell flat on her face. The resurfacing of the parking lot work began long after hours, when the halls of the prestigious advertising firm had emptied. The blasting of concrete, the shaking of walls, floors and desks may unnerve some, but not Molly McKenna. The unsettling noise suited her mood just fine. She, herself, was feeling a bit unsettled. It proved a welcome distraction from the high-pitched voices in her head telling her to take those diamond encrusted Louboutin's off and abort this crazy scheme she had somehow gotten herself into. How could being on the arm of the man she had shared a passionate love story with for the last three years possibly be a mistake?

The fact that, until now, that love story happened solely in her head or that the only thing she had shared with him was a mere two seconds of eye contact most days, seemed somehow insignificant. How did she agree to deceive the man she loved? How could she think she could pull off a charade as preposterous as this? After all, Sebastian Tate was bound to recognize her as his faithful assistant of three years.

This undoubtedly was an error in judgment, a temporary lapse when the brain didn't connect with the heart.

Trying to reconnect her brain, she quickly decided that abandoning the mission was her only option. She grabbed her purse off the desk and took two hurried steps toward the door before it opened. There he was, his piercing blue eyes and distinct dimples lighting up his face like fireworks. Quickly throwing the glasses behind the desk, she leaned against it to steady the quaking of her twig legs as they teetered on top of her heels.

"I apologize for the late notice. My assistants tell me none of my friends were available for a last minute date to the Manning's Gala. I'm just glad they were able to hire an escort in the eleventh hour," he said, not looking up from the pile of papers. Then he glanced over and stopped dead in his tracks. His eyes traveled from her head to the tips of her Loubis. A slow smile crept across his face. "You're my date?"

"Mayday, mayday, abort mission," resounded in her head. He knows it's me. How silly—of course he would, just because I'm under a pound of makeup and my hair is down from its usual ballerina bun, without glasses and the fact that I look completely different than my work self isn't going to fool him. He loves me too. No, she stopped the dialogue rolling in her head, maybe not love, but undeniably he knows it's me, Molly McKenna, faithful assistant. It's true she thought after three years he still didn't really know her name, but he knew her soul, she had convinced herself. In fact, he came amazingly close to knowing her name on a few occasions.

"Yes, that's me," she said quietly.

"You're beautiful," he said, walking closer. "I mean I didn't expect the agency to send over such an exquisite woman. This evening just got a whole lot better. If you'll excuse me, I'll call my driver to pull the car around." He disappeared to the hall and her pencil legs swayed beneath her, threatening to give way.

"Told you it'd work," said Hunter, her friend and coworker of three years who was waiting just on the other side of the door.

"I can't do it," Molly said, attempting to walk in heels with the grace of an elephant.

"Yes you can. Just put one foot in front of the other, and soon you will be walking in heels like every other woman in New York City," said Hunter.

"Not that part, maybe a little bit that part, but I'll never pull off a sophisticated beauty hired to date the most eligible man in the city."

"Sure you will Red, you are doing awesome and you have no choice. If we don't find a woman to be on his arm we're both fired. Remember old man Price's promise?"

"I'm no good at dating, and I think it is fairly evident that lying and deceit are better left for those who, I don't know, have experience in that sort of thing."

"Red, you have been dreaming of this moment since the day you stumbled into your interview three years ago. This is your dream come true!"

"True, he is so Sebastiany," she said, her eyes closing dreamily.

"Ok, that's not a word, now let's focus. Say as little as possible. Stay away from the bitch, and most importantly—leave by midnight. We need to get those shoes back to the studio before the actors get in. Kyle and I will be nearby in the car if you need to escape."

Scratching the row of hives emerging around her neckline, Molly repeated, "Midnight," and stared down at the crystal encrusted stilettos.

Chapter One
Three Years Earlier

Molly felt her blood pressure mounting with each flashing light as she watched for the elevator to make its descent to the first floor. Waiting for the mirrored elevator doors to open, she caught a glimpse of her reflection. She realized it would probably be a good idea to remove her knee length hooded parka which her mother referred to as an "Alaskan ice fisherman's coat."

She remembered her mother's rant about how brutal New York winters could be. After removing her parka she again checked the reflection in the mirror. She couldn't help but wonder if she was what they were looking for. Questioning her choice of black polyester stretch dress pants with matching blazer from JC Penney, now seemed like the wrong decision. Her crisp white button down and sensible ballet flats somehow seemed so perfect in the dressing room mirror despite the sleazy seventeen year old salesgirl who asked if she was attending a funeral. Little did she know, Molly's bathing suits had more fabric than the spandex napkin the salesgirl was wearing as a skirt.

"It's Beginning to Look a Lot Like Christmas" rang out from her purse. Fumbling, Molly answered, "Hello."

"Hey little Sweet Potato, you ready to go get that big New York job?" asked Maxie, the middle of three McKenna sisters.

"Maxie, I'm not sure what I'm doing here."

"Molly, you are brilliant. You have earned this. Just relax."

"I know, but New York? I'm sort of a small town girl, or at least I was until the uptown move."

"Molly, New York is where the best marketing firms are located. I know your real dream is Holiday Village but learn from the best and then put it to work for you."

"Thanks Maxie, for talking me off the ledge. I love you."

"Love you Sweet Potato. Meggie and I want a call as soon as you know anything."

Molly silenced her phone and began her ritual. "This is it. Your big chance, the thing you have worked painstakingly for, for the last six years. You can do it. Breathe," she whispered to herself as a bead of sweat bubbled under her collar.

The bell rang signaling the arrival of her elevator. Molly climbed in hesitantly. She repeated her self-imposed pep talk at a quickened tone as she climbed the towers of Waters and Price Marketing firm. Armed with a fresh Master's Degree and a resumé highlighting her many accomplishments, this was her shot to break into the extremely competitive world of advertising.

Floor ten blinked once followed by a sluggish stop. The doors opened and a curvy brunette in five inch heels and a form fitting sweater dress stepped in. Chomping hard on her gum, she hiked her dress a few inches further up her thighs. Examining her image in the elevator mirror, she bent over from the waist and flung a mop of over-teased hair into Molly's face then applied a swipe of frosted lipstick.

Who even wears frosted lipstick, snow angels? thought Molly.

Turning to Molly, Frosty gave her the once over, asking, "Were you looking for accounting? You missed it—floor seven," she said, swooshing her berry flavored gum forward with her frosted lips before blowing a bubble.

Again, with a quick check in the mirror, Molly pushed her

heavy rimmed glasses back on her nose and made absolutely sure every strand of her auburn hair was neatly contained in its ballerina bun.

"No, actually I'm going to Waters and Price," said Molly, wondering what she meant by that.

"Really?" said the girl, smacking her gum as the elevator doors opened onto the twelfth floor.

She made it. She survived the elevator ride without pushing the button for the first floor and high tailing it out the massive front doors. Nothing could stop her now. Not even frosted lip girl's negative tone.

Her idol, Evan Waters, would be just on the other side of those doors, waiting to welcome her into the firm. Evan was known in the industry as the leading expert in all things advertising. She had studied him in school, followed him in seminars and read everything she could possibly get her hands on about his profile. Called "The Shark" for the sometimes underhanded tactics he used to land a campaign, he'd created some of the biggest campaign slogans of all time. Mr. Waters was her mentor, her guru, and hopefully, soon, her new boss.

In her head she practiced those all too important first two minutes. "Hello, Mr. Waters. I'm Molly McKenna, graduate of Wharton School of Business, cum laude."

Too much. "Mr. Waters, I'm Molly McKenna, it's an honor to meet you." Too kiss uppy.

"Hello, I'm Molly McKenna, here to interview for the ad exec position."

Her mind raced and her heart pounded as she stepped off onto the black marble home of Waters and Price. The walls, painted a stark white, were adorned with framed images of past slogans. White leather sofas with black and white patterned chairs greeted clients. A single five-tier chandelier hung over the waiting area. No Christmas decorations, not even a single string of lights, no

Christmas trees, no garland, no holly, not even a glimmer of mistletoe. Molly found this extremely unsettling

Molly loved Christmas. Her birthday fell on Christmas Eve. She had always considered this her lucky month. She couldn't imagine a better time to interview at Waters and Price.

The staff, who appeared better suited for a modeling agency, stopped and took a full length check of Molly. Unfazed, they quickly returned to business. A slim brunette with sky-high cheekbones greeted her.

"May I help you?"

"Mr. Waters' office please," Molly managed to choke out.

"Down the hall, make a left, first office on the right."

"Thanks."

Perfect. Everything seemed to be just as she had imagined. Now that they knew she wasn't delivering flowers or takeout they seemed mildly interested in her. Holding her head up high, she tried not to notice the staff giving her an uncomfortable onceover, followed by muffled whispers.

None of that would bring her down. Mr. Waters was the only one she needed to impress, and with a resumé like hers, it was a slam dunk.

Turning the corner, she took a deep breath before heading down the next corridor.

"First door on the right," she repeated to herself. Before she could take another step that very door opened. Out popped a deranged looking Mr. Waters—his white wavy hair ruffled, his cheeks the color of a blood orange and his eyes wild. In his hands was a large potted plant. He began the approximate ten foot track toward her. A hive the size of a golf ball emerged on her lily white neck, followed by a small colony not far behind. This was not exactly how she envisioned their introduction, but she went for it.

"Mr. Waters, my name is Molly McKenna." It came out sort of like a whisper.

Stopping just short of her, he said, "You! I should've known. You've been after my job for years. You slimy bastard," he growled, his eyes even more demonic than just seconds ago.

With the emerging hives, her neck was nearly as red as his face.

"No, I, actually, I..." Nothing was coming out despite her attempt to connect her brain with her mouth. She clawed mercilessly at the hives.

Mr. Waters took the large potted plant and slammed it hard to the marble tiled ground. A plume of dirt engulfed her. Wiping the remnants of dust from her now fogged glasses, she noticed he was looking past her. She hadn't realized someone had come up behind her, and in fact, was the person to whom the rage had been directed. Turning, she saw him. Sebastian Tate, in the flesh. Not actually in the flesh, that would be more than she could handle, but in an Armani suit. His dark wavy hair and crystal blue eyes twinkled. Mr. Tate had visited as a guest speaker her last semester at Wharton. Intelligent, gorgeous and sexy, he left a lasting impression on her, as well as every other girl and a few guys in that room.

A half-smirk crawled across Tate's face, revealing one incredible dimple, and then, the voice. In his impeccably sexy Australian accent he said, "Sorry old man, but you brought this on yourself. Greed is an ugly thing, mate."

With that, Mr. Waters lunged at Sebastian, Molly tangled smack in the middle before two guards grabbed and restrained Mr. Waters.

"You are coming with us," said one of the guards.

Sebastian took a look at Molly, her dust covered face with glasses on sideways. Her now less-than-perfect suit was rumpled, resembling someone who just survived a twister. He noticed she was carrying a briefcase and reached out his hand.

"Hello, I'm Sebastian Tate. You must be here for the job. Price told me someone was coming over."

"Yes, I, my name is Molly. I, you…" she said babbling gibberish.

"Sorry you had to witness that. Our Mr. Waters had a little embezzling problem. My new office is right this way. Hunter will get you set up. You will need to stop down on the eleventh floor to fill out some paperwork," he said, barely making eye contact. She followed him down the corridor to his office. Outside sat two desks.

"Hunter, my good man, please set Kelly here up with a desk and show her around."

Hunter Bentley stood to greet her. His wavy brown hair, tousled like a surfer who just spent a day at the beach, fit with his relaxed vibe. Dressed in khakis and a blue button down, a tad wrinkled, with an orange tie, he gave her the once over. "Sure thing, Mr. T."

"Do you moonlight as a chimney sweep?" asked Hunter casually.

Dusting off the dirt on her shoulder, she pulled a tiny chrysanthemum leaf from her hair.

"No, Mr. Waters broke his planter and…"

"Yeah, lot of drama today, but welcome to Tate and Price, formally known as Waters and Price. Apparently, Mr. Waters will be facing some pretty big charges for embezzlement," said Hunter.

"I didn't know. But I got the job. I got the job. No interview, no resumé. It's a miracle. I need to call my mother and father and sisters and my boyfriend, of course." She fished out her phone and pecked in Maxie's number.

"I got it. It's really happening. I'll call you tonight."

"I knew you would. Love you Sweet Potato."

"About that, before you start your victory speech you might want to slow down a bit. Not sure what job you think you got, but the one you did get is assistant to Mr. Tate, a.k.a. 'glorified secretary,' or in laymen's terms 'Sebastian's bitch,' 'slave' if you will."

A dreamy look washed over her face. She had just finished the second book in the "Fifty Shades" series and found it not her cup of tea, yet somehow the title "Sebastian's Slave" seemed wildly erotic at this moment.

"There it is—that look. The goo-goo eyes look that graces the face of every girl in his presence, but you don't have a chance in hell with him," said Hunter.

"You must have misread my face, I have no interest in him at all," she said as she clawed the hives on her neck. "I'm simply here to advance my career, and besides, I have a boyfriend."

"Really? Yes you did mention that. What's his name?"

Hmm, that was weird. His name escaped her for a moment. It must have been the craziness of the day. She loved him. He was perfect for her. Everyone thought so. A fabulous catch as her parents reminded her daily. After a brief pause she answered, "Thomas. Yes, that's it."

"You sure about that or do you need a minute to think about it?"

Frosted lip girl sauntered up just as Mr. Tate appeared from his office.

"Hi, Mr. Tate," she purred. "I heard you were interviewing a new hire, so I took the time to bring the human resource paperwork up for you."

"Wow, that was thoughtful of you. What's your name again?"

"Chrissie," she said, batting her spider-like lashes.

"Right, thanks again."

After he disappeared down the hall, Chrissie dropped the papers on Hunter's desk.

"Here," she said before slinking away.

"What's her story?" asked Molly.

"Check the book."

"The book?"

"Mr. Tate has a little black book. Although in this case it's more like a big black book. You'll become very familiar with it. Chrissie, let's see if we can find her," said Hunter, opening the drawer of the desk across from his. "Tate spent quite a bit of time with her when he was a consultant. I'm fairly sure she didn't slip by his radar."

Thumbing through the pages he stopped on Chrissie. "Let's see. She's filed under 'Airhead from HR.' It comes with helpful notes, like a check if she is worth calling or an x if she's a definite no go."

"You mean he takes notes on his girlfriends?"

"You could say that. He uses the book if he needs an impromptu date for a work function. He'll say call Anna or Jackie, good dates."

"You mean good arm candy?" asked Molly.

"That would be unfair to say since they are all good arm candy. Mr. Tate has dated every woman in New York except my mother, Big Ethel, you know the lady who sells fish fry on the corner, whose legs are worse than a Sherpa, and I'm guessing you?"

"That's all very disturbing."

"Not really. Some chicks are better dates. They don't get too drunk or start stripping. You know, the man has to set some standards."

"No, I mean the whole rating system."

"Yeah, well get used to it. And welcome to Tate and Price."

"One more question. Where are all the Christmas decorations?"

"Don't know, never been any in the two years I've been here."

"Sad, we'll have to change that."

"Now you better get that golden career kick-started," said Hunter.

"I better get those papers down to HR. I don't care what you say, this job will advance my career. It's a stepping stone. A year tops and I'll be in that ad exec position."

Chapter Two

Three years later, Thanksgiving weekend

"How much do you need for a weekend, woman? In addition to your three bags and Henry's bed, I packed protein bars, granola, chocolate, an eighties dance party CD, Henry's dog food and his toys," said Hunter, packing the last of Molly's things into her compact car.

"You're a lifesaver, Hunter. What would I do without you?

"Suffer, which is probably what you are going to do for the next seventy two hours." He smiled.

"Please don't remind me. Promise you will have hot cocoa and mini marshmallows with our first Christmas CD of the season waiting for me as I try and forget my awful trip."

"Your wish is my command."

"You spoil me, Bestie," she smiled, throwing her arms around him.

"I think 'Bestie' is reserved for your girlfriends."

"Nope, you're my Bestie, kisses," she said, waving as she crawled into her car. "Are you sure you can't come? You know how much Benadryl is required to make it through a family weekend with Silvia."

"Sorry Red, Kyle and I are preparing a feast, and I packed you two extra bottles of Benadryl for those pesky nerve hives. Mittens, I should have packed you mittens to keep the clawing down to a minimum."

"Again, I simply would be a mess without you. If you must abandon me to deal with her by myself, you better rest. I have big plans for the decorations at work this year."

"Of course you do."

In the years that had followed her joining the firm, Hunter had in fact become her best friend, confidant, eighties dance party partner and Monday night football buddy. He knew her strengths, weaknesses, fears, insecurities, allergies, and above all, how to calm her down when the hives erupted. He made her laugh and had become her family here in New York. A family she had grown more comfortable with than her own.

Hunter knew her hopes and dreams and allowed her to believe she could someday catch the man of her dreams, Sebastian Tate. Catching a man like Sebastian would be no easy task, and the fact that he still didn't remember her name after three years might have discouraged some, but not Molly. She knew the importance of patience. She would wait for Sebastian until he was ready or at least until he realized she was alive. She knew it wouldn't be long before he recognized her full potential and gave her that promotion, and then they would fall madly, hopelessly in love.

Driving in torrential downpours on the busiest travel day of the year seemed to be the highlight of the dreaded Thanksgiving holiday for Molly McKenna.

Endless scenarios of painstaking conversation with Silvia played in her head. "You're twenty five years old, which is practically thirty. You're sailing right through your baby-making years. Thirty, for God's sake, you might as well join a convent. Then you'll never give me grandchildren. Who am I kidding, what are the chances of you marrying and bearing children before forty? Are there no men in New York? Are you having confusing thoughts about your sexual orientation? We have people for that."

"Why do I put myself through this agony year after year?" The whole point of leaving Greenwich, Connecticut was to free herself of the constant judging, the need to keep up pretenses for the family name. Here she could finally prove to Silvia she was good enough, if there was such a thing. "For God's sake you would think I'm a leper the way she treats me," she said to Henry, her faithful dog of five years. Slobbering a long wet pile of drool on her lap, he brought her back to reality.

"Thank you Henry, for acknowledging I'm not a leper," she said as she patted her pleasantly plump Pug on the head. Henry, not exactly a looker, sported a rather severe under bite. His short legs caused his belly to almost skim the floor. Silvia hated Henry, just another perk of bringing a girl's best friend along. It would at least limit her time alone with Silvia.

"Yes, with any luck the traffic will detain us for several hours before we face the interrogation squad."

B101 had started playing its annual homage to Christmas with twenty four hours of holiday music. Singing along to "Santa Baby," she thought about Sebastian, his dreamy smile, those piercing eyes and that body, not to mention the Australian accent. "Hmmm," she sighed.

Yes, it was true. Her boss of three years hardly detected she shared the same oxygen as him with the exception of the two seconds of eye contact she received each morning. Pathetic, she reminded herself. The only relationship of substance she had since Thomas left her for Carey White nearly three years ago, was a two-second flirtation five days a week. Okay, maybe not exactly a flirtation, but acknowledgement, definitely acknowledgement. There was no chance of a broken heart when you steer the ship. Yes, she was in control of those two seconds. She could count on them. "When you say it out loud, it does sound sort of pathetic," she said to Henry, who gave her a long pitiful gaze, showing the whites of his eyes in agreement.

Perhaps that was exactly why she was secretly content with

having a lusty affair with Sebastian silently in her head. *Who needed men?*

Thomas Landon III made that perfectly clear that fateful Christmas Eve—Eve. He and Carey White were caught making out backstage when the curtain accidentally fell at the annual Ms. Winter pageant. Just like that, Molly lost her boyfriend, her dreams and her dignity, all in front of the entire town of Greenwich. Silvia's first concern was not for her humiliated daughter Molly, but rather that the unfortunate debacle would somehow overshadow the crowning of Megan, Molly oldest sister. She was about to become Ms. Winter for the second year running.

Molly's two older sisters took after their mother with long dark hair, curves that should come with danger signs, big boobs and bigger butts. They shared her olive complexion with eyes the color of a rich mocha latte. They could easily have hailed from the Kardashian clan. Silvia never missed an opportunity to remind Molly of her drawing the short straw in the gene pool. Molly inherited her father's Irish genes, with a thick head of cork screw curls in burnt orange, fair skin with a dusting of freckles squarely across the bridge of her nose. Her eyes of green would be the envy of even a leprechaun. Molly seemed more likely to be a member of the Claus family than a Kardashian.

The sound of a horn blaring as an SUV passed her with the driver flipping her the finger, interrupted her self-loathing.

"Why do I do this horrible drive each year?"

Henry responded with a snarl and blob of drool. The drive that should have taken approximately an hour now entered its fourth hour. Exhausted, she turned into the spiral-shaped driveway that led to the massive house on Winthrop Lane. She stopped the car and took a deep breath. The house, which was nothing short of a mansion, boasted four large columns in the front, flanking massive double doors that sat squarely under a five foot semi-circular window.

"How bad could it be? After all, they are my family, right? Just hold your head up high. Embrace your single lady status. Be proud you don't need a man. Yes, I can do this. It's no one's business but my own whether or not I choose to date, right Henry? You're the only man I need in my life, period. We got this," she said as she patted the dog's head and fixed her pink glasses.

She gathered Henry and her suitcase and headed toward the heavy doors. Inside she put down her suitcase and heard the echo of marble in the hollow foyer. Ah home, cold, impersonal, yet beautifully decorated. Yes, its message screamed, model home, staged for sale, not comfort. Come in, sit down—but not too comfortably—rather take your shoes off, God forbid anything gets on the white rugs. Sit down, but don't mess the pillows—again, they are staged perfectly. Have a drink, but for heaven's sake use a coaster. Yes, home sweet home. She was distracted by a tiny voice, yelling down the hallway, and the pattering of small bare feet on the marble.

"Molly's here," yelled Sophie, her four-year-old niece, rushing to the door to greet her. With her thick black hair and large doe eyes she looked like the poster child for Burberry Kids. The two hugged and the little girl snuggled Henry.

That went well, thought Molly humming, "All the Single Ladies."

Alright, maybe she doesn't count as a member of the firing squad, but I'm in the door, step one.

A flood of McKennas stormed the foyer.

"Molly-O-Golly," yelled Megan, her oldest sister. At five foot nine, she towered over the crowd.

"Sweet Potato, Henry, you made it," said Maxie, the middle sister. Maxie, equally striking, was homecoming queen and a shoo-in for this year's Ms. Winter.

"Baby Doll you made it," said Dad. "How was the drive?"

So far, so good, here she comes, take a breath. Molly hummed the refrain of "All the Single Ladies" over and over. It had proved to be an independent woman's anthem as well as a remarkable distraction. She was strong, fierce, independent.

Silvia did a long once-over before she went in for the kill. "Molly, you look so pale. Have you lost weight? You know that weight comes off your chest first. God knows you don't need that. They make wonderfully padded bras for those who are cup challenged. And why do you always wear those God awful sheep hunting shoes?"

"They're Uggs, Mom. They are made of shearling, not used for sheep hunting."

"Awfully testy, dear. You know, if you had a man in your life you would be much happier. If you took that hair out of that ballerina bun and maybe tried contacts. You know I have a doctor who will do that eye surgery and get rid of those awful school-marm glasses. I'm sure there is some man out there who would find you attractive. Maybe your sisters could help you with some makeup tricks."

Molly pushed back her glasses and stuffed a few loose strands back in her bun, pushed out her 32B boobs and reminded herself it was just seventy two hours.

"Mom, that's enough," said Megan. "She is beautiful the way she is. Maybe she doesn't want a man." She picked up Olivia, her fifteen-month-old who just toddled in.

"For heaven's sake, say it isn't so, are you a lesbian?" Silvia whispered.

"No, I'm not gay, Mother."

"Dear, if you are I'm not saying we wouldn't be disappointed and need to do major damage control at the country club, but we would get you help."

"*Help?* I don't need help. Even if I was gay I wouldn't need help," shouted Molly, whose Irish temper had run dangerously close to its boiling point.

"Defense mechanism, that right there, that's what that is. Molly, we have always known you were different…" Silvia started.

"For your information Mom, I do have a boyfriend if you must know," said Molly. It just sort of rolled off her tongue. *Crap, what happened to being a single lady, embracing my independence?* She broke under the pressure.

The room fell silent, all eyes on her. Then a burst of questions engulfed the room. *And the interrogation begins.*

"What's his name? Where does he work?"

His name, his name, oh boy she hadn't thought this through very well.

Henry drooled a large puddle of slobber right on Silvia's shoe.

I love that dog, thought Molly.

"For God's sake, I thought that damn beast died already," said Silvia.

"Sorry to disappoint you, but Henry is as fit as a fiddle," said Molly, thankful for the momentary delay in the interrogation.

"Name, Molly, he has a name, right?" said Silvia.

"Of course," Molly said with a rash of hives brewing under her scarf.

"Well?" said Silvia with the gaze of a professional private investigator waiting to break a criminal under pressure.

"It's Sebastian, yep Sebastian." *Whew, that just sort of popped out,* she thought as she clawed at the hives beneath her scarf.

"Sebastian, as in your boss?" asked Silvia, eyes wide.

"Sebastian, as in your sexy hot Aussie boss?" asked Megan.

"Can she at least get her coat off and then you can nose your way into her business?" asked her very level-headed father.

What have I done? Molly asked herself silently as she reached in her bag for Benadryl.

Thanksgiving Day

Thanksgiving Day came with no smell of turkey wafting in the oven. No pies warming on the counters. No Macy's parade, not even one chore. No setting the Thanksgiving table, no slaving over a hot stove. No, just the new version of a McKenna holiday, a more upscale, more elegant affair, as far as Molly was concerned, more fake and sadly disappointing. The food catered from Allberry's, delivered precisely as the football game ended, filled the counters. The table was set with scads of candles in various heights, all cream colored. The fine china imported from Italy would make even Martha Stewart jealous. Tiny cornucopias, each wrapped in burnt orange ribbons sat in the center of each plate. Every seat was set with a proper place card scrolled with a male Pilgrim for the boys and, of course, a female Pilgrim for the girls. Silvia took care of the décor. It had to be perfect. The food would be carved and doled out in precise portions almost scientifically equal.

Molly, being the only sister without a husband or date, sat at the end of the table between her nieces. She felt them to be better company anyway.

Silvia started by saying grace, then dug right into grueling Chinese water torture games, such as *Tell Us About Your Love Life*.

Passing the gravy, Silvia's face lit up as she bragged about Maxie's fine catch in a boyfriend, Alex Dolan. Alex was handsome in a seersucker, boat shoe kind of way. He was meticulously dressed with every one of his sandy-colored hairs close cropped with the exception of a few pieces spiked in the front. Theirs was an arranged dating scenario. Maxie, the rebellious daughter, went for bad boys. Not bad as in murder, drugs or the like, just bad as in attitude, motorcycles or tattoos. Silvia needed to nip this in the bud when the family moved to their new zip code. So one day over tea at the country club she pulled out pictures of the beautiful Maxie and sold her like cattle to the Dolan clan. Before you knew it an arranged family get-together found the two of them seated next to one another while awkward conversation surrounded them. Maxie wasn't naïve, she knew the game. He was hot and rich and "Well, why the hell not?" were her exact words. Eternal soul mates, no way, but comfortable and tolerable certainly.

"Molly, did you know that Alex here is studying medicine? Just like Thomas. Alex is in his residency now dear."

Molly sighed.

"Alex has been a remarkable influence on Maxie. She is going back to school to get her degree in accounting. I'm just saying when Thomas was in your life you seemed so driven. Not quite sure what this Sebastian fellow is doing for you. Thomas is a fine young man, Molly."

"Really, Mom? Which part is so fine, the part where he humiliated me or banged a skank in front of much of Greenwich?"

"That was a simple indiscretion, a momentary lack in judgment. He's different now. He grew up, dear. Men aren't perfect, but a work in progress. From where I sit, he is pretty close."

"Mom, stop!" Molly yelled before grabbing her plate and heading to the kitchen. Silvia stomped behind her.

"Where are your manners? You certainly have gotten snippy since your move to the big city."

Molly shook her head as the sound of the front door chimes rang Happy Holidays. "Saved by the bell." Molly took the opportunity to escape the unpleasant banter and made her way to the front door. *Maybe it's flowers or a candy gram*. She smiled, allowing her mind to whisk her away momentarily.

When she opened the door, there he stood. Thomas. Damn it, he did look good, impeccably dressed with his short, spiky cut and big green eyes. His smile big and bright hid the beast within.

"Really Mom?" she said.

"Molly, what a surprise. To be honest, Mom may have mentioned you were coming in."

"Mom? You call her Mom?"

"Old habits are hard to break Molls. You know Silvia and I have patched things up since the oversight. I wish we could do the same."

"Oversight? Is that what you call screwing someone in front of the whole town when you are committed to someone else?"

"Okay, I see we are still a little testy Molls, but how about we grab some dessert and talk. Mom did say there was apple pie."

Her phone vibrated in her pocket, giving her the reprieve she so desperately craved.

"Happy Thanksgiving, Red. I wish you were here. Kyle and I set off the smoke alarm and cleared the building but managed to save the beast. The turkey is charred on the left side but we did each get a slice. I pulled out all the Christmas decorations like you instructed," said Hunter.

"Oh God, it's good to hear your voice," she said before realizing all eyes were on her.

"Sebastian, love, I so wish you were here to meet my family."

"Did you start dipping into the eggnog early this year? Has your imaginary love affair finally made you go mad?"

"Mad, yes. I'm very mad you couldn't be by my side, Sebi."

"They think you're gay, right? Oh no, it's all coming to me. You panicked and the imaginary boyfriend suddenly became real, hmm, hmm, hmm."

"You know me so well, lovie."

"Woman, I can't leave you alone for a minute."

"I'm dying here."

"Tread lightly Red, we know how good you are with lies."

"Kisses," she said before hanging up.

Silence hung in the air as the group stared at her, faces awash in astonishment.

"Shall we have dessert?" asked her father.

The crowd quickly agreed dessert was just the thing they needed to break that dreadful silence. Thomas rarely backed down from a challenge and in true form took the seat directly next to Molly.

"So Molls, did you get that big promotion you have been talking about for three years? Silvia keeps me up to date."

"As a matter of fact," *oh God, here it comes, stop, stop with the lying,* she pleaded with herself. "I did."

Everyone gasped and then all started talking at the same time. Her sisters yelling cheers of congrats, her father praising her for her patience, but Silvia kept a cool tone.

"That's funny dear, you forgot to tell us?"

"Not forgot, just looking for the right time, which happens to be now."

"Your title is?" asked Thomas.

"Vice President of Marketing." *Oh my goodness, it just keeps getting worse. Curse the white lie Gods.*

"This deserves a toast," said her father.

"To Carrot Top, her new love, new career and continued success and happiness."

"Cheers," said the girls.

"While we are celebrating, may I share some good news with the fam?" asked Thomas.

"Surely dear," answered Silvia.

"My official physician ceremony is tomorrow, and I'd like to invite you all to a party at my place afterwards."

Everyone clapped except Molly. *Why, why did he have to upstage her moment? Fake as it may be, it was still her moment.*

"We can't think of a place we would rather be. Isn't that right Molly?" said Silvia.

Oh let me think, where would I rather be? I don't know, maybe having a double root canal, maybe acupuncture where they stick those little needles right into your eyelids, or maybe the Himalayas with no coat, yep she could think of a few.

Molly paused for a moment and then said, "I thought maybe tomorrow we could decorate. You know, since the little ones are here. It could be fun."

"Molly, since when have we decorated?" Silvia said with a chuckle. "You know the Stanwicks have been doing our decorating for years. I already have them scheduled for December 13th. You need to book those guys early. Everyone in the neighborhood uses them."

"I know Mom, but isn't it more fun to do it ourselves?"

"If by 'fun' you mean pulling up all those boxes of rubbish we used to call 'ornaments' from the old house and grueling over prickly pine needles, no, I don't think so. And besides, those hideous things are most likely gone. I asked your father to get rid of them. I honestly don't know why we hang on to those junky little Christmas ornaments, or for that matter, the house. Nothing compares to the Stanwicks decorations. We've won first place every year for the last five in the Greenwich Holiday Home tour. Honestly, sometimes I wonder if you really are a McKenna."

"You and me both," said Molly under her breath. She had forgotten that everything in life was a competition. First place trumped everything else. Molly didn't miss that one bit. She did however miss how Christmas used to be before Dad got his big promotion and they moved to the high rent district. Life was simpler. Money and appearances weren't important. Back in New York her apartment was the size of a postage stamp, but Hunter and his roommate Kyle were two doors away. It was small, but had character, it was lived-in, not staged. Mis-matched pillows and colorful fluffy afghans welcomed everyone who entered. It was perfect for her and Henry.

"So what time Thomas?" asked Silvia.

"Eight p.m. sharp. Bring your dancing shoes. And Molly, I hope you save a dance for me," said Thomas before clearing some dessert plates and heading toward the kitchen.

"Honestly, Molly you need to rethink things and consider giving Thomas another chance. I mean how serious are you and this Sebastian fellow? You know dating the boss undermines your value in a company. Some may even wonder if you got that promotion by sleeping with the boss."

Sleeping with her boss sounded like a fantasy to her right now, no promotion required.

"Mother, usually I'd let you get to me, but not this time. I don't need to rethink being humiliated. I'm good."

Molly helped Maxie clear the table and found Thomas in the kitchen flirting with Megan. Megan, married for five years now always needed the validation of another man. She loved her husband, but as mother's pageant-ready daughter she thrived on a good compliment or ten. Thomas, a pro at making a woman feel like she had just been named "female of the year" never missed a chance to worm his way into the good graces of a McKenna. He would use any tool necessary.

"Should have been a lawyer, that snake," Molly said to Maxie. "He's got them all eating out of his hands. I hope you're not falling for his song and dance routine."

"Nah, I can spot a charmer a mile away. He seems like he is determined to win you back, though. I hope you're up for the fight. He has Mom eating out of his palm. Sebastian has big shoes to fill. He will be joining us at Christmas, right? I'd love to meet the man who stole my little sister's heart," said Maxie, collecting the cloth napkins.

"Um, Christmas, sure he is, wouldn't miss it. I'm glad to hear you're so happy with Alex. I know when Mom brought him around you were not really feeling it. Maybe Mom does know something about relationships, but not when it comes to me."

Maxie turned her eyes downward. A certain sadness washed over her face. "Yeah, Alex is a good man. He'll make me happy. You know Sweet Potato, I've learned life with a happy Silvia is much easier than the alternative. I envy you really, getting away, making your own decisions. Who knew my kid sister would be the brave one?"

"I do miss it here. I'm not really a city girl. If I were going to do the whole Holiday Village thing someday, there is nowhere else in the world I'd want it to be."

"Are you still thinking about it?"

"Every day of my life. Few people love Christmas the way I do. People grow up and it becomes a chore, a chore to decorate, a chore to get Christmas pictures with fancy little matching outfits for their brood, a chore to try and make sure each kid gets exactly what he or she has on their list. They lose the feeling of Christmas. It's a feeling deep inside. I wish I could give adults the feeling of what Christmas was like as a kid again. If I could help them remember, it wouldn't be a chore."

"Aw Sweet Potato, that's what I love about you. You're a dreamer, an adult with the ability to live life through the eyes of a child. You should do it. I'm serious. What's stopping you?"

"Me, I guess. I have the marketing plan down. I have the design down, but the capital, the staff, all the technical nitty-gritty, not so much."

"I could help, with the finance stuff. I could help you secure a loan. Staff, hell there are enough kids in Greenwich to staff the North Pole."

Molly's face brightened with hope. She felt alive and energized with the thought of her dream being a reality.

Then her face tightened, her eyes pensive and her mouth taut. "And then there is Silvia."

"So what, Silvia? She has her dream of living the perfect fake life of wealth and country clubs. You do your thing. It's not up to her. Remember, you're the sister who had the guts to go."

Molly grabbed Maxie in a bear hug. "Thanks sis. I'll think about it. For now I'm not feeling so well. A bit of Thomasitis. If you don't mind, I think I'm going to turn in early," she said, kissing Maxie on the cheek.

"Sure Sweet Potato, get some rest. Apparently we are all going dancing tomorrow night."

"'Night all. I'm exhausted, turning in early," said Molly.

"Molls, I look forward to that dance. Wear something special," said Thomas before sneaking a quick kiss on the cheek.

Rolling her eyes, she and Henry headed upstairs. Retreating to the comfort of her room, she opened the door and grinned. It hadn't changed much from when she left for New York. As a matter of fact, it hadn't changed much since she was a kid. Despite the offer for an interior decorator to give her the room of her dreams, Molly insisted on keeping it exactly as it was in the old house. She had the walls painted in the same warm violet called, "Lavender Fields." On the bed was a lavender floral and white eyelet comforter she brought from her old room. Silvia hated it, probably why Molly insisted on keeping it, but her father was stern about letting the girls do whatever they needed to make the move an easier transition.

Her sisters took full advantage of the designer. Megan had a mural of a runway on her wall with a closet that you could hold a fashion show in. Maxie loved sports so she had a softball themed room. The two girls both covered their walls with Vogue models and Chanel bags but Molly chose a simpler approach, her own artwork. Molly loved sketching ideas, jingles, anything that allowed her creative mind to soar. The room faced the circular driveway in the front of the house. She watched through the massive three pane glass as Thomas got in his Jag. He was handsome and successful, and of course, came from a wealthy Connecticut family. But he was also a liar, showy, arrogant and fake. In her defense, Sebastian too was fake, but only the part about being in love with her. After three years he still couldn't get her name right. "Molly," it really wasn't that hard. Still she would never give up her dream of becoming VP of Marketing even if her dream of being Mrs. Tate remained pure fiction.

She crawled in her four post bed and dialed Hunter.

"Hey," she said.

"Hey yourself little Ms. Liar, Liar pants on fire. Tell me, did you at least plan a horrific breakup scene?" he said.

"No, not exactly. I might have said he's coming for Christmas," she mumbled.

"Oh Lord, she's on a roll. How, pray tell, do you plan on pulling that off Red?"

"That's not all."

"Good Lord, you're not fake pregnant are you?"

"Heavens, no. You are watching too many of Kyle's soap operas. This is serious. I'm in over my head. Somehow I sort of implied I got the promotion to VP."

"By implied do you mean said you're up for it?"

"More like I got it," she said softly. "It sort of just slipped out. Yay me," she said, her voice trailing off.

"Holy Shit, you should come with a muzzle."

"Crap, I know. Why did you let me come here? You should have taped me to the couch. You know I'm not good under pressure, and Silvia is a high pressure cooker," she said, this time her voice squeaking higher with each word.

"Breathe. You're hyperventilating, aren't you?"

"A little, maybe, yes I am. Oh no, what have I gotten myself into?"

"Things will look brighter tomorrow."

"Oh yes, I'm sure they will. Did I mention my ex-boyfriend, the one who broke my heart and humiliated me in front of the whole town stopped by?"

"Must have left that little nugget out. You know, who needs soaps when you have such juicy material."

"Hunter, this is serious."

"Okay, he stopped by. Did you kick him in the b…?"

"I'm going to a party at his place tomorrow night to honor his becoming a doctor."

"Wow, I kinda saw that going in a different direction."

Whining, she moaned, "Help me. I hate it here. I'm never good enough for Silvia, a constant disappointment. Now she is practically planning Thomas and my wedding."

"Two-timing whore, what about poor Sebastian?"

"Hunter, I do not know why I called you."

"Yes, you do, because you love me. I'm your bestie. Now, let's get a good night's rest and develop a plan in the morning. Try not to bump into Silvia in the night. You may be running for governor by morning."

"No, no more lies. I need to start repairing this mess. Tomorrow night I'll be firm. I'll let Thomas know he isn't worming his flirty self in and that I'm done with him and his kind. In forty one hours Henry and I will be hitting the road."

"You go girl. Give that bastard hell. Let him know no one messes with Red. Speaking of Henry, how's my boy?"

"Sophie and Olivia fed him turkey under the table all night. He is currently in a tryptophan coma," she said, looking over at the pudgy pooch laid out on the bed, snoring.

"Give him a kiss for me. Remember stick to your guns. Don't bring any with you though. You're sounding a bit feisty on this trip. I don't have bail money. Talk to you tomorrow."

"Single and loving it" was the plan she was going with. How did she get so far off that path? One more night and then she could put this dreadful weekend behind her until one month from now when the whole ugly nightmare of Christmas awaited. Two things she knew for sure, Thomas's charms weren't working on her and she had a better chance of bringing home Santa Claus himself than Sebastian. She snuggled Henry as she stared out her window before falling asleep.

The next day breakfast in the dining room had an icy tone to it. Dad read the paper and Silvia moved the fresh fruit frittata around her plate and swirled her mimosa. It was clear Molly had disappointed her again. She hadn't minded her manners and played nice.

"I'll go."

"Pardon me," said Silvia knowing exactly what Molly was referring to.

"To the party. I'll go, but don't expect me to be all gushy with the bastard."

"Molly, have you never made a mistake in your life? How about your decision to follow in Maxie's steps and try softball despite our suggestions that it may be disastrous? Yes, I recall you regretting that decision every time you took the plate and swung at the sky, never even causing a breeze to pass the ball. Every time the fans booed you, you wished you had thought of the consequences. And how about the decision to go to sleep away camp and you cried every night you couldn't come home? You regretted that as well. Not everyone makes the right choices all the time. Just think about it."

She thought about it for two seconds then said, "I didn't hurt anyone except myself with my bad decision making skills. Thomas, on the other hand, crushed me with his inability to think with his head instead of his male parts. There is a difference."

"Not true, I believe you hurt everyone on that softball team by losing every game."

"Thank you for that vivid reminder. And I don't think the decision of an eight-year-old can compare to that of a grown man."

"Ladies, can we agree that tonight is about celebrating a young man's accomplishments and nothing else. Let's try to go as a family and enjoy the time we get to spend with our Molly."

"Thanks, Daddy," she said before collecting her bowl of now soggy cornflakes and retreating to the kitchen. Edward McKenna was, if nothing else, a peacemaker. As the sole male in a house full of estrogen, he brought reason to the craziness. Molly glanced at him for a second and thought of his quiet demeanor, despite his high-level career. He was soft-spoken and knew better than to ever push his opinion over Silvia's. Yes, their marriage worked because he was the silent partner in their agreement.

"Hey, Molly O'Golly, do you want to spend some time with your favorite nieces today?" asked Megan.

"Can't think of anything else I'd rather do."

"Great, but first, the girls are home with Chase and I need some adult time. Are you up for some shopping? I need something to wear tonight."

"Perfect, I'll be down in ten." Molly headed upstairs, down the hall and heard Maxie's voice. She was giggling and flirting shamelessly on her cell.

Molly smiled and thought that's what she wanted with her fiancé someday, to flirt shamelessly like he was the only man in the world. She dressed in practical jeans, a green turtleneck and Uggs, partially to piss off Silvia. Her phone rang and a picture of Hunter popped up. She smiled and swiped her phone. "Hello."

"How's it going? I'm almost afraid to ask. You didn't proclaim you are getting a Nobel Peace Prize for ending world hunger or starring in a new Quentin Tarantino film?"

"No, I've kept the lies in check but did have a rousing discussion about how I ruined the lives of an entire team of eight-year-olds during one awful softball season."

"Okay, you are a bad ass after all, huh?"

"She's insufferable. She can't fathom that I won't give Thomas a chance. She thinks I should just break it off with Sebastian and pick up where I left off."

"To her credit, breaking it off with Sebastian wouldn't technically be that difficult. So what is this Thomas's deal besides screwing another girl? Is he an axe murderer, homeless, penniless, could double as the Hunch back of Notre Dame?"

"I'm in love with Sebastian. I'm patient, that's all. I believe true love will find its way in time. It always does. As for Thomas the Loser, he's a cross between the boyish good looks of Brad Pitt and the swagger of Leonardo DiCaprio. The bastard is a doctor. He just bought a mansion on the green and his family is worth more than Bill Gates.

"Christ, what a freakin' loser. I can see why you wouldn't want to be hooked up with that."

"Shut up! You don't know him. He's a getter."

"A whater?"

"A getter. Some people are wanters, but not Thomas, he is a getter. He always gets what he wants. Sometimes just for the sake of saying he got it, not because he really wants it. You know."

"But maybe he's genuinely sorry, and he really does want a second chance. You said it, true love always finds a way."

"Impossible, he is incapable of genuine."

"If you say so, Red. Just be strong then and don't give the getter his prize."

"That's why I love you. You always understand."

"That, and my boyish good looks."

"Oh yes, that too."

"Good luck."

"Love you."

Molly and Megan jumped into Megan's white Lexus SUV, a "mommy car" that still said "sexy." Megan may have been a mom, but few men saw that when they looked at her. She somehow defied the laws of pregnancy and came through with a flat stomach and even bigger boobs. Bigger boobs were about the only thing Molly found intriguing about pregnancy. Henry was her child and she felt quite content with that.

"Do you mind if we check out a new set of boutiques over on the other side of town? It's near Chase's new office complex."

"Fine with me, you're the one shopping."

"Oh come on, why not get something fancy for tonight. Make

Thomas eat his heart out. I find it's the best form of revenge, and Mom will never see it coming."

"Intriguing, I'll see what they have."

The fifteen minute drive turned into twenty five with traffic, but Megan insisted the drive would be worth it. From Megan's description, the shops were a delightful mix of designer boutiques and gourmet eateries.

"Wow, Chase travels here every day? I imagine with rush hour it takes a bit longer."

"I swear I never see the man. He leaves early, stays late and rarely calls. He travels about three times a month."

"That sucks."

"I guess it's the price you pay to keep up with the Dolan's. Ask Dad how his life changed with the big promotion. Remember we went from dinner at five thirty as a family seven nights a week to a weekend meal with Dad if we were lucky. It's all what you get used to."

"Are you lonely? I mean do you have time for, you know, husband and wife time?"

"Sex, Molly, you can say it." Megan laughed in her hearty raspy sexy laugh. Yes, she even laughed sexy. God, Molly wished just one sexy gene had been left in the pool by the time they got to her.

"Okay, sex, is there time?"

"Not very much. He's always tired, you know with the travel and late hours. But it's cool, we're good."

Molly wondered what "good" meant. If that was good, Molly wanted great. If she were with Sebastian they would never be apart.

They pulled up to a swanky development with a mix of restaurants, upscale shops and high-rise condos. It was exactly the type of place Megan would shop. She followed in Silvia's footsteps when it came to the finer things in life. The move had been much easier on Megan than the other two, partly because she was older, and partly because she secretly wanted that zip code as much as Silvia.

Maxie took the move worse than her sisters, not for the same reasons as Molly but for her own reasons, reasons that seemed silly to Silvia. Maxie was experiencing her first love. Antonio Delvecchio, a fellow student at the Moor school. They shared their love of sports—Maxie All-County softball pitcher and Antonio All-County baseball pitcher. Antonio, a skinny olive-skinned boy with remarkable dimples, lived on the opposite side of town. His father left when he and his two brothers were young, leaving his mother, Angie, alone. Angie, a round Italian woman who still spoke in Italian mixed with broken English, worked as the cafeteria lady at Moor during the day and cleaned offices in the evenings. The family shared a two-bedroom home that on the outside told the story of Angie's financial struggles yet the inside told a different story. A home filled with love and delicious Italian meals. Silvia hadn't learned of the relationship until one day when Maxie's bike tire caught a nail after a visit to Antonio's home. Silvia pulled up to the modest house with a missing shutter and tall overgrown shrubs and yanked Maxie out, forbidding her to see him again.

When Silvia learned Angie was a cook at the school she tried to have her fired. Maxie, a true McKenna, had a fighting spirit of her own. She ignored her mother's wishes and continued her relationship with Antonio without Silvia knowing. It wasn't until Silvia announced the family would be moving the week before Christmas to Greenwich that Maxie freaked. Although the move was just a few miles away it would change everything. She begged her dad not to take the job. Her friends were here, her ball team and most of all the love of her life.

Megan pulled the SUV into a tight spot, flipped down the driver side mirror and applied a thick layer of gloss to her full lips. Smacking them together, she fluffed her hair. "Molls, let's get gorgeous."

Bev's Boutique sat square in the middle of the shopping center. The two made their way through the large glass doors and were greeted by a pretty salesgirl.

"Hi, welcome to Bev's. How can I help you?"

Molly looked around at the stark white design of the shop. The chairs made of steel with fur pillows said anything but "sit on me." It felt cold and snooty. But Megan was in her glory.

"Oh, yes you can. We are going to a 'new house/I'm a doctor now party' and we need to look fabulous."

This caught the attention of a tall icy blonde whose eyes were botoxed so tight she may have been squinting or not, Molly was unsure.

"Hello, I'm Bev. This seems like a party that just may require my help Sadie," she said to the salesgirl who appeared relieved. The icy woman led the two to the back of the store where rows of party dresses lined the walls.

"Whom do I have the pleasure of working with?"

"This is Molly, she needs a dress that says eat your heart out you slimy bastard. I'm Megan and I need a Hot Mama dress."

"Now Megan, let's see what we can do for you," the owner gushed, grabbing her hand as though they were best friends. Molly wondered why her slimy bastard dress didn't trump the Hot Mama but also felt a small wave of relief she could browse unbothered.

Megan and Bev disappeared into a dressing room giggling and dishing about everything from Chase to the girls. Megan emerged in a black backless dress made of straight spandex painted on to every curve of her body, especially her butt.

"Oh hell yes, I do believe this says 'eyes over here.' Right Molls?"

"Yep, that sure says that and a few other things."

"Molls here is a bit more conservative."

"We can do a *quite sexy conservative eat-your-heart-out you cheating scum* dress, you know," said Bev.

"Okay, I guess."

Molly took the three dresses Bev came back with into the dressing room alone. There was something creepy about a total stranger dressing her.

"How's it going Molls?"

"The first two aren't really sending the right message, if you know what I mean. Not quite what I'm going for. I'm trying the last one on now." She slipped the ivory colored dress over her head. It had a nice high neck line but the short length gave it an edgy look. She looked at her pale skin beneath the fluorescent lights and decided she looked translucent, something she seemed to wear well.

"Come out, let us see," said Bev. "Hmmm, Nicole Kidman can pull off pale, but darling you're downright pasty. Have you tried Glow-Me-Perfect on Main? Take that off, let's try a different color."

She returned with a mint-colored strapless dress. "Not much upstairs," said Bev, pointing to her chest. "But you have beautiful collarbones and shoulders. Let's accentuate them."

Molly took the next dress from her and marched back into the dressing room shaking her head. *Why did she care what Thomas the cheating scum thought anyway?* Bev and Megan were flipping through brochures of Christmas and New Year's dresses when Molly now standing in front of them cleared her throat.

"Holy sexy mama, that is the one that will make him regret ever even breathing near another woman," said Megan.

Bev, equally as ecstatic, spun Molly around and showed her herself in the mirror. A few snooties stopped to look. She had definitely gotten the attention of these fashionista women, maybe this was the one.

Looking at herself she smiled slightly. "Okay this is the one.

Wait, how much is it?"

"Doll, no dollar amount can ever be a deterrent when it comes to revenge dressing," said Bev.

"I got it Molls. Chase gave me his card. No limit, just wants to make me happy because he can't go tonight. Poor guy, he probably won't even get to eat. He always has working dinners.

"Are you sure?"

"Take it off and meet me at the counter."

The two followed Bev to the front of the store. Megan pulled out her card, a peculiar design made of clear plastic with a swirl of prism through the center.

Bev held up the card, marveling at its original design. "I thought certain I'd seen every one out there." She wrapped up the two dresses and promised to call Megan when the Christmas dress she had picked out arrived in stock.

"Bye Dolls. I hope tonight is everything you desire."

They checked out a few of the other fancy shops and stopped at Salad Works for a quiet lunch before heading home to the chaos of Megan's young daughters.

Inside they were greeted by Sophie who was wearing her mother's tiara and a frilly dress with a tutu underneath.

"Hey baby, where is Daddy?"

"I'm Princess Sophia," said the small girl, the spitting image of her mother with her dark hair and big brown eyes.

"Sorry Princess Sophia. Where is the royal king?'

"He is busy. Leave him alone."

"Did he say that?"

The little girl, barely fazed by the comment, said, "Yes, he's always busy."

Molly stepped forward and asked, "May I have a tour of the royal kingdom?"

"Thanks, Moll. I need to talk to him. He is probably late for work."

Aware of the tension between the two, Molly knew she needed to get her niece far from the argument. Shouting seemed not to deter the little girl from merrily knighting plants and furniture in her kingdom.

"Where is your sister?"

"She is napping in her royal bedroom."

The door opened and Chase barreled out, not even acknowledging Molly's presence. Megan's eyes were red and swollen. She shook her head and ran past Molly to the stairs. Molly took the princess to the kitchen and whipped up some tasty snacks. Megan returned fifteen minutes later as though nothing happened.

The little princess headed back to the playroom.

"You okay?"

"Oh yeah, it was nothing. I sort of hoped I could change his mind about tonight, but it was a long shot," she said, her eyes still red.

"Hey listen Megan, why don't you take a little time for yourself. I didn't get much time with my favorite nieces. We have much catching up to do."

"You wouldn't mind. I don't get much time to think with these two."

"My pleasure." Molly loved kids, there was simply something about their ability to just enjoy the wonders of life without all the analysis that adults used to crush those moments. Christmas would be here in a month. The joy and magic of the season was exactly what she loved the most. The time before adults grew up and compartmentalized Christmas into work. Yes, spending time with the very imaginative little princess and her sister was a gift.

A few hours later, a very exhausted princess had settled in front of the TV to watch Cinderella. Olivia played quietly with her blocks. Megan came in smiling and refreshed.

"You ready to bring out the revenge dress, Molls? Come on,

let's get beautiful. I have some great makeup upstairs."

Upstairs the two talked and laughed like when they were kids. Molly watched her sister as she began the process of making Megan magic. The whole thing took hours, but in the end, as usual, Megan had reached supermodel status.

Molly took a pass on the makeup and just put a swipe of lipstick on and changed her glasses to tort shell black and gold ones.

"Hey Moll, why don't you consider contacts?"

"I don't know. I can't put anything in my eyes."

"Here, let me do your hair," Megan said, pulling it down from its tight bun. She brushed it and left it in a low pony. "You look great Molls, eat your heart out jerk!"

They were interrupted by a knock on the door. It was the sitter, Lea. The girls eagerly ran to hug her.

"Okay, let's do this," said Molly. They kissed the girls and left for Thomas's.

They headed to the upper Moorlin area and turned onto Dalton Lane. "There it is, number five, on the right," said Megan.

"Holy crap, this is his house?" asked Molly.

"Yeah, he is loaded."

"Of course he is."

Inside, the home was as extravagant as the impressive exterior. Mother waited in the living room with Maxie.

"What took you girls so long?" she snapped.

"Making an entrance, Mother," said Megan, who trotted across the room toward the bar. In less than two seconds a hoard of men surrounded her. Maxie grabbed Molly's arm. "Come on, girl, we need a drink too."

"Molly, remember—be nice. He really has changed," said Mother as the two disappeared into the crowd.

Maxie's phone rang as soon as they found a dashing young stud carrying a tray of drinks. Maxie grabbed one, downed it and excused herself.

"Really Maxie, you're leaving me?" Molly said, politely thanking the stud. She sipped her drink and made her way back to the living room where Thomas stood in a sea of women, telling his latest medical saga. The dreamy-eyed women swooned over his every word. Molly needed more than a drink, she needed Hunter. She slipped into what she thought was a room, turned out to be the closet, and pecked at her cell.

"Are we behaving? How's the party?" said Hunter when he picked up the phone.

"Ugg, it's awful. Thomas lives in a mansion. Silvia is salivating and practically has the hydrangeas picked for the wedding. Maxie bailed, and Megan is in, well, Megan-mode. Did I mention I'm in a closet?"

"Alone?"

"Yes."

"Of course you are. Why exactly are you in a closet?"

"It feels really weird. Most of the same powerful socialites that were there the night we broke up are here."

"I'm sure they have forgotten all about that. I mean people break up every day. Not exactly newsworthy," said Hunter reassuringly.

"Did I mention when the curtains opened and I saw Thomas kissing her my fingers froze like lead balloons on the piano keys, dragging out a long dong sort of sound that silenced the audience. I panicked, got up to run and caught my shoe in the front of my dress and sort of swan dived, mosh pit style into the orchestra pit."

"Might have left that part out."

"Trust me, there isn't one person who was there that night who doesn't remember. What am I going to do?"

"Remember, he is the enemy. Have a drink, be cordial to the guests, but stay away from Thomas and leave early. Good plan, right?"

"Right, got it. One drink, stay away from Thomas and leave

early. Oh and Hunter, I miss you."

"Enemy love, remember."

She slipped out of the closet to see a room filled with Connecticut's finest all gathered in the vast living room, all eyes on Thomas. She inched her way closer to see what was going on. A studly waiter asked if she wanted a drink. Without hesitating she grabbed one.

"Thank you everyone for coming. This is a big night for me. I'm about to embark on my dream of becoming a doctor. Funny thing about dreams, they are nothing if you can't share them with someone."

Molly grabbed the stud and took another drink, slamming it down in one gulp. Now holding a drink in each hand, she waited for the other shoe to drop.

"Tonight I would like to do something I should have done three years ago."

She linked arms with stud and emptied another from his tray.

"You see three years ago I made the biggest mistake of my life. I was young, under a great deal of stress and still figuring out life's meaning. I hurt the one person I loved by losing her trust on a meaningless indiscretion. I was hoping to make Molly McKenna my wife and I was a fool. Molly, where are you Molly?" he asked, panning the crowd.

At this point she had found a column that would prop her up and was sort of sliding down it. With all eyes on her she slowly raised her hand to about her chest.

In a grand gesture he rushed to her, grabbed her hand and pulled her into him. "Molly McKenna, older, wiser and not one to allow something cherished to get away I ask that you give me the chance to win you back. Let me prove how sorry I am," he said, batting those long spider-like lashes as the women in the room sighed. Without warning he moved his face closer to hers.

She knew it was coming. She wanted to move, like in the horror movies when you yell at the screen for the victim to move, but they never do. Neither did she. His lips approached hers like a butterfly landing on a daisy, soft, gentle, sweet. She felt her head titling to lean in deeper. Damn she thought, *this feels nice*. To be honest it was a whole lot nicer than nice. Lost in the kiss she realized it felt good. It may have been the drinks, she couldn't be sure. Then she panicked. *Oh no, this couldn't be happening, not with the enemy*. Pulling away, she regained her composure, angry she had allowed that kiss at all. She convinced herself it would have felt the same with a gorilla, after all she couldn't remember the last time her lips met someone's except for the unfortunate mouth-to-mouth she received from fireman Bill last Halloween after a mishap with an apple bobbing bucket.

She studied him. He was beautiful, like he just stepped off a Ralph Lauren photo shoot. He was rich, successful and one of Connecticut's most eligible bachelors, but he was a liar and a cheat. Although she didn't know Sebastian intimately, her heart told her he was a good man. The dialogue in her head was abruptly interrupted by Silvia taking the lead.

"Congratulations kids. What took you so long?"

The crowd cheered and Thomas invited everyone to enjoy the catering by Tony. Molly, relieved Silvia took the pressure off her, quickly pulled out of his embrace.

"Molly, I'm glad you've come to your senses," said Silvia, grabbing a Chardonnay as stud strolled by.

"Mother, Thomas, I have no idea what you two have been up to, but I said no such thing."

"Molly, what is wrong with you? It's not exactly like men are falling out of trees over you. It's time you settle down and be grateful Thomas is willing to give you another chance."

"Grateful? Did you really say grateful? Give me another chance?"

"Ladies, let's table this for now, shall we? It's a party and I by no means wanted to put Molly on the spot. Take time to think about it."

Silvia gave Molly an icy stare, and the room temperature dropped by twenty degrees. She turned in disgust and moved to the kitchen.

Molly shook her head. *He didn't want to put me on the spot by calling the crowd to pause and look at me as he ravaged me, sure, that was exactly what he wanted.* She moved in the opposite direction, looking for Maxie. Hunter was right. Leave early. That was a good plan. She moved in and out of each room scanning for Maxie. She tried her cell, five times.

Then a text. "I'm busy Sweets, can you give me a few?" A few translated into an eternity as Molly and stud man became best of friends. After her fourth or fifth drink she couldn't remember why she started telling him how Thomas had humiliated her in the first place. "How does he think I'm going to just fall back into his bed, right?"

Stud listened politely.

Preposterous, the man was so damn arrogant. The crowd thinned as she waited for Maxie. Her head started feeling a bit like it had filled with helium, light and as though it may just float off her body. Stud man suggested she lie down.

An unusual sound made her stir. It was a buzzing like a cell phone. She rubbed her eyes and tried to focus. Jumping up she surveyed the room. Lit only by the shadows of the street light outside she first examined the sheets, then lifted them up, to find herself wearing only her bra and undies. She gasped then rolled over and hit something. Realizing it was not a something, rather a someone, she sat straight up.

"Oh my God," she whispered as she recognized the man in the bed as Thomas. Again, she peeled back the sheets to find him completely naked.

"Oh no, no, no, this can't be happening, enemy, one drink and

leave early. What happened? Crap. I had casual sex. I'm a slut. No, of course I'm not a slut. People do it every day. It's normal, liberated and my generation. Nope slut, drunken slut."

She scurried to find her dress crumpled in a ball at the bottom of the bed. She imagined a rousing sexual tryst with clothes flying, body parts flailing. Oh, what did she do? She found the buzzing. It was a text from Maxie, asking where she was and if she was okay.

Panicked, she opened what she thought to be the bathroom door and found it to be yet another closet. She slipped inside and dialed Hunter.

"Hello," said a very groggy Hunter.

"Hunter, I think I screwed up," she whispered.

"What? Where are you, and why are you whispering?"

"I'm in a closet at Thomas's."

"Still?"

"No of course not. This is a different closet."

"Of course, my bad. Why are you still there? It's four a.m.?"

"I tried to do what you said, one drink, stay away from the enemy, leave early."

"And how did that work for you."

"Not a hundred percent like I had planned. I may have or may not have had sex with Thomas."

"How does that work actually?"

"I can't really remember."

"Moll, people forget if they locked the door, let the dog in or charged their cell, most people actually know if they had sex."

"Well, I had a few drinks."

"A few? What happened to one?"

"I stopped counting after five or six—the waiter was so damn cute and a great listener. I think he was listening. Ohhhh, I'm so mad. He did it again. The getter always gets what he wants."

"Red, how did the getter get to you?"

"When I stepped out of the closet..."

"This closet, or the first one?"

"Not relevant."

"Just trying to clarify since someone is a little fuzzy on the details."

"Anyway, he had assembled a crowd. He pronounced his undying love and devotion to me along with an apology for the mistake he made three years ago."

"Damn, that's why he's a getter, he's good."

"I know, right...and there's more."

"More?"

"A kiss, he planted right there in front of the crowd."

"Did you whack him?"

"Not actually."

"Red, what happened to he's the enemy?"

"It was sort of nice. I don't know, I was drunk for heaven's sake."

"What's the plan now?"

"I'm not that good with plans, so I think I'm going to get dressed and sneak out."

"Get dressed?"

"That is the evidence that lead me to believe I may have had sex. That and the fact I was in bed with a very naked Thomas."

"Nancy Drew I think you have figured out the clues. That must mean something. You aren't the kind of girl who goes around having casual sex."

"I know, right? It's been," hmmm she paused, "three years."

"Oh good Lord, are you telling me you haven't had sex since Thomas?"

"Kinda."

"There you go again being hazy in 'the did I or didn't I' department."

"Technically at least, I did kiss fireman Bill last year at the Halloween party."

"Really, the one who rescued you from nearly drowning in the apple bobbing bucket?"

"It happens."

"No, really, it doesn't."

"He was cute."

"It wasn't a kiss, woman. Mouth-to-mouth is a life saving measure not foreplay."

"Anyway I'm going to my mom's and packing to come home. Are the Christmas things ready? I need Christmas."

"Do you think you can stay out of trouble for say twelve hours?"

"I hope so."

She pulled on her dress and slipped on her heels. Not without taking notice of the clothes in his closet. Closets say a lot about a person. The pants neatly hung by color, black, navy, Kelly green, beige and white. The shirts crisp and pressed, hung in dry cleaning plastic wrap alongside his blazers. A few pairs of jeans lay folded neatly on a shelf near his vast array of cable knit sweaters. At the end hung his white coat. She moved it into the light and read his embroidered name—Dr. Thomas Landon III. He did it. He went for it and got it. Also a house and wardrobe to complete it, all he needed was a wife. This closet said "Thomas is a getter."

She didn't want to be a conquest, rather a soul mate. That was what Sebastian would be to her, as soon as he realized she was alive. Molly crept down the stairs and out the front door. The first signs of daylight were just peeking through the clouds. Pulling out her phone she dialed Maxie. Right to voicemail. Next she tried Megan.

"Hello."

"Hey Megan. What are you doing?"

"Molly? Do you know what time it is?"

"Nope."

"It's five a.m."

"Okay, so funny story—I may have spent the night with Thomas."

"What? What happened to 'eat your heart out you lying sack of shit?'"

"I honestly don't know. I looked for Maxie, she went into the kitchen and disappeared. I had too much to drink, and I woke up in his bed. All I know is, I need to get home."

"I would come, but Sophie is in bed with me. She threw up all night. It was rough. Chase never made it home so I have no one to leave her with."

"It's perfectly fine. Mom's house is only about ten blocks away. Worst case scenario, I walk."

"Why not ask Thomas for a ride? It's the least he could do."

"No. I need to get out of here now. I can't face him."

"Moll, it was just sex. You didn't marry him."

"I don't have just sex."

"Maybe you should."

"I hope Sophie feels better. Pray for me."

"Will do, Lolita."

"That was helpful."

Molly slipped off her heels and felt the chill of the November morning on her bare feet. She started the ten block trek back to her parents' house. The streets were quiet. A few cars hummed by, breaking the silence of the eerie morning. She knew it was safe to walk and maybe a little fresh air would clear her head. Why did Thomas do this? She knew she wasn't his type. He liked girls like Carey, the blonde bitch he cheated on her with. Carey was bold, outspoken, undeniably sexy and driven. Driven like Thomas, she was a getter. She always wanted Thomas and his family's money. He was in her sites, she set the bait and caught the fish. He was quite a catch and it lasted for about a year until their competing priorities made it impossible to compromise. Carey would settle for nothing less than climbing the social ladder. If she needed to step on someone or sleep with them, whatever worked. Molly, by the town's definition, was sweet, wholesome and faithful, until tonight of course. *Holy crap, what did I do?* "Is it technically considered cheating if you cheat on the boyfriend who's not even yours yet?" she rambled as she rubbed her temples.

A low siren droned behind her. She turned to see Jimmy Cregar in his police car.

"I'll be! Is that Molly McKenna in the flesh? What are you doing in these parts?"

"Long story." She decided against going with the drunken slut and just said she was heading home.

"Hop in. It's chilly out there."

She hadn't even noticed the cool November air, until she slipped into the toasty warm police car. Her head felt like a bowling ball and she wanted to disappear into her bed. She hopped in the car and asked if he could kill the siren and flashing lights. Nothing says "slut enduring the walk of shame" like a cop car flashing the scarlet letter.

They shared small talk and in about five minutes pulled into her parents' home. Praying with every fiber they would all still be blissfully sleeping, she attempted to go around back and enter through the kitchen. No luck. Molly walked right into an argument between Maxie and Silvia in full rage.

"Molly, what in the name of God?" asked Silvia before peering out the side window to see Jimmy's police car pull away.

"Did you spend the night in jail? Oh Lord, where is your father? We need damage control."

"Calm down. I spent the night with Thomas. Jimmy just drove me home."

Silvia's face lit up like the Christmas tree at the lighting ceremony. Silvia would be proud of her daughter wearing a scarlet letter if Thomas was involved. "Well that is spectacular news. Come dear, sit down, tell us all about it," she said, putting the box of oatmeal on the counter and pulling up a stool.

"Really, I get a high five for sleeping with Thomas after three years when I have a boyfriend."

Maxie said, "At least someone is doing what mommy dearest wants."

"Maxie, watch your tone."

"Did I miss something?"

"Maxie here seemed to get lost last night and also appeared rather early this morning, but the curious thing is her boyfriend did manage to show up here last night looking for her."

Grateful she was not the only slut at the table, Molly remained silent, just thankful for the moment's peace from interrogation.

"Mother, for the last time, I do not owe you an explanation. It is between me and Alex. I'm almost thirty years old, I do not have to answer to you," screamed Maxie as she marched out of the room.

"I also must go. I have a dreadful headache and have had no sleep," said Molly as she dragged herself to a standing position.

"I hope you will stay another day so you and Thomas can make some plans."

"*Ugggg*, I'm leaving today mother. I have a job and a boyfriend. His name is Sebastian, not Thomas."

She crawled in her bed and pulled the covers over her head. She would need to face Thomas, but hopefully not until Christmas. Christmas always meant so much to her. How did this whole mess become so complicated? Christmas was a time when she felt like a child, filled with wonder and surprise, a magical world where little elves happily made toys, a world where you could send your wish out to the universe and wait and see if it would be granted, a place where good was rewarded. She crawled out and moved over to her massive closet. Unlike Megan and Maxie's that were filled with clothes, shoes and bags, hers was filled with a dream. She stepped inside and turned on the light. There was her rendition of Holiday Village covering the ten by ten foot wall. There would be massive gates with the letters NP for North Pole monogrammed on them. The road leading to the village would be called Mistletoe Lane. Inside, a village filled with childhood memories lit with millions of lights. She would have shops, a restaurant, Santa's workshop, a toy store with life-size toys and a large carousel in the middle, a monorail with sleighs that carried you high above the village, a mailroom where you could write a letter to Santa. There would be a naughty/nice board where you could search for your name. A wrapping station, hot cocoa café, and Candy Cane Lane, a spiral walkway lined with eight foot candy canes lit with white lights that led to Santa and Mrs. Claus's cottage. Inside a warm glowing fireplace would be lit and Christmas stories would be read to the children. Treats of cookies and milk would be handed out before getting a chance to sit on Santa's lap. Every door would be topped with Mistletoe. And each night at eight o'clock there would be caroling around a massive tree in the square. The lighting would not be complete until the Angel was set on the top of the tree. This would be a place where every person could feel like a child again. She ran her fingers across her enormous drawing and smiled as she imagined each piece.

"Sweet Potato, are you in here?" asked Maxie.

"Closet."

"Why?'

"Seems like I've been spending a lot of time in closets as of late."

Maxie stepped in and did a once over of the masterpiece. "Do it. What's stopping you Moll?"

"I don't know. Maybe it's because I went to New York to prove to Mom and everyone I could be successful in the Big Apple. Mom thinks this is a joke. A fall back plan if I fail."

"No way, Molly. You have been dreaming of this since you

were a kid. How many people get the chance to make their dreams a reality?"

The intercom beeped loudly with Silvia practically singing on the other end. "Molly, you have a visitor."

She ran to her window and looked out to see Thomas's car. "Crap, I'm dead. Please, I can't see him."

"You have to face him sometime. It'll be different when you come home at Christmas. You'll have Sebastian by your side."

"Right," said Molly, scratching her neck.

Henry trotted alongside her to the living room where an arrogant Thomas sat with an "I won" getter grin plastered all over his face.

Henry snarled.

"Hey there babe."

"Babe? Really, did we?"

"Did we what?" he asked, playing dumb.

"You know what."

"You can say it Moll, we have had sex before you know."

"Thomas," she said, her eyes narrowing.

"No we did not. Naturally I had to fight you off because I'm a gentleman. I figured I'd wait until you know, you beg."

"Why are you here?"

"To give you this," he said before leaning in for a kiss.

"Stop that! I have a boyfriend."

"So you've said."

"You'll see at Christmas."

Chapter Three

Christmas being just three weeks away, Molly decided the office badly needed some holiday cheer. She had started the planning in August. She enlisted Hunter's help. As a good bestie, he dutifully indulged her Christmas crazy. This year she borrowed two hand carts from Jerry down the hall and loaded each with five boxes of decorations.

"Oh there you are. What took you so long? These decorations aren't going to walk themselves up to the twelfth floor," Molly said, eyeing up a slightly disheveled Hunter.

"I'm sorry, the tree you had sent over arrived early. I had the unfortunate luck of being the one to go down to sign for it and then lug it up there."

"Now that does not sound like Christmas spirit to me," she said humming, "It's beginning to look a lot like Christmas."

"Really, I often wonder if you have pointy ears tucked in that bun."

"I admit it, I'm a Christmaholic. I'm utterly hopelessly addicted. If you're implying I'm an elf, maybe, Christmas cheer doesn't spread itself, so Santa needs a few helpers. Call me an elf if you must, but I love this holiday and having the Tate and Price expense account to purchase the stuff only makes it sweeter."

She merrily went about the business of decorating as her coworkers gave her the same awkward stare they had since day one. Didn't matter, it was impossible to get Molly McKenna down this time of year.

She started with a large tree with white lights and gold ornaments in the entry hall. Next the hallways were strung with garland from one end to the other. Stockings with each employee's name hung by the water coolers. The only thing missing was mistletoe. Try as she may she was unable to find a single strand of mistletoe in all of Manhattan. She would not accept defeat, if not for the office she would definitely need it for her apartment. Christmas would not be Christmas without mistletoe.

*****

Buzzzzzz.

The sound of Mr. Tate summoning Molly was music to her ears. "Ms. McDermott, my office please."

"Girl, you look like you just got asked to the Junior Prom by the football captain," said Hunter.

Pulling a mirror from her top desk drawer, she wiped her teeth with her finger, checked her tightly wound bun for any stray hairs and did a quick spritz of perfume.

"How do I look?" she asked Hunter, smiling with wide open clenched teeth, the kind of face you make the day you get your braces off.

"Like you're a mini Chihuahua trying to pass a peach pit," said Hunter.

"Thank you, that's exactly what I was going for."

"I'm just saying it's been three years and the dude doesn't even know your name."

"It's not a common name, you know."

"Yeah, that's it," Hunter said, tapping to his earphones.

Buzzzzzz.

"Ms. McKnight, now."

Jumping up, she banged her knee hard on the corner of her desk. "Ouch, son of a…"

"You really ought to think about investing in a round desk."

"Ha ha," she mumbled as she made her way to his office.

"Mr. Tate," she managed to choke out.

Those big blue eyes peered from under black lashes, long feathery, so thick, the kind that breathed, "I have eyes only for you."

"Focus," she instructed herself.

"How do I look?" he asked.

Oh God, loaded question. She could speak eloquently about the market, stocks, CEO's, but this was bound to be a disaster.

"Um hum look you how..."

"Yes Ms. McKenzie, are we speaking Chinese? Do I look good?"

"Yeeeesss, like a sultry hero on the cover of a romance novel," she breathed softly in a purring fashion.

Raising his eyebrows, he said, "Um, that's great, I think?"

"Oh, did I just say that out loud?"

"Victoria is coming by."

"Of course, nasty gold digging hoe," again allowing her inner thoughts to escape.

"What?"

"I said like gold rolling in the doe. You know that Victoria is one classy girl," she said as a bead of sweat dripped down her brow.

"It's an important date. We haven't seen each other in a week."

Why was he so smitten with the spawn of Satan? Why, he was so kind and smart and beautiful. Why her?

"Next week we have the Manning's Gala. I bought her this." He pulled out a bag and in it a vintage Versace gown in Kelly green. "What do you think?"

"She doesn't deserve it."

"What?"

"What?" she repeated, realizing she just said that out loud. "It's perfect."

"That'll be all Ms. McKenzie."

"Molly, you can call me Molly."

"Okay, great."

"The wicked witch of Manhattan is coming," she grumbled as she returned to her desk.

"When are you going to give up this ridiculous fantasy that he will give her up and choose you?"

"She doesn't deserve him."

"He is doing mankind one giant favor taking the bitch off the market."

"What would you know about that market?" she said.

"Hey I happen to be selective, nothing wrong with wanting perfection," he answered.

The sound of the stilettos crashing against the tile floor sent shivers up her back.

Hunter started humming dun da dun da dun da. "Look out for falling houses."

Victoria entered the room as if confidence were her middle name, wearing a white skin tight knee length Gucci with a tiny black belt cinching her ridiculously small waist, making her massive breasts swell unnaturally. Her blonde hair, Gwen Stefani white, was cut into a blunt asymmetrical bob. Her stilettos were nothing short of five inches and her bag was more suited for carrying a small horse than the tiny bug-eyed Chihuahua that peeked out of the top. She was the ice queen.

"Secretary!" Like clockwork she snapped at Molly. "Announce me."

"Yes, ma'am."

Hunter cowered in his corner as Victoria leaned into Molly's face. "What did you call me?"

Umm, stumbling over her nerves she blurted out, "Ms. Cromwell, Mr. Tate has a surprise for you."

"Nice recovery," Hunter whispered under his breath.

The look of a lioness before she ate her prey softened slightly.

"A surprise?" she asked.

"Yes," Molly answered with a forced crooked smile, one corner of her lip quivering, the other side trying to fake enthusiasm.

"Ms. Cromwell to see you sir."

"Listen up peon, hold all business, and I mean all. Do you understand? I mean all business," the lioness warned.

"Thanks Nelly," Sebastian responded.

Sneering at Hunter, Molly wagged one finger and gave her most threatening stare, "Don't."

With that, Victoria disappeared behind the doors of Mr. Tate's office and the room temperature returned to normal.

"Hey girls," said Jackson the mail person, addressing Hunter and Molly.

"Oh that was a great one," said Hunter sneering. Hunter despised Jackson and the way he drooled all over Molly as if she were a melting ice cream cone.

"Important document for Mr. Tate, will you sign for it Molly?" Jackson said with an ear to ear grin.

Pushing her black glasses back on the ridge of her nose, Molly answered, "Yes Jackson and thank you for knowing my name. Are these all the Manning's papers? Mr. Tate has been waiting for them to be messengered over. I wonder why they arrived via regular mail."

"They didn't," smirked Jackson. "I paid the guy to let me deliver it so I could see you again. How about we get coffee today?"

Hunter gagged into his trash can. "If only I could change the channel from another episode of "As the Losers Date."

Ignoring Hunter, Molly awkwardly said, "Well I…"

"Should I play some soft music, maybe light a candle?" Hunter asked.

Buzzzzzzzzzz.

"Oh wow, that was intense, I better get in there, sorry Jackson, duty calls."

"Saved by the bell." Hunter laughed.

"Don't you have something better to do? Like crawl back in the hole you came from?" said Jackson.

Grabbing the paperwork in its folder Molly jumped up, slamming hard into the same corner. Bang, the same knee met its familiar fate.

"Rounded corners," said Hunter.

Barreling through the doors to the office, she tripped on a man's shoe and fell flat on her face in front of the desk, papers flying like a windstorm in the desert. She popped up to see Ms. Cromwell naked on Mr. Tate's desk. Sebastian's tie dangled around his naked chest. The thought of what he had on underneath that desk forced her to keep her eyes fixed to the ground.

"Oh God!" She stumbled to get the papers and hit her head on the desk, sending her glasses sailing.

Staggering to her feet, she attempted to straighten out her blouse, and said, "I, I, I'm so sorry, the buzzer it was going on and on and I…"

"Sorry, awkward one, I must have sat on the buzzer when Sebi here was going down on my…" said Ms. Cromwell.

Molly coughed loudly to cut her off.

Victoria didn't bother to grab her clothes. Her body was even more amazing than Molly imagined. Those breasts larger than life were even perkier and rounder than a brand new softball. Must be fake and the stomach the result of endless crunches with a personal trainer, no doubt.

"Kelly!" yelled Mr. Tate. "If you are done cluttering my office with a plethora of papers, can we have some privacy please?"

"Yes I, I can't seem to find my glasses."

Then a slim, long leg with a red stiletto stomped hard on the plastic frame.

"Oops," said the voice from above.

"There they are. I'll just get them later." Don't look up, don't look up she repeated to herself. Grabbing as much paperwork as she could head down, she reached up and laid the Manning's folder or what was left of it on the desk.

"The Manning's paperwork you have been waiting for was rushed over." Then blindly she hightailed it to the door. Slammed right into the door jam.

"Crap," Molly said, reaching for the two inch bump now protruding from her head.

"Ouch," said Sebastian. "Are you okay?"

"Yes, I have a very bad astigmatism. I've had glasses since I was nine. Blind as a bat, didn't see a thing, honestly," she squeaked as she felt the hives mounding on her neck. Two more steps to safety and she slammed the door behind her. Leaning hard on the wall, she attempted to regain her breath. Raking her neck, she stumbled to her desk.

Squinting one eye, Hunter did a once over. "Is that a bump on your head or did you spontaneously sprout a unicorn horn? Where are your glasses? Do you have Chicken Pox? What the *hell* happened in there?"

Rambling she went on, "naked desk hit head, butt on buzzer."

"Do you need some ice, a drink, a shrink?" asked Hunter. "Start from the beginning, Pookie, this should be rich."

As her story reached its climax, Hunter burst into tears. "Very bad astigmatism, smooth.

I really need to drill a hole in that wall," he said, grabbing his side from laughter.

"You're not helping," she said as she attempted to slick back the loosened hairs from her bun.

"I knew she had work," said Hunter. "That nose, classic Belton. All the a-listers go to him for work."

"What are you, Joan Rivers? I don't care about her work. My retinas are forever seared with that image. I'm not feeling so good. I think I may need to go home," she said, again scratching the red raised hives on her neck.

The door flung open and the perfectly manicured Victoria strolled out, every hair in that bob perfect. Not one piece out of its precise place. She smirked as those stilettos crushed against the floor like glasses breaking at a Jewish wedding. With a flush on her face, she dropped the bent glasses on Molly's desk. "I had a surprise for him too. I asked you to hold all business. Do you have a hearing problem as well as a sight issue? Is that Amish hairstyle pulling on the few brain cells that keep you breathing?"

Flinging her bob, she strutted to the door, but not before warning Molly, "You better not have screwed things up, or you will pay." The door to the elevator closed as Molly let out her breath.

"What did she mean by that?" asked Molly, still shaken up.

"I don't know, still marveling over no sex hair," said Hunter.

"What just happened there? She threatened me. What did she mean?"

Hunter stormed over to her desk. "It means, Pookie, that she doesn't want him reading those papers for some reason. This is Tate's big chance. She's up to something and she has him right where she wants him, weak, confused, in a testosterone coma. You know everything about that account, go in there and tell him what you think," demanded Hunter.

"I can't, it's not my place."

"Not your place? You have an MBA from Wharton and you run around here like a temp in high school."

"I know I could do so much more," she said, trying to fix her glass rims. "But this is the business world, you must work your way up."

"No, you have been here for three years, you should be up by now! Admit it, you won't leave because of him."

She knew it was true, she graduated cum laude from Wharton. Yes, the economy was bad when she took this job, but the chance to work at Waters and Price was every business student's dream. With that on her resumé, she could go anywhere. Marketing could be a fickle field she told herself. Learn the business from the ground up. Mr. Tate still hadn't given her any real important assignments, but she knew every merger, every deal and every potential client on the map. After all, she did her homework. Above and beyond the call of duty, she researched each client, read all the major magazines and stayed current on trends in the field. Her social life was non-existent. Every weekend she spent working in her sixth floor studio apartment with one goal only, the hope of impressing the one man who she idealized.

Buzz. "Mandy," said Mr. Tate.

Darting from her desk, she tried to bend the mangled glasses now resting sideways on her face.

"How do I look?"

"Girl, do you really want me to answer that?"

"Never mind," she said as she ran to Sebastian's office.

"Ms. Cromwell was in such a hurry to leave she dropped her datebook on the floor. Can you hurry and catch her please?"

"Datebook? Yes, sir. I'll do my best," said Molly, running out the door.

"What's that you're clutching so tightly? American Idol results?" asked Hunter.

"Better," said Molly.

"Intrigued, tell me" said Hunter as he pounced from his desk to hers.

Barely releasing her tightly clenched hands, she laid the book on her desk.

"It's the witch's datebook. She was in such a hurry to go she didn't realize she dropped it."

"Jackpot," said Hunter, reaching for the book.

Slapping his hand away, she pulled the book back.

"We shouldn't. It's not right. I'm going to take it downstairs and try and find her."

"Weak," he said.

Rounding the corner, she caught the elevator right before it closed. Three other people who avoided eye contact stepped inside. *Good, now I can't look, not that I would want to.* At floor ten two stepped off. There still stood one lonely traveler who would keep her honest. Floor six, as he walked away, so did her conscience. The door was barely closed before her hands ravaged the leather-bound cover.

Meeting with Collins Real Estate Agent Todd Burns December 9th, 12 pm.

Dinner with Amelia at the Randling Inn, December 10th.

Dr. Belton's December 11th, 10 am.

"Damn, Hunter is right about the plastic surgery guy."

Francesca's Salon December 12th, 8 pm with Tia.

Mani Pedi Lola's December 13th.

Meeting about M with W 9:00—Saturday. The Lizards Lounge December 13th.

Lola's dog grooming appointment December 14th

"Tough life," Molly moaned as her fingers frantically paged through the datebook.

Nothing glaring stood out about what Cruella was up to. Maybe Hunter was wrong about her. No, he was right and she knew it. Victoria was sneaky and up to no good.

The elevator door opened and Molly slammed the book closed.

"Hey, Walt, did you see Ms. Cromwell?" asked Molly.

"Sure did, she just got into one of Mr. Waters' limos," said Walt the doorman.

"Mr. Waters? Are you sure?"

"Bastard got away with the charges and fired me from his fleet of drivers. Everyone attached to him at the time was let go. Randy, a buddy of mine, took a position there about two months ago. We just spoke a few minutes, you know catching up, and he said he was working as a limo driver for Mr. W."

"Thanks Walt," Molly said before she strolled back into the building.

Hunter was right. That snake was playing Sebastian and the Manning's deal was square in the middle of it. Should she tell him? Tell him what? She had no proof. Yes, proof was what she needed.

The floor had all but cleared out. With just weeks until Christmas, the usual holiday madness had descended on the city. Momentarily getting lost in the elevator music that had turned to all holiday, she began thinking about Christmas. Her shopping was finished, just some last minute wrapping left to do. Hunter had promised beer, pizza and a ridiculous caroling fest while helping her wrap. Her gift for Hunter was safely wrapped and tucked under the tree. She learned the hard way from Christmas's past that he was a snoop. This year she was ahead of him. The elevator doors opened to Sebastian with his black wool coat and gray scarf.

"Still here, Collie?"

"Molly, and yes sir, just need to finish up a few things," she answered as she slipped the book under her blazer and ran her nails across the hive on her neck.

"It's Friday night and I'm sure you have some plans. Don't stay too late."

"Plans, yes, of course, I do have plans to go out. Yep, out on the town. That's what I do on Fridays."

Oh my God! How lame did that sound? she screamed in her head.

Casually walking away from the elevator, she moved to a sprint to get back to Hunter.

"Holy Crickets, you won't believe what happened," she said, slamming the book on his desk.

"Holy crickets? Really?"

"Focus, the witch is working for Waters."

"Now you have my attention."

"Walt told me. We need to find out what is going on, but how?"

"You still have the book, don't you?"

"Yes."

"It's time to work it, Sherlock Holmes."

"I'm not very good at that type of stuff."

"You don't say. Bring it tonight. Wrapping just got a whole lot more interesting."

"I have a bad feeling about this."

"You need to go in there and read the Manning's papers. Find out what is so urgent about the campaign rules."

"Are you trying to kill me? I'm not good at stealthily breaking into someone's office," she said, wiping her forehead.

"Really, the door is open and the man is gone. Pebbles Flintstone could crack this case."

"Fine, but this goes against my principles," she said, walking ninja-like, looking side-to-side.

"Did you ever break a rule before? Forge Mom's signature, took your parents' car, snuck a boy into your parents' house?"

"No, for heaven's sake, why would you ask?"

"Remind me not to choose you as a partner in crime."

She opened the folder and skimmed the paperwork. "Not seeing anything yet. Wait, there are pages missing. Cruella took them. How did she do that without him seeing?"

"Sex coma."

"What does that even mean?"

"It means he has been rendered completely useless. It's up to you now, Red."

"It's true I don't want him to be hurt. I couldn't stand to see those big blue eyes sad."

"Well for you it's all about protecting your fake boyfriend from heartache, for me I need to protect my job. Now let's get moving.

I'll see you at seven."

This was a bad idea, but if Cruella was working for Waters she needed to warn Sebastian. He would be eternally grateful and ask her to dinner. After dinner he would take her dancing and maybe out for a nightcap. Who says "nightcap"' she asked herself, interrupting her perfect scenario.

She packed up and headed home to Henry.

"Come here my little lovebug," she said, snuggling the droopy faced pup.

A kiss, albeit a wet slobbery one, but a kiss nonetheless, always waited for her behind her door. *Dogs aren't a man's best friend, they are a girl's substitute boyfriend. Dogs never lie, never humiliate you and never cheat on you. Really, they are the answer to the whole dating mystery thing.*

"Knock, knock pizza's here. No garlic for my little vampire, extra pepperoni and ranch dipping sauce," Hunter said, carrying pizza, beer and a stack of DVD's.

"You are the best. What would I do without you?" Molly asked. "Where's Kyle?"

"Fighting with Jeffery, he'll be here in a few."

"So, do we decorate first or dissect the book?"

"Oh we are going in on that book first," he said, grabbing three plates and a stack of napkins.

"Okay, but I must warn you, there isn't a whole lot of information to go on."

"Fear not, the great Kyle is here. I'm known for my decoding of information. Hand over that juicy little tidbit," said Kyle, entering the apartment with bells around his neck.

Molly handed out the plates and grabbed a slice.

"Where is the garlic?" Kyle barked.

"You know Molly is allergic," said a very protective Hunter.

"My bad, never remember that dear."

Flipping through the book, Kyle mumbled, "Let's see what we

have to work with. Dog grooming, blah, blah, meeting with real estate agent, blah, Dr. Belton, bitch has good taste, dog grooming blah, bingo!"

"What, what does it say?"

"It says we are scheduling you for an appointment at the very exclusive Francesca's."

"What are you blabbing about over there?" she asked.

"Our girl has an appointment for a wax with Tia at Francesca's, we need you in there. Waxers are like hummingbirds, ask them anything and they will sing like a canary on Red Bull."

"I do not even know what that means," said Molly.

"It means you go in and pretend you're good friend Vicky recommended Tia to you. You know, say, 'She just raves over your waxes girl.'"

"Have you met me? What would indicate to you I would be able to pull something like that off?"

"Maybe because the love of your life is about to get screwed royally by the ice princess, and you could be the heroine that prevents that," said Hunter.

"He would probably be so grateful to me." She sighed, floating around the room. "Okay, I'm in. I'll do it."

"Atta girl. We will convert you to the dark side yet little one," said Kyle with a sinister laugh.

"But for now we are wrapping presents and singing Christmas songs," she said, dancing merrily across the room to the CD player.

"As festive as that sounds, Jeffery is coming over. We need to talk about things," said Kyle.

"He's a jerk. You're too good for him. There are plenty of men in Manhattan. Why do you take his nonsense?" asked Molly.

"Sometimes we go for the bad guy. Love is tricky, you can't always pick who you fall for," Kyle said before grabbing a beer and throwing a piece of crust to Henry. "Have fun, you two."

"He's right you know, you can't help who you fall for," said Hunter.

"Are we talking about Rachel?"

"Yeah, kinda, whatever."

"You're mumbling, that's my job. Is there trouble in paradise?"

"No, she's great, is that the Beach Boys Christmas?" he said, changing the subject.

"She's beautiful and built, even if she is a bit of a dodo bird," said Molly.

"She's okay. Now let me see that music selection."

"We have Bing and The Carpenters and…"

"You know I must love you to spend my Friday night in wrapping with you while listening to the Carpenters."

"I know you do," she said, singing her version of Karen Carpenter's "Merry Christmas Darling."

Molly mixed up a few Mistletoe Martinis and the two giggled their way through wrapping.

"Is there even a present in that one?" she slurred, holding a clump of paper with a few strands of tape and a mangled bow on top.

The two fell into the couch giggling. Hunter put a bow on Molly's head and asked, "What would you like for Christmas, little girl?"

"I must have mistletoe, new Uggs—pink please, new glasses—maybe yellow and Sebastian under my tree."

"Why is that darned mistletoe so important?"

"When I was little, my mom used to tell us fairytales about the beautiful princess who found her true love at the stroke of midnight. That is when the magic happens. She will know him by his kiss. My birthday being on Christmas Eve and all I sort of rewrote my fairytale, so that the princess will know her true love by his kiss under the mistletoe. Always been a Christmas geek."

"But the cutest Christmas geek I've ever seen," he said. "Then mistletoe you shall have little girl."

"Have I told you yet today how much I love you?" she asked, resting her head on his shoulder.

"No, but it never gets old," Hunter said, wrapping his arm around her shoulder. The two fell fast asleep wrapped in a snowman afghan while watching *It's a Wonderful Life*.

The next morning Molly jumped up in response to the buzzing of her alarm. Stumbling over Hunter, she managed to slap the button to turn off the humming of "Jingle Bell Rock" blaring from her phone.

"Who sets an alarm on Saturday morning?" said a still groggy Hunter.

"I'm sort of regretting that decision now. My head feels like it spent a few rounds in a shrinking machine. It's those darned Mistletoe Martinis, how many did I have?"

"Not sure, but if the wrapping is any indication, a few too many," answered Hunter.

"Christmas is going to stink. I don't have my fake boyfriend to bring to the family holiday. My presents resemble the remains of a failed attempt to compact them with a trash truck. I don't have a real tree and I have no mistletoe. It is not Christmas without mistletoe. Do you realize what this means?"

"I'm afraid to ask."

"Christmas will come and go with no mistletoe and my fairytale will never come true."

"Red, you're growing a hive the size of a small cantaloupe on your neck. Calm down. We will avert the crisis. Make some coffee and give me a minute to make a plan."

She hurried into the kitchen and brewed up some high test coffee. Throwing two bowls on the table, she grabbed the Captain Crunch and spoons. "Okay, what have you got?"

"Captain Crunch? You expect me to be brilliant on Captain Crunch?"

"Stop whining. Do you have a plan or not?"

"Sebastian, being an important businessman will be stuck overseas on a weather delay. Yes, that works. The gifts, well, look at it this way, we get to unwrap a bunch of gifts and then rewrap. Yeah, that sounded better in my head. Mistletoe, we will find. New York is a big city, but first you need to get your appointment with Tia."

"What do I ask for? Silvia always said I should shape my eyebrows. How bad could that hurt, right?"

"Right, make the call."

Hesitantly, she pecked away at her cell phone trying to muster up her best undercover skills.

"Ello Francesca's Salon," answered a woman with a broken accent.

"Umm, hi, I'm looking to get a wax," Molly mumbled. Putting the phone down she whispered to Hunter, "that sounded awkward right?"

"Nah, not at all."

"Jes, when would you like to come in?"

"I would like to schedule with Tia, if that's possible."

"Jes, she is in this afternoon. One o'clock, jes?"

"Jes, I mean, yes, that is perfect."

"Name?"

"Molly, I mean Kelly, Kelly Hunter."

"Okay, see you at one."

"Thanks," Molly said as the woman hung up on her. "Jeez, that was weird. I could hardly understand her and today, really? I'm not sure about this."

"You'll be fine. Just act like Victoria is your best friend and she talks so highly about her and blah, blah, blah. You know what Kyle said—she'll spill all the details about her fabulous client."

Pulling at her eyebrows in the mirror, she repeated, "I don't know about this."

"It's for your love. If she is working with Evan Waters, she is undermining our company and we are all collateral damage."

"Why can't you do it?" Molly asked.

"I don't know, I kinda like my brows."

Throwing a Santa pillow at him, she filled her Captain Crunch with milk and sipped her coffee.

"I tell you what, while you get the info, I'll seek out some mistletoe."

"You would do that for me?"

"Since you did prepare me this fine breakfast, it's the least I can do."

Kissing him on the forehead, she headed to her bedroom to change. Today green glasses were her choice to complement her crème cashmere sweater and black corduroys. Crème Uggs, a black fur trimmed coat and houndstooth scarf finished her look. She headed down fifth toward the swanky salon. The stores were filled with scurrying shoppers. Carolers stood by the vendors selling roasted chestnuts. Santas rang bells, collecting for the Salvation Army. So filled with the holiday spirit, she almost forgot the task ahead. But there it was right in front of her, the upscale salon. The windows filled with fluffy white snow, twinkling white lights and large silver stars. Peeking into the salon, she took notice of the clientele. Dressed in leather pants, sheer blouses and heels she suddenly felt even more awkward about trying to pull this off. Reminding herself Sebastian needed her, she adjusted her scarf to tug at the new pinkish hive brewing. She pulled open the door and entered. A dark-haired young woman greeted her from behind the desk. She took her name and offered her sparkling water or a glass of wine. She instructed her to take a seat on the white leather sofas. Tia would be with her soon.

Molly studied the women as they came out. Her nerves started to stir. A large framed article on the wall above a glass table caught her eye. The article talked about the five sisters who came from Brazil to start the best waxing salon in the city. She sighed and felt a wave of relief. Her fear of leaving with one eyebrow suddenly melted away as she listened to the soothing melodic music and daydreamed about Sebastian's undying gratitude.

"Hello, Ms. Hunter," said a short, stocky, gruff looking woman.

For a moment she had forgotten that was her undercover alias. "Yes, that is me. Kelly Hunter."

"This way," said the woman, waddling to the back down a dimly lit hallway. The whole spa experience was quite relaxing. Molly was beginning to see why people spent the money. The woman opened a door and pulled out a large white fluffy robe.

"You can undress and put on the robe on."

Strange, she thought all this pampering for a couple of eyebrows. The rich really knew how to live.

The woman entered and quickly headed toward a pot filled with hot wax. She stirred it gingerly with a wooden spatula and collected a pile of strips. "Here you can lay down right here on the table. Soothing hypnotic instrumental music mixed with the sounds of water filled the room.

Before Molly knew it she had relaxed onto the table and started in for the information. "I requested you because a dear friend of mine, Victoria Cromwell, suggested you. She says you're the best."

"Victoria is your friend?"

"Yes, we go way back. We met when she got Lola, her dog."

"Oh jes, she is very lucky lady. Things are really going her way."

"Yes absolutely. She has it all," said Molly, eying the woman opening the robe.

"Did you see the rock Evan gave her? That diamond must have cost him a cool million," said the woman as she pulled Molly's leg over and spread a large dollop of hot wax on her inner thigh.

So stunned by the rock announcement, Molly temporarily hung her mouth open unable to speak. Then the sting of the hot molting wax adhering to her thigh snapped her out of her shock. "I, I wanted my eye b…" Without acknowledging her pleas, Tia placed the waxing strip on her thigh while ripping at the same time. Before she could finish screaming, another blob of hot wax was dropped dangerously close to her lower parts.

Molly let out a death curdling scream, saying, "Rock, as in diamond?"

"Yes, they are picking their new penthouse out and planning the honeymoon all at the same time."

"I, I…" and then another rip. "Holy crap," shrieked Molly. "What the hell was that?"

"We specialize in Brazilians, Vicky told you, right?"

"Umm she, I, I don't feel so well. I think I need some water, a washcloth, a…"

Molly opened her eyes to a soothing cloth on her forehead. She heard the sounds of water falling in the distance and felt a cool breeze blowing in her face. Then she realized what had happened.

"I continue?" asked Tia.

"Nooooo, I'm good. Thanks."

"I only did half of your…"

"Nope, that is exactly what I wanted. I'm sort of bipolar that way, one side and done. Perfect," she said, looking down at her red bumpy half stripped body.

"You are the customer. Tell Victoria I said hi. Are you going tonight?"

"Yes, I am going tonight with Victoria," answered Molly, hoping the canary on Red Bull would start singing.

"The Lizard Lounge is the hottest place in town. After she and Mr. Waters have that business meeting there, I think they are going to announce their engagement to a few close friends, so nice, right?"

"I can't wait. I love the Lizard," said Molly, trying to swing her half dead thigh off the table.

"I see you next month?"

"Yes, yes you will," said Molly, trying her best to sound convincing.

If she thought she felt awkward entering the salon, now her off kilter gait dragging one leg behind her made that pale in comparison.

After she left, she quickly called Hunter.

"They are the Brazilian masochists. They don't do eyebrows!"

"Breathe. What are you babbling about? More importantly did she give you any clues about Victoria and Waters?"

"Oh God, I almost forgot. They are getting married."

"You forgot? Holy mother of mercy what is Cruella up to? She is hanging around Sebastian for a reason, and we need to find out what it is."

"Yes, tonight they are going to a business meeting at the Lizard Lounge."

"Get home, Nancy Drew we are going dancing tonight. And dress sexy, the Lizard is the hottest club in town. Brazilian, huh?" Hunter said before hanging up.

Molly waddled into her apartment and flopped wearily on the couch. Henry snuggled up next to her, resting his head on her lap. She grabbed the plump dog by the slouchy jowls and asked, "Henry, what am I doing? I can't let the bitch hurt Sebastian, but this is crazy. I already lost the first three layers of skin on my left thigh. I don't have a good feeling about this."

His droopy eyelids mirrored exactly how she felt. The Pug nestled up closer against her and let out a snort. Yes, staying on this couch with Henry would certainly be safe but looking around her apartment, taking a quick life survey, she realized where safe had gotten her.

"No Henry, I'm going to do this."

After all, this was for the man of her dreams. Molly went straight to her closet. *Something sexy huh, that part may prove a bit challenging.*

She didn't exactly have a section designated as such. Her rows of black pants, white shirts and endless rows of flats didn't exactly scream "siren." Then, in the back of her closet, she spotted the dress she bought for that fateful New Year's Eve when Thomas broke her heart. She never actually got to wear it, but saved it just in case. Black three quarter sleeve knee-skimming dress with a leopard peter pan collar. Yes, she would pair that with black stockings and black flats, of course. After all, sensible shoes made sense in the event it turned into a late night. Glasses were easy, leopard large-framed ones with a touch of gold.

"What do you think Henry? Does it say va, va, voom?"

Henry snorted loudly before falling back to sleep.

"Hey, guess who's joining us on this mission?" Hunter said, calling Molly from the living room.

"I'll be out in a minute Hunt, putting the finishing touches on sexy."

Opening the door, she twirled into the room. "Voila."

"Wow," said Hunter with one eyebrow raised high.

"Wow, as in you look sexy, wow?" asked Molly.

"Wow, my fifth grade teacher Sister Lynette showed more skin."

Joining the two, Kyle darted through the door.

"Party people, are you ready to dance?" Then abruptly stopping, he leaned back on the door with this eyes squinting.

"Oh, please tell me that outfit is like an onion. That outer layer peels off and underneath is where the real outfit lives."

"No, no sadly, that is it. It's more of a double duty outfit, by day, great for the library, and then by night, well I got nothing," said Hunter.

"You two do know I'm in the room right?"

"You see Molls, this is the Lizard Lounge. It's hip, sexy, wild, you know all the things that outfit isn't."

"Alright already, I got it, but this is all I've got."

"Heels, you don't own heels?" asked Kyle.

"Well yes and no. I have one pair, but we all know I'm not that good in them. You remember my last attempt yielded a broken heel, not to mention nearly a broken ankle."

Kyle placed one hand over his mouth, took a deep breath and said, "I think I have an idea."

"Please say you can magically zap that into something resembling sexy," said Hunter.

"Let's get moving. We can stop at the studio on the way. I have shoes in every size, shape and style. We can dust on some makeup and maybe revamp that frock. Time's a wasting," said Kyle.

"He has that look on his face. That scares me," Molly said, grabbing her fur-trimmed parka.

"What do you think you're doing with that?" said Kyle, whipping the coat from her hands.

"It's twenty five degrees outside. Do sexy people have more insulation?"

"No girl, we just suck it up and freeze."

Talmen Studios outfitted some of Broadways biggest shows. Kyle worked as a makeup artist on the set. He also helped Jeffery with costume design. Having keys to the studio was a perk he earned after ten years on the job.

The three entered the studio through the back doors.

"Wow, this is amazing," said Molly, examining the endless rows of shoes, dresses, gowns, coats and just about anything one could imagine.

"We have every major designer in here. It's like a little piece of heaven," said Kyle. "Sit down, my little starlet." He leaned back and sighed. "Okay first thing's first—that hair." He pulled the tightly wound bun out of its knot. Cascades of coils tumbled down her back.

"Wow, that is some crazy-ass hair. I love it. It's perfect, just as wild as it is!" said Kyle, running his fingers through her spirals.

"Are you nuts? I look like a mangy poodle!"

“Trust me, I got this,” he said, dusting her face with a bronzer. “Now go in the dressing room and flip your dress around. I need the zipper in the front. Meanwhile I will pick out a fabulous belt and matching shoes.”

Doing as instructed, she looked in the mirror at her unruly mop and the sight of her dress on backwards and felt that overwhelming feeling of a hive brewing.

“Oh yeah, and ditch those black tights,” Kyle said.

“It’s cold! What do I wear on my legs? Where is Hunter?”

“He is fetching a belt for me, dear. Now hurry along.”

Kyle took one look at her and said, “Yes, a huge multi-chain gold necklace should lay right over the exposed skin we will achieve by unzipping that to about here.”

“Hold on cowboy. That is a bit low,” Molly said, zipping the dress back up.

“Good Lord, woman, are we going to Sunday school or the hottest club in town?”

“Got it,” said Hunter, running down a flight of stairs and locking his eyes on Molly.

“Wow, you look, dare I say—a little sexy?”

“Not what I’m going for here,” said Kyle, proceeding to cinch the waistline of the dress with a thick black belt and pulling the dress up around four inches above her knee. Now slip these babies on,” he said, handing her a pair of red stilettos.

“Oh no, no, no. We’ve already discussed how my last heel adventure went. “I have no time to hobble around on crutches for a month?”

“True,” Said Hunter.

Ignoring her completely, Kyle went about fluffing her curls and spraying a fog of Aqua Net through them for more volume.

Standing back, he examined his work. Cocking his head to the left, he let out a sigh.

“Now what?” Molly asked.

"I'm not feeling the glasses."

"Need them to see, Einstein."

"We can take them off when we get into the club."

Molly clumsily crawled into the back of Kyle's car and the three headed toward the Lizard. "Does this wretched vehicle have heat? I feel like a naked Eskimo protesting clothes."

"Really, stop the whining, hot people just warm from their inner goddess. Work it, girl," said Kyle.

"Working it here, still feels like my goose bumps have grown goose bumps of their own."

"See, that will thicken your skin," said Kyle as he attempted to park on a side street.

"Come on Rebel Eskimo, let's get that goddess going," said Hunter as he pulled her from the back seat.

The club was everything Molly imagined and then some. Her heart thumped from the pounding of the bass. The large open room lit with only beams of lighting on the dance floor and large glittery balls of light that sporadically dangled from the ceiling opening to five levels above. Balconies surrounded the dance area, each filled with club goers. Women wearing little more than their underwear shook things Molly wasn't even sure she had. Her feet stuck to the surface of the black and white tiles.

"So, what do you think?" asked Hunter.

"I imagine this is how one feels awakening from a near death experience. My chest feels like I have danced with the electrodes of resuscitation paddles, my ears are bleeding, rendering me deaf and I lost my eyesight back when you fools took my glasses."

"Fun night, right?" said Kyle.

"How in God's creation do you expect we are, A: going to find them? and B: ever be able to hear a blessed word they say?" asked Molly.

"Oh ye of little faith. I, The Great Kyle, have thought of everything. Do you guys remember Landon?"

"Landon, the paranoid obsessive compulsive boyfriend you barely escaped with your life from, Landon?" asked Hunter.

"Yep, that's the one. Remember how he bugged the whole apartment, elevators, even the cat to find out if I was cheating?"

"Yes, he listened in to your every move, including bowel movements," said Hunter.

"Is there a reason for this conversation?" asked Molly.

"He works here. He is the hostess. Yes, I said 'hostess.' He prefers to be addressed as such. He takes reservations, books tables etc. He diligently spent the day on the lookout for Waters' reservation. Turns out he has booked the fourth floor for a private meeting at nine and then at ten it opens to their engagement party."

"Still not following how we are going to get in that room or hear anything," said Molly, rubbing her heel, which had now formed a blister.

"Landon, luckily for us, still dabbles in eavesdropping and still finagles the little bugs into the darndest places. He has set one under all the seats. The sound waves travel about fifteen feet. The problem is the table is thirty feet from the door, so that wasn't going to work."

The conversation stopped abruptly when Victoria and Waters entered the large double doors and headed toward the hostess stand. Landon, calm as a cucumber, greeted his prey and led them to the glass elevator, first giving a wink to Kyle.

"Oh my God, they really are together. I can't believe it…"

Molly stopped when she saw Landon coming back. He walked nonchalantly past them to greet a man they didn't initially recognize. And then at the same time they said, "It's Bigsly from Manning's firm they are meeting!"

Landon rushed the three to the elevator and disappeared.

"What's the plan? Hurry," said Molly.

"That's the part I'm not sure you're going to love. Here are earpieces. Once you get in range they will sort of squeal first before the sound clears," said Kyle before handing each a small earbud.

"Ok, how the hell do you expect us to get up there and not be noticed?"

"That's the thing. Landon reserved a cage for you to get up there," said Kyle, half squinting.

"I'm sorry, it sounded like you said a cage?" said Molly.

"Nope, he said an open air elevator," said Hunter, winking at Kyle.

"Yep, that is it. Kinda funky way of getting up there but open so you can stop on that floor and listen."

"Alright, let's do this," said Molly.

"Hunter, here is a hat for you so they can't recognize you or see your earpiece."

"I can't see three feet in front of me. Three fourths of my face is covered with hair, I don't think we need to worry about them recognizing me," said Molly, whose knees banged mercilessly against each other in her wobbly heels.

Kyle opened the door to the cage. A brass pole was centered inside.

"At least they had the good sense to put a rod to hold onto for balance in this thing. I'm not even sure if this is safe," said Molly.

Locking the cage, Kyle pushed floor four and released. "Good Luck Hunter, you're going to need it."

"Yes Molly, that is exactly why they put that pole there. What other possible use could there be?" Hunter smiled, hoping she wouldn't notice the scantily clad women riding the poles in the cages next to them.

"Woo, I can barely get my footing. This doesn't seem too safe." And then, like clockwork, she spotted the woman next to them upside down, legs spread wide in the air and another woman under her straddling the pole.

"Wait for it," he said.

"Awwwwww, oh my God, do you know what these poles are for?"

"I had a sneaking suspicion."

"Now what? What are we supposed to do in here? Do you have hand sanitizer? If I had my parka, I would have gloves."

"Oh shit, I don't know, but you better start busting a move quickly. We are eye to eye with Victoria."

"No, no, no. I agreed to spy—that even sounds horrible—but stripping, that is off the table."

"I'm pretty sure you can keep your clothes on Sandra Dee, but you better use that pole for something that resembles sexy or our cover is blown."

Hunter started dancing to the sexy thumping of the techno beat as Molly watched, jaw hanging.

"Where did you learn to move like that?"

"Come on," he instructed as he put his hands on her hips and gyrated them with tiny thrusts back and forth.

"I feel like I need to go to confession," she said, awkwardly twisting and thrusting like she was having a convulsion.

"Feel the music. Let it take over. Hold onto the pole, swing yourself around and I'll catch you."

"I don't know about this," Molly said before flailing around the pole. Her ankle twisted and she lost her balance. Hunter threw his arms out and caught her, ankles bending, dress flying, hair flinging over her face.

"I just gave the whole world a show," she said, shaking and holding onto him.

"I'm pretty sure the show they are watching is not in our cage."

A squeal indicated they had reached a safe distance to hear and as promised the conversation clearly erupted in their ear.

"So Victoria set up Sebastian to take the fall for losing the campaign. Price will fire him. I will offer a buyout and you, Mr. Waters, will once again be the owner of Waters' advertising.

The plan is simple. Tate uses the false information I leaked to him suggesting that the theme for the Winsor campaign is sexy, wild, and sleazy. Once they announce Winsor decided to go for a more wholesome campaign, they will show Tate's entry first and his inappropriate push the limits ad will bury him. Price will most likely fire him on the spot, leaving a perfect entrée for your pitch," said Bigsly.

"Did you hear that?" Molly said, adjusting the earpiece.

"I sure did, but we have bigger problems. Waters is staring directly at us. Start dancing."

Molly began a jerky version of the hokey pokey. Left arm in, shake it all about, her lips moved silently as she recited the song in her head.

"Are you seriously doing the hokey pokey?"

"Yes, you know how I get when I'm nervous. It's all I've got."

Without thinking, Hunter grabbed her by the waist, hoisted her up on his thigh and began grinding on her, his hands traveling up and down her back.

Her face crimson red and her eyes like saucers, Molly spoke not a word but hung on for dear life. For a moment she completely forgot why they were there. She gazed into Hunter's big green eyes and thought how remarkably handsome he looked in that hat.

"Push the button," he said.

"Hmmm?" she answered.

"The button to get us out of here, push it."

"Oh yes, that button," she said sliding down his thigh and adjusting her skirt. Her mind a bit rattled, she lurched toward the button and pushed the down arrow. It must have been the rush of being a spy, the loud music, the euphoria of the whole club scene that made Hunter look so damn sexy. Crazy, she reminded herself as the cage dropped down a floor. A couple opened the door and asked, "May we?"

Neither Molly nor Hunter peeped. The couple entered and

started working the pole. The man slid his hands up her shirt and pressed her tightly to his chest. In response the girl wrapped her arms around his shoulders and jumped onto his hips. Straddling him, she leaned into a backbend, her skirt riding dangerously high. Molly slapped both hands over her eyes and flattened herself to the outside of the cage. Hunter turned away and faced Molly, blocking her view.

"Hey, you can come out now," he said as the metal box came to a stop.

Kyle waited at the foot of the cage. "So?"

"We've got to get her out of here. I think she is hyperventilating," Hunter said, pointing to a flushed, panting Molly. She struggled to balance herself as the thick crowds of people pushed and shoved. An overzealous, large man carrying two drinks plowed into her, sending the drinks down the front of her dress. Startled, she jumped, losing her footing, sailing across the slick floors, landing on her back.

"Watch where you're going dork!" said the burly man as he stepped over her.

Wiping the front of her dress, Molly stared up at Hunter. "You see, this is why I don't go to clubs. Do you see any Christmas spirit here at all?" As she attempted to stand, her ankle gave out from under her.

Scooping her up in his arms, Hunter carried her to the safety of the car.

"We need to act quickly. You saw the campaign Sebastian has ready to go, spring breakers going to a nudist camp wearing only their sneaks. It'll blow up in his face," said Hunter.

"But how? He is dead set on that campaign, the music and the actors. We don't have time to shoot a whole new one," Molly said.

"Tomorrow is Sunday, we work on a new pitch," said Hunter as he helped her out of the car. He bundled her up in his arms and carried her into the apartment building. Inside the elevator, he swung her around to push the button. "See that, we make a great team, Red. Now come on my little sexy dancer, let's get that ankle up."

"Sexy dancer, really, you're going to make fun of me after the night I had?"

"Oh, come on, Sport, you were fabulous," Hunter said, shaking one arm in front of him while singing the hokey pokey. "No, really, there is something to this. It may catch on, you know the next trendy dance sensation."

Throwing a large pillow at him, Molly tried to grab him and lost her balance, falling squarely into his arms. He bundled her up and their faces were inches from one another. Suddenly, feeling uncomfortable, the two pulled back.

"Hey, what do you say I get you some ice for that ankle?"

"Yes, please. I warned you and Kyle about me and heels, but no one would listen."

Molly put on her p.j.s and curled up in bed with Henry. She rubbed the Pug's rumpled skin and nestled him close.

"This, Henry, is what I call enjoyable. Who needs loud clubs with unfriendly people?"

The dog let out a long snort in agreement. Hunter entered the room with a bag of frozen peas wrapped in a pillowcase.

"Girl, it's a good thing you don't eat veggies or you'd be screwed."

"Ice machine's not working again," she moaned.

"Tell the landlord. It's been like two months."

"Hunt, can I ask you a question?"

"If I answer, will I have to kill you?"

"Ha ha, no, this is serious."

"The dead ice machine wasn't?"

Molly sat up in her bed, propped lots of pillows behind her back and asked, "Am I a dork?"

"Is this a trick question?"

"Hunter!"

"No. Why do you ask? Because you never leave the confines of you apartment? Or because your only friends are Gus and Lou from the homeless shelter? Or because you spend most Saturday nights cooking for them and rounding out the night with a rousing game of bingo?"

Feeling a tear well up in her eye, Molly hopped out of bed and hobbled to the bathroom, shutting the door behind her.

"Hey Red, I was joking. Come out of there. I'm sorry. You are the sweetest, kindest, funniest most wonderful girl I know. If that's a dork, get me one of those tee shirts that says, 'I Love Dorks.'"

Gradually, Molly peeked out the door. "Do you mean it?" she said, sniffling.

Hunter pushed open the door. "Come here," he said before wiping her tears and enveloping her in a bear hug. "You know I do. What's really going on here? Since when has the great Molly McKenna ever cared about what other people think?"

Limping over, she slumped onto the bed. Henry grunted.

"All this, this craziness tonight, was for him. I just want him to notice me. I'm not his type. You even said so when I first started and every day since. Sebastian likes sexy, worldly women, not dorky girls who like hanging with the homeless crowd. I don't know what I was thinking."

"Hey, you were thinking you like the guy and don't want to see him get hurt. Keeping our jobs is another perk. Seriously Red, you are a great girl. Any guy would like you if they got the chance to know you."

Hunter picked up her pea-wrapped ankle and propped it on a pillow, pulled her blankets up tightly and kissed her forehead. "Get some sleep, tomorrow we must be brilliant."

"Hunter, we are the best team in the business. We will create a perfect campaign. Selling it to him will be the hard part."

Hunter left Molly and her frozen pea bag all alone to think about what the hell she was doing.

The next day Hunter tapped lightly on Molly's apartment door, then let himself in. He was greeted by Henry. "Afternoon sir, are you ready for a big day? Hey Red," he said to Molly coming out from her bedroom, red glasses on. This meant business. "We gonna do this thing?"

"We're going to try with everything we have. Although I'm not entirely sure that is much."

"We have plenty of time, it's only three o'clock."

They pulled up all the information they had on the Winsor Company, that for years used a marketing plan where their shoe sold concepts of sexy, youth oriented, brilliant and successful to it's consumer. Molly wondered why they had changed their image to include everyone regardless of age. That didn't matter. What did matter was a kickass campaign that sold wholesomeness, family and reached across all age ranges. Five hours later covered in papers, Molly lay upside down on the couch, hair scraping the ground with a face of defeat.

"We're doomed. What made me think we could do this in one day? It took the firm months of data collecting, image boards and collaboration to create that add.

The apartment door opened with Kyle on the other side. "Here to see brilliance in action."

"Wrong apartment." Hunter sighed.

"Nonsense, you two are like two brains separated at birth. You just need to get your minds in sync. Do you want the witch to win? Were all my efforts for nothing? I think not. Get up off that couch and start brainstorming. The night is young."

"He's right, we can't let her win," said Molly, piping up.

"Kyle, we need caffeine and a lot of it," Hunter said.

The two worked together as though they shared one brain. Ideas were flying and ten hours later they had finished a campaign that was sure to blow Sebastian's socks off.

"Now we have exactly two hours to sleep before we have to knock this pitch out of the park. See you bright and early."

Chapter Four

The pounding on her door jarred Molly out of a sound sleep. She rolled over to find her ankle soggy from thawed peas. Her eyes were swollen from her mini meltdown and her ankle still throbbed. Not two minutes later Hunter barreled in.

"What are you doing in that?"

"That, as in my bed, or my p.j.s?"

"Do you know what time it is? We need to be in the office in twenty minutes. With the holiday crowds on the streets we'll barely make it if we leave now."

"Crap, I must have forgotten to set my alarm. Here, help me up. Grab my black pants and tan blouse. Flats, I'm gonna need flats.

"Do you have super powers that can weld that mess on your head down?"

"Crap, get me my industrial hair gel."

She brushed and slicked and smushed and gelled and finally some semblance of a bun appeared.

"Let's go."

"Hunt, you know I can't think without my cereal."

"Way ahead of you, grabbed a few of Kyle's makeup donuts he bought for Jeffery."

The two pushed and squeezed their way through throngs of holiday shoppers. The streets were filled with vendors selling just about anything one could think of. They slammed through the glass doors and yelled for someone to hold the elevator.

"The twelfth floor please," said Molly.

"My decorations really set a festive tone, don't they?"

"Not really noticing them at the moment."

"There he is," said Molly breathlessly. "Such a perfect creature. We need mistletoe."

"Yeah, yeah, let's get Mr. Wonderful's attention."

Molly only now realized that speed walking on a sprained ankle may have been a tad premature as she struggled to walk toward Sebastian in a sexy sophisticated manor. Ethel from graphics sped around the corner spilling a tray of Christmas powdered donuts on Molly. With two smudges of powdered sugar squarely on her nose and red and green sprinkles smeared with a touch of jelly on her blouse she managed to get out, "Mr. Tate, may we have a word with you?"

"Yes Milly, I need to speak to the two of you as well. My office in ten."

"Did you hear that? Milly, oh my gosh do you even know how stinking close that is to Molly. One vowel my friend, one vowel. This is progress. This is good. I need lipstick or perfume or..."

"A mirror would help Milly," said Hunter.

Pulling the small eyeglass shaped mirrored compact from her desk, she flipped open the lid and screamed.

"Good gravy, no one could bother to tell me I looked like the Pillsbury dough boy before I approached Sebastian?"

"Yeah, if that powder wasn't on your nose everything would have been different."

"This is the single most important pitch of my life. It's not just a career changer, it could be the start of a beautiful romance."

"Your endless optimism should be a benchmark for all, yet somehow its sounds so, what's the word? Ridiculous?"

"Laugh now, but when I am Mrs. Sebastian Tate, Vice President of Marketing, you will eat your words."

Buzzzz. "Milly, Hunter, my office now."

"When he says it that way I think he actually is saying Molly, just with a thick sexy accent."

"Yep, that's it Milly."

Collecting herself, Molly grabbed the large pile of notes and sketches the two had worked on feverishly all night. She could do this. Her campaigns always gained major attention in college. Her professors named her the campaign queen. Executing a pitch was child's play, but she had never really pitched an entire campaign to Sebastian, though certainly he had used many of her ideas that she subliminally passed on to him. Molly knew how to change his mind without him knowing she had, but to actually show him what she was made of drove the knocking of her bony knees to a deafening decibel. Hunter was great—he listened to her pitch and drew the sketches of each slide of the commercial. He even put the whole thing to music on her iPad. But Hunter was different. They shared a bond. Nothing ever felt uncomfortable. She had flaws, of course, but Hunter never cared. He hung on her words. He finished her thoughts. They were two peas in a pod. And now he would stand by her side and give her the strength to impress the man she adored.

"Ready, Red?"

"No, but here goes."

Knocking once, Hunter opened the door. There he sat, eyes sparkling, teeth gleaming, five o'clock shadow beckoning her touch. "Focus," she reminded herself.

"Hello, team. I know you mates said you needed to talk to me so you have the floor. Please remind me I also need to talk to you after."

Molly set up her iPad and connected it to the projector. Hunter set up the sound. Sebastian stared blankly.

"Ok, so I know the Winsor campaign is just about wrapped, but if you will hear me out I think it will be worth your time."

"I'm all ears."

"The campaign is without a doubt sexy. You know spring breakers at a nudist beach in just their Winsor's."

"Genius, right?" he said.

"Maybe, but if we look at the demographic that wears Winsor's, the age spans from infant to senior citizens. This campaign will reach high school and college kids but may fall short with young parents, the baby boomers and seniors. I think a message that will embrace people of all ages while showing the shoe would be marketing genius."

"Hmm, I'm listening."

"Roll it, Hunter," Molly said as she walked up to the screen.

Passing Sebastian, she got a whiff of his woodsy cologne and felt her brain softening.

She needed to get it together. Stand tall, speak with authority.

"First scene, a grandpa and grandma in their rockers on the porch, their twelve-year-old grandson sitting beside them asks, "Pops, how'd you get the girl?" Grandpa looks down at his Winsor's and smiles.

We see a series of events play out in Grandpa's head. First Grandpa running track in college wearing his Winsor's, Grandma smiling as he goes by.

Second, Grandpa at the middle school dance along the wall. He takes the floor in his Winsor's and starts breaking it down. A young girl (Grandma) smiles. He motions for her to join in.

Third, a young grandpa in kindergarten sees a little girl with a bow in her hair crying because her doll is on the other side of a puddle. Grandpa bravely hurdles the puddle (close up of the Winsor's) to rescue her.

And last, Grandpa as a newborn in the nursery next to a little baby girl in pink smiling at him, camera goes to the bottom of his blanket and he has on tiny Winsor's.

"Grandpa gives the boy a wide grin, reaches for Grandma's

hand and then points to his Winsor's and says, "Son, you need to have game!"

Whew, she did it, her hands sweaty, knees banging and a hive the size of her fist mounting just under her bra strap, but she did it. Hunter shot her an expression of pride and managed to slide a small thumbs up under the table.

Silent at first, Sebastian pushed his seat away from the table and clapped vociferously.

"Milly, that is probably the best campaign to come out of Tate and Price to date. Get the creative team working on it. We need actors, music and the film crew. Tell the graphic design team we need the baby grandpa to wink. I love it. I'll call and let them know we are sending over our campaign by noon tomorrow."

"You, what, okay, great…" she stammered.

"Not tomorrow," interrupted Hunter. "We think you should keep this under wraps, say, until maybe the night of. The committee views and decides right then and there, right? Why tip your hand?"

"Hmm, you may have a point. We will stall as long as possible."

"Oh, and Mr. Tate," Molly said in a whisper.

"Yes."

"Maybe don't tell Victoria. I'm superstitious and all. You don't want to ruin anything, right?"

"It will be hard not to share this with her, but you might be right. We need this win. This is the biggest contest in Marketing. The winner will skyrocket to fame."

Packing up their iPad, the two, beaming ear to ear, headed to the door.

"I almost forgot. Milly, what are you doing Saturday night?"

"Saturday? Me? I?"

"I would like you to join me at the Sentinel Children's Hospital for the dedication of the new orthopedic wing."

"I, me?"

"I'll take that as a yes. And Hunter, I need you there also. Milly, take the business credit card and get something festive to wear for both of you. You'll be handing out the coloring books and crayons we've ordered for the kids. We will also be donating a substantial amount to the wing in our name."

"Yes, of course. What time?" Molly said dreamily.

"Be there by six, bells on. It is Christmas, you know. Tate and Price will be spreading holiday cheer in a big way this year."

Molly floated out of the door and dropped to her chair. "My dreams are coming true. My love is taking me on a date. A real date."

"Hmm, why then, am I coming?" asked Hunter.

"I don't know. I suppose you will be giving out the gifts while I'm linked arm-in-arm with Sebastian as we donate the check."

The smile plastered across her face quickly vanished with the sound of clinking heels on the tile.

"Oh God, she's here. What if she recognizes us from last night? How can I look at her when she is trying to hurt my man? What will she do when she learns he is taking me instead of her?"

"Announce me, minion," said Victoria, her bob swinging perfectly.

"Mr. Tate, Victoria is here to see you."

"Splendid, send her in."

Victoria waltzed in like nothing was wrong between her and Sebastian.

"Scheming witch deserves to get dumped, even though she isn't really going out with him," said Molly.

Not two minutes later the two appeared at Mr. Tate's door engaged in a lip lock that would have Michael Phelps gasping for air. Molly, dumbfounded, couldn't break her gaze from them.

"Until Saturday night, my love," breathed Victoria. "We make such a lovely couple. The picture for the paper with us donating to charity will be divine."

She moved slowly and deliberately to Molly's desk. "Try not to mess up handing out the gifts. Can you handle that and stay out of our way? I do see why he would have picked you for Mrs. Claus," she said, throwing her hair back while enjoying the sound of her own cackle.

After Victoria marched out of the office, Hunter slid over to Molly's desk.

"You okay?"

"She is using him, that harlot. How can she lie like that right to his beautiful face? Why can't he see it? I would never deceive him like that," she said, her face a deep shade of scarlet.

"Harlot? Red, he's not thinking with his head. Men tend to be extremely gullible when it comes to beautiful women. We'll get her. When we foil her plan, he'll see her for who she is."

"Why are men so stupid?"

"Age old question Red. Now let's get this campaign rolling."

Hunter and Molly went about the business of setting an entire commercial in the works.

The week passed quickly and Molly set out Friday to get some outfits for the two of them.

She remembered seeing fabulous Christmas outfits in the Christmas Boutique on Fifth. She did love Christmas, and giving gifts to children in the hospital certainly constituted true Christmas cheer. Doing this alongside Mr. Tate, a gorgeous, intelligent, sexy and charitable man would be icing on the cake.

Inside a pimple faced teenager in a monotone voice greeted her. "Welcome to The Christmas Boutique, how can I help you get your cheer on?"

"Why hello. Merry Christmas, and thank you for offering to help. I so want to get my Christmas cheer on."

The boy turned his back, rolled his eyes at the girl at the cash register and then turned back. "What do you need?

"I need to look festive, so maybe something red and green."

“That’s thinking outside the box,” said the boy who led her to the back of the store to what looked like an “ugly sweater party” exploded. “If you need me, just jingle,” he said, handing her a tiny set of bells.

“Jingle bells—I just love that. Thank you. I’ll have a look.”

There were sweaters with lights that blinked, sweaters that said “Ho, Ho, Ho” when you shimmied, sweaters that appeared three dimensional, and sweaters that even jingled with every step. But she wasn’t feeling anything until she turned around and saw it. There it was. *Perfect*, she thought as she grabbed a small for her and a medium for Hunter.

She worked her way to the sales girl and returned the bells. “These will be perfect.”

“Great,” said the girl, ringing up her total.

“Thank you and Merry Christmas,” said Molly.

“Christ, why don’t they get Ms. Merry Pants to work here?” the purple haired cashier said to the pimple faced boy as Molly walked away.

Walking down the busy New York streets, Molly hummed “It’s the Most Wonderful Time of the Year,” to herself. She smiled at fellow stone faced New Yorkers and thought how proud Sebastian would be to see her and Hunter dressed so festively to represent the company. Mariah Carey’s “All I Want for Christmas” chirped from her hand bag.

“Hello,” she said, smiling. That song always got to her.

“Hey Molly, we still on for Saturday night?” asked Gus.

“Saturday night, oh my gosh, I completely forgot.”

“It’s ok Molly, we at the shelter appreciate any time we see your smiling face.”

“No Gus, I will be there. I promised I have some surprises for everyone. I just may not get there until around eight. Is that okay?”

“Molly, I don’t know if you realize this, but homeless people don't exactly have busy dance cards."

"You will have the sing-a-long all set up, right? I dropped off song sheets and hot cocoa and marshmallows. Tell Lou I couldn't get a Santa this year, everyone was booked."

"No problem, sweetie, we will make it work."

Molly hurried home. There were so many presents to wrap and tag, it would be a long night. Lucky for her, Friday nights were usually quiet.

Saturday night came in a hurry. Time always seemed to fly around the holidays, despite Molly's attempts to stretch the season as long as possible. Truth be told, it couldn't get here fast enough. The chance to see Sebastian out of work and more than the normal two seconds of flirtation once a day was a dream come true.

"Knock, knock, you ready to go on your date?" asked Hunter, walking through her door.

"Sure am." Molly met him in the living room.

"Wow," said Hunter, his eyes bulging. "That is, wow, a whole lot of festive.

"Glad you like it because you are Mr. Claus," she said, throwing the packaged suit at him.

"Oh no, you want to be Mrs. Claus that's on you, but I'm all dressed for my date with Rachel after, so it's a no on the ho, ho."

Lowering her wire rimmed glasses and tucking the strands of gray hair back into her bonnet, she laid her head on his shoulder and stared up at him. "Pleaseeee, it's for the kids and a little for me."

Five minutes later he was donning a Santa suit and heading to the elevators. He opened her car door. "Your sleigh awaits you, Mrs. Claus."

"I must say you are looking fine, Mr. Claus."

They arrived promptly and met Mr. Price in the hospital foyer. "I say you two look marvelous. Here are the bags of gifts. The kids that can, will make it down. The others may require you two to visit their rooms."

The three headed to the new wing together. There they met Sebastian, alone. Mr. Waters entered through the opposite door.

"What the hell is he doing here?" asked Sebastian.

"I don't know but looks like he brought his own elves," said Price, referring to a group of leggy girls who could double for the Rockettes in tiny elf skirts with fur boots.

Molly looked at Sebastian as he eyed up the sexy elves, then turned her glance toward her puffy full length dress trimmed with fur up to the neck. Again, she had failed to get his attention. She blended in like the wallpaper. Victoria strolled in with a full length fur covering a red satin gown. *And there it is. Now I'm reduced to the woodwork.*

Molly watched the well-orchestrated dance between Victoria and Waters. She wondered if Sebastian even noticed the stolen stares.

"Mr. Tate, would you like to talk to some of the children?" asked Molly.

"No, Twit, that is what you and the other loser are for," said Victoria.

"Yes, she's right. I'm not much for kids. But Hunter seems to be doing a great job over there."

Could she have been wrong about the man Sebastian was? No, she decided, the bitch had a hold on him and he couldn't think straight, just like Hunter said. Then she turned to Hunter and her expression softened as she saw a little girl struggling with her walker to kiss his cheek. He "ho, ho, hoed" merrily, giving each kid plenty of time to share their wishes. Under the fluffy white face full of hair she could see the corners of his eyes smiling. He truly was one of the good guys. He motioned to her to join him as he visited the patients confined to their beds. She watched as he high-fived the boys, winked at the girls, listened to every Christmas wish and spread a glimmer of hope among the children. As they left the last patients room, Hunter's phone rang.

"I better get this. It's been blowing up all night," he said.

He answered the phone, and although she couldn't make out what he was saying, his face contorted to the color of Santa's hat, and she knew only Rachael could evoke that face.

"Sorry, I gotta bounce. Do you mind if we pick up Rachel on the way back? We are going to a holiday party with her agent, and she's a little testy. You know she thinks she's going to be the next Jennifer Lawrence."

"No problem. I need to get going to."

"Hot date with Henry?"

"No, if you must know, I have plans with Gus."

"Girl, you need to find a man who has teeth."

"Gus has teeth, for your information. I can't say that for everyone there, but yes, Gus does."

Sebastian and Victoria interrupted them at the end of the hallway. Sebastian's face was blazing angry.

"Waters brought game systems for the kids and he donated twice our amount. Bastard," he said, wringing his hands.

"Mr. Tate, the kids don't care about all that. You brought them joy tonight. That's what truly matters," Molly said.

"She's precious, right?" Victoria said, wiping the tears from her eyes. "Really, my side hurts when you speak. You ought to try standup comedy, dear."

Sebastian, so involved in his defeat, paid no mind to either of them.

The two walked toward the car, Molly's face red with frustration. "She is too much. We should tell him what she is up to. He is going to be crushed."

"Hold on there, Sassy Pants. Think about that. We aren't one hundred percent sure what she is up to. What if she is working with Sebastian to bring down Waters? Do you even know what kind of fools we will look like?"

"Oh my gosh, is that even possible?"

"I don't know Red, but I know the campaign you designed will put Tate and Price at the top of the advertising world. Everything else is a guess."

"I guess you're right. It just feels wrong knowing about her and Waters, if she is with him. But Sebastian would be angry if we spied on her and it was all his plan. I'm so confused. This night has been awful."

The two left the party and went to pick up Rachel, who brought a whole new level of holiday angst to the night. After ten minutes of ranting about not being able to make an entrance, she motioned to Molly and said, "Is this why you were late?"

Molly, still in her costume, slunk deeper into the back seat.

"We did a nice thing, babe. You ought to try it sometime. You know the holiday giving thing kinda feels good."

"Not my thing."

They pulled up to the apartment building and the group headed upstairs for Hunter to change clothes.

Molly gathered her presents. She lugged all three bags of gifts to the elevator.

Kyle, heading toward the elevator, asked if she needed help. "Where are you going with all those gifts Mrs. C?"

"I have some very special friends who need these tonight."

"Tonight?"

"Long story, but yes. I have some friends that I have very important gifts for. The weather forecast is calling for a nor'easter tomorrow. These may come just in the nick of time."

"I got you. You really are Santa's helper, aren't ya?" said Kyle, grabbing two bags.

"Something like that."

The two packed her small Honda to the brim.

"Thanks Kyle, you're a lifesaver. You going with Hunter to Rachel's bigwig party?"

"Yep, I just can't help but celebrity watch. Hey, wish those friends a Merry Christmas for me."

"Was that Molly heading out?" said Hunter as Kyle held the taxi for them.

"Yep, she packed her sleigh and is headed somewhere that she has a tremendous amount of friends. Still in costume, too."

"I think I know where she is going. Do you guys mind if we take a quick detour?"

"I mind," said Rachel, eyes like daggers.

"No, seriously, I think she is going to the homeless shelter on Broadway. We could help her unload."

"Really, homeless shelter? Have you seen how I'm dressed? I think sequined shorts and a satin cami are a bit overdressed for the bums."

"Did you really just call them bums?"

"Ok kids, let's simmer down here a minute. Hunt, why don't we drop you off? I'll take Rach, we'll pick up Jeffery and Molly can drop you at the party when you're done. Sound good?" said Kyle.

"Whatever," said Rachel, fixing her makeup.

"Great, thanks," said Hunter when they pulled up. "Look—there's her car around back. Kyle hand me that Santa suit. I was going to give it to Molly and ended up bringing it by accident, but I think I may just need it after all."

Hunter had a key to Molly's car, apartment, desk, so he used the car key to open Molly's trunk. He hurled a big bag of gifts onto his back.

*****

Molly worked her way through the kitchen toward Gus. "I'm here. Sorry, just Mrs. Claus this year. I have a few more bags in the car. I'll be right back."

"You look fabulous! Who needs Santa when you have Mrs. C?" said Gus. "Kids are all inside ready for the sing-a-long. Can I give you a hand?"

"No, I'll just go grab them. Be back in two. Before she could get to the door, the main doors swung open and in waltzed Santa carrying the rest of the bags.

"I thought you said you couldn't get Santa," said Gus.

"I couldn't."

"Ho, Ho, Ho and Merry Christmas friends. I see a lot of good little boys and girls here. Does anyone have a Christmas list?"

That voice, she knew it all too well. Tears rolled down her face when she recognized Hunter.

"What are you doing here?" she asked, sitting down next to him.

"I thought you might need a hand with that bag of cheer. What is all of this?"

"Nothing, I just got them each a coat, hat and mittens."

"Them, as in all of them?"

"There are only twenty one adults and ten kids."

"How did you pay for it?"

"Christmas bonus."

"You're too much, Mrs. C,"

"Right back at you, Mr. C."

Hunter snuggled each of the kids up in his lap and listened to their wishes, wishes that were so simple and different from the kids at the hospital. Each kid asked for one thing only. Molly stood by his side handing each kid a wrapped jacket and a candy cane. Shortly after, Gus rallied the troops to the center of the room for the sing-a-long.

Molly handed out the sing-a-long song sheets. Hunter made his way over to her as Gus started strumming his guitar.

"Thanks Hunt, that is the sweetest thing you've ever done."

"My pleasure, Red. You really are an elf, aren't you?"

"Just love the holidays and seeing a smile on people's faces."

Reaching into his pocket he pulled out his phone and excused himself. A few minutes later he returned. "Hey, Kyle said Rachel is freaking. You good here?"

"I sure am. I hope Rachel isn't too mad at you."

"She actually just found out she got a small part in a Broadway show. She's so pumped she probably forgot I'm not there."

"Not possible." She kissed him on the cheek. Thanks, Hunt," she said before joining in a rousing rendition of "Rudolph."

After the sing-a-long, Molly handed out the rest of the coats, gloves and hats to the adults. She and Gus warned of the severe weather coming their way and urged them to stay the night. Gus walked Molly to the car. "So who's the Santa?"

"My bestie."

"Is that all?"

"What do you mean?"

"I don't know, you must mean a lot to a guy for him to give up a portion of his Saturday night to play Santa to the homeless."

"We do mean the world to each other, but not that way. He has a girlfriend. He is really picky and this one has been around for a couple months, so I'm thinking there is something to it. Besides, he knows my heart belongs to someone else."

"If you say so Molly, but sometimes the things we are searching for are right under our mistletoe," said Gus, kissing her on the forehead. "Now go on home, you look beat."

"I'm sort of spent. Thanks—you sure you can handle the cleanup?"

"Absolutely sure, and I have Lou to help."

"Good night, Gus."

As Molly walked to her car, she thought about what Gus meant by, "right under her mistletoe?"

She picked up her phone and dialed Maxie. "Hey there, you

guys all ready for Christmas?"

"Sweet Potato, it's good to hear your voice. Mom is in Silvia mode, so the Christmas decorations rival Macy's but other than that we're ready to see you and more importantly meet your man."

Chapter Five

Molly would leave for Connecticut soon and the disappointment would begin. She and Henry would head home for the Christmas holiday sans boyfriend. The week rolled by and before she knew it, Thursday had arrived. Just two days before the big event. The chance for her campaign to make history for Tate and Price was right in her sights, but there was still the sticky little no boyfriend dilemma that dampened her enthusiasm.

A car accident—Sebastian was healing and couldn't make it. No—a break up, it was too much working together and all. No, face it Molly, you stink at lying. It would be easier to just fess up and say she made the whole boyfriend thing up so they would get off her back. *Molly the loser, Molly the only McKenna to die alone. Molly the sexual orientation challenged McKenna. Oh God, this would be horrible. The humiliation of that awful Christmas pageant would pale in comparison to this.* Molly headed to work alone this morning. No signs of Hunter. She sat at her desk wondering how she got herself in this mess but knew Hunter could help her figure it out.

Hunter strolled in with a huge smile on his face.

"You're late," said Molly.

"I know, Rach and I celebrated a little early this year. She leaves to go back to her folks' house this weekend."

"So you're going to be alone for Christmas?"

"I've got Kyle and Jeffery," he said, plopping a cappuccino latte with extra whipped cream on Molly's desk.

Taking a big gulp, Molly's eyes closed as she licked a dollop off her lip.

"I'm in heaven," she sighed.

"Uh oh, you must have slipped off a cloud because I'm pretty sure you're heading to hell in three, two, one," Hunter said, looking over Molly's shoulder toward the elevator. "The bitch is back."

This time, Victoria didn't even stop to berate Molly. She just stormed right in to Sebastian's office.

As any good employees would, the two plastered their ears to the door, hoping to catch a snippet of the yelling.

The door opened and the two nearly face-planted, trying to get out of Victoria's way. She didn't bother to pay them any mind, she just stormed her way to the elevator. Sebastian appeared, his eyes tearful and his face heartbroken.

"Mckenzie, please inform Mr. Price I will not be attending the gala Friday evening."

"Mr. Tate, why not? We have the campaign nearly finished."

"It doesn't really matter anymore," he said, his shoulders slumped.

"What doesn't matter, Tate?" asked Mr. Price as he rounded the corner.

"Nothing matters."

"Tate—in your office now," said Price, looking less than pleased.

Pacing back and forth, Molly alternated between wringing her hands and scratching the hives on her neck.

"She did it, broke his heart. I knew it. We should have told him. He is crushed. I just want to hold him and wipe away the tears from those sultry baby blues. How can I call myself the love of his life and allow him to have found out this way?"

"First of all, no one knows why you call yourself that. Secondly, one wonders how you have any skin left on your neck with that scratching. And third, we weren't really in the position to tell him. Trust me, we saved his ass from sabotage. We did our job. We aren't Match.com."

One long, agonizing hour later, the door to Sebastian's office opened, and he walked past the two without muttering a word. He headed to the elevator and disappeared.

"See that. He looks better to me," said Hunter.

"Really, that is the look of devastation."

A few minutes later, Mr. Price peered his head out of the office.

"You two, in here now," he said with heat in his voice.

"Oh God, he knows we knew. I need Benadryl. I can't take it. Maybe we are the reason she dumped him. Maybe we were spotted at the club."

"Pull yourself together, woman. It could be something entirely different. Let's go."

Mr. Price instructed the two to sit on the couch. He paced back and forth several times before speaking. "As you just witnessed, Mr. Tate is going through an awkward—if you will—break up. He feels as though he can't represent our company and face Victoria with Waters. She played him, but she won't bring him or my company down. That's where you two come in. He will need a date for Friday night. Not just any date but one of the hottest women in the city kind of date. He must walk in there with a first class beauty on his arm. Am I making myself perfectly clear?"

"Yes sir, but where would we find that type of woman in less than forty eight hours?" asked Molly, now slapping the swollen lump on her neck.

"The where isn't my problem, but it will be your problem. If you want to have a job come Monday you better get working."

He turned and walked casually out the door and down the hall. Molly threw herself on the couch face down and sobbed.

"Now, not only do I not have a boyfriend to take home, I'm jobless too."

"Hold your horses there, Ms. Negativity. We haven't lost anything yet."

"Where, where the hell are we going to find a gorgeous woman who will be available days before Christmas and just agree to go? They don't grow on trees?"

"No, but they do live in a certain little black book."

"You're brilliant," said Molly.

"Yes I am, if I must say so myself."

"Where do we start?"

"Okay, we run this like a job interview. We set up times with these beauties and we pick the perfect one from the bunch. It sounds like a slam dunk. Hardest part will be narrowing it down to one."

"Ok, we set up the appointments for tomorrow. How about Maggie's coffee shop on Lexington?"

"Perfect. I'll start with the first few, you take the next few."

Hunter started in the A's. "Hello, may I speak with Abigail?"

"Speaking."

"My name is Hunter Bentley. I'm an assistant to Sebastian Tate…"

Buzzzz.

"Hey, I think we go disconnected."

Dialing the number again, Hunter started with, "Hello this is Hunter Bentley. I believe we just got disconnected."

"If you said 'Sebastian,' it was not a mistake." Click.

Molly didn't have much luck either. "Do you think there is a coincidence here?"

"I think he pissed off a few ladies. Here, look at this. Written under a girl named 'Ann' he has the notation 'a real angel.' This is her. I can feel it."

"Hello," said a sweet voice on the other end of the phone. Ann did sound like an angel and agreed to meet with them the next day at eleven. They set up seven appointments in all. This would work. It had to, if they wanted to keep their jobs.

"I have a bad feeling about this. I wish I could be the one on his arm making him forget about that awful witch."

"Look Moll, we meet a girl—send her on her way and Monday we still have a paycheck. Stay focused."

The two packed up their belongings and headed to the elevator. They had one day to pull this off. Hunter kissed Molly on the head and left for his apartment. Molly opened her apartment door and plopped down next to Henry who was warmly snuggled against the heating vent.

"I don't think I get a *Christmas happily ever after* Henry, like in my fairytale. Who am I kidding? Sebastian doesn't even know or care I'm alive. Look at me," she said, pulling her tight bun out of its clenches. I'm not in their league. Maybe I was meant to be alone."

Mariah rang loudly from her purse. "Oh no, no, no, it's Mother," Molly moaned. Henry raised one eye and then rested his head on her lap.

"Don't give me that guilty look. She is relentless."

"Hello, Mom."

"Dear, we are all so excited to meet Mr. Tate, Sebastian, right? The house is perfectly dressed and we are just waiting for you to arrive. Did I mention the pageant is going to be spectacular this year? Your sister is sure to take first place. Keep it in the family. Molly, are you even listening to me?"

"Yes Mom, sounds great. I'll see you Sunday."

"Don't you mean we'll see you? Honestly, you don't know how long we have waited for this."

"Actually, I do. Bye, Mom."

"Ugg," she said, snatching a pillow from the couch and burying her face in it. "Henry, pray for a snowstorm that will bury the city."

Chapter Six

Molly climbed from her bed and rushed to the window. "Yep, nothing. Not even a flake. Damn it. Henry, today I get to go meet all the beautiful women who have come before me, all the women who have shared Sebastian's affections. Specfreakintacular!"

She slicked back her hair into its all too familiar bun and chose black plastic frames. Yes, it felt like a black day. Slipping on a black turtleneck she said, "Cut to the chase, I already know a hive will emerge at some point in this day."

"Ready, Red?" said Hunter, slipping his head into the apartment.

"Well, aren't you perky?"

"I'm the envy of most of the men in New York. Today I get the pleasure of meeting New York's finest ladies."

"Yay, yippee."

"Moll, where is my Christmas elf?"

"I'm trying, but this is not my idea of fun."

"We'll be in and out in no time. Hour tops."

They headed down to Maggie's, walking briskly in the wintery winds. The cold stung Molly's face and made her eyes water but helped divert her attention away from the grueling task ahead. Maggie's windows were a hodge-podge of Christmas decorations from eras gone by. A vintage Santa holding a slightly yellowed scrolled list with large multicolored bulbs strung window to window, a toy train set, wrapped presents, a red and white shovel, a table with cocoa and a tray of cookies. The regulars knew Maggie's was the place for homemade Christmas cookies. Each year she announced the cookie of the week. That week would highlight cookies from around the world. Not the largest place, but cozy and a place you could nestle into with a laptop or book and no one would rush you out.

Hunter opened the door and the obnoxious bells rang out loudly playing, "Have a Holly Jolly Christmas." Inside, Hunter pointed to a gorgeous brunette in a low cut sweater and said, "Bingo, I think Ann is the girl for us!"

He headed straight toward her and extended his hand. "Ann, Hunter, we spoke yesterday." The woman slammed her laptop closed and grabbed her coat. "Pervert," she said before heading to the door.

Two tables away a nun eating a croissant listened to the conversation. She wiped her face, shifted her habit back and threw up a hand, waving to him.

Hunter scratched his head, noticing the nun out of the corner of his eye. "Don't look now, but is there a nun waving at me?"

"Yes it appears so. Do you know her?"

"No, how would I know her?"

"You went to Catholic school, right?"

"In New Jersey. They don't have ESP."

The nun waved him over.

"I better see what she wants. It's probably a sin to ignore a nun."

"What could it hurt?"

"Hello, Hunter, right?" said the nun.

"Umm, yeah? Crap, they do have ESP."

"I'm Ann, we spoke yesterday."

"Jesus, you're Ann? Crap I'm sorry, father forgive me..."

"Nice to meet you," she said, smiling at him and pulling out a seat. "Join me. I'm interested in hearing what sort of favor Sebastian needs."

"You're a nun. I thought you dated him."

"Yes, I am a nun. You're quite observant. And yes, I did date him. He was actually the reason I entered the convent."

"That bad?"

"No, he was sweet and kind when I told him I felt conflicted about taking our relationship to the next level. We ended as friends. Can I help?"

"I doubt it unless you have any hot friends. Sorry. Damn, you are difficult to talk to."

Molly interrupted. "Excuse him—we are just in sort of a bind." She explained their plight.

"I wish I could help but all my friends are sort of spoken for by the big guy upstairs." She winked. "Good luck, you seem like good friends to Sebastian," she said as she headed to the door.

"This is a bad sign," said Molly, stretching the fabric away from her neck.

"Look, we got that out of the way. You know the worst is over. Right?"

"Holly Jolly Christmas" rang out as the door opened and a blonde carrying a ton of presents pushed the door in with her butt.

"That's Bally," said Molly. She said she would be wearing a red coat with black fur trim.

"Thank God," said Hunter, looking at the platinum locks that fell to her waist.

"Don't thank him so soon," said Molly as Bally turned around to reveal a watermelon sized bump under her jacket. She was more than willing to help but warned her water could break at any moment. Things didn't get much better. There was Colleen, the waitress who snorted when she laughed and whistled when she said 's,' due to her new braces. Then there was Danny who was midway through her transition to a male, an awkward mix of boobs and a beard, she made Ann look better and better. Elle, a fashion model, was perfect except she brought her body builder boyfriend who dangled Hunter above the toy train threatening his life if he contacted her again. After four hours, a large woman with three chins walked over and greeted Molly and Hunter with a bear hug guaranteed to crush a spine. She sat down and immediately started reminiscing about Sebastian. Hunter's eyes glazed over as he studied the rotund woman.

"You look surprised?" said Farrah.

"I didn't expect you to, well to…"

"Be so big?" Farrah laughed.

"I'm not the girl he dated, but she is still inside," she said, pointing to her stomach.

"You ate her?"

Kicking Hunter hard under the table Molly listened as Farrah told her love story with Sebastian. Lovely, funny and sweet, Molly wished Farrah would meet the approval of Price, but sadly she knew this was not the woman he spoke of. Farrah explained she would love to help but quite honestly wasn't interested in going backwards. Hunter sighed with relief. Molly applauded her strength.

After Farrah left, panic crept in. With one possible contender left, things were looking bleak. Then the door of Maggie's swung open and in walked one of the most beautiful women Molly had ever seen. Her long black silky hair shined in the twinkling lights. Her body was simply outstanding. Every eye in the coffee shop was drawn to her like a magnet. Hunter quickly flipped open the little black book to refresh himself on any notes. "ROG" written in red across the entire page signaled this was one hot woman. The acronym stood for something. Really, outrageously gorgeous, ridiculously outstandingly, great, the possibilities were endless, but the bottom line was they had found their girl.

"Hello, my name is Gina. I believe you called me about Sebi. I must admit I was surprised at first but if anyone can help him it's me. We were engaged and shared a home. Our history is deep. If he needs me, I'm there. Name it."

"As strange as this sounds, we were wondering if you could accompany Sebastian to an event tomorrow night. I know it's sort of short notice, but it would mean a lot."

The brunette's eyes lit up, her smile spread slowly across her face as she closed her eyes and sighed. "Finally, he came to his senses."

"Hmm, what did you say about senses?" asked Hunter, his eyes squinting a little.

"We ended quite abruptly. One day he mentioned his best friend had recently gotten married, so naturally, I took that as a proposal. I realized it seemed soon to some people given we had only known each other for two days, but I ran with it."

Molly stretched the turtleneck down, swabbing her neck with ice water on a napkin to slow the developing patch of hives.

"Long story short, that day I bought a wedding gown, broke my lease with my landlord and had all my belongings moved into his place."

"Naturally," said Hunter.

"Here's the crazy part," said Gina.

"We didn't get there yet?" asked Hunter.

"I arrive back to our home and the police are there to escort me out, slapping me with a restraining order. Crazy, right? It states I'm not allowed within fifty feet of Sebi. I'm glad to see that has been lifted, right?"

"You know, for your safety we are going to make sure of that, and we will call you with the details. Thanks for your time," said Hunter, ushering her to the door.

"No, no no! What have we done? This is insane. We introduced a psycho back into his life. This is bad, bad, bad, bad," said Molly, grating her neck, swigging Benadryl from the bottle like a flask.

"ROG, Restraining Order Gina, crap, that was a hard one," said Hunter.

"Now what? It's nearly six o'clock on Thursday, the day before we need a freaking date."

"Pipe down there Red. We still have time."

"Time for what?" she said, pacing while scratching. "We've tracked down everyone in that damn book except Marcy, who is out of town."

"Let's go home. We'll get something to eat, regroup and start calling every agency in the city."

The two braved the cold, crowded streets, stopping at Minnelli's for dinner. Molly's neck, now frozen, settled a bit from the row of hives.

A small Italian man greeted them. "So lovely, this young woman is. You take care of your girlfriend, my friend."

"Oh no, she's not my girlfriend," said Hunter, following him to the table.

"Why not?"

Molly blushed.

Hunter tripping over his own words answered, "She's my best friend."

"Exactly, my wife is my best friend too," said the little man handing them two menus and walking away.

"That was weird, right?" said Molly.

"Very. Could you imagine us?" He laughed.

"Let's eat so we can muster enough energy to make some desperate calls."

After a delicious pasta and chicken meal the two headed back to the apartment. They cracked a few bottles of wine and then picked up the phones. They dialed away explaining their plight to every escort agency in the city. Every girl was booked. They didn't give up. Around midnight, they started leaving messages for the New Jersey agencies. Night turned to day without the two realizing they had fallen asleep on the couch, phones in hand. Startled by a knock on the door, they popped up, banging heads.

"What, where are we?" Molly screeched in full on panic mode as she jumped to her wobbly feet.

"The door, the door," said a groggy Hunter.

Hunter opened the door to see Kyle with coffee and bagels. "All-nighters, not as easy as in college, eh?"

"What time is it?" asked Hunter.

"Noon. Did we drink a bit too much last night?"

Molly's phone sang Mariah. Flipping the couch cushions, she struggled to find it.

"Hello."

"Ms. McKenna, this is Price. I trust you were successful in finding a beauty for Tate. I need her here at the office by six. I believe Tate bought a very expensive dress for Victoria. You can stop by and pick it up for the young lady, size two. Hope she's a fit one. That is all."

"No, no, no," she said, lying face down on the couch.

"This is bad," said Hunter.

"What's the problem?"

"We need a girl by six o'clock tonight to escort Mr. Tate. We have six hours. We failed. We are going to be on the unemployment line on Monday."

"Wait, why?" asked a very intrigued Kyle.

"Where are we going to find a girl in like, ten minutes?"

Kyle looked sheepishly at Hunter and then diverted his eyes to Molly flung on the couch with one leg over the back and her hand over her eyes.

"She's a girl," said Kyle.

"This is not a time for joking," said Hunter.

"I'm not joking. Do you need a girl or not? Last I checked Molly had all the parts to qualify as one. Sure, she needs a little—well, a big overhaul but that is why you two have me."

Molly peeked out from behind her hands. "Oh, hell no!"

"Molly, look at me. We don't have a choice here. We are out of options. Do you want to let Price down, the company down, and more importantly, the love of your life down?"

"This is a bad idea, very bad. Have you two thought this through? I can't walk in heels, need glasses and in case you haven't noticed, I'm not exactly a beauty."

"Get your coat Molly. I've got just the guy who can change all that," said Kyle.

As Molly retreated to the bedroom, Hunter pulled Kyle aside. "Are you sure about this?"

"Sure as ever, my friend. You go pick up the dress you speak of and meet me at the studio. Leave the rest to me."

"Hey Moll, what are you doing in there? Hunter is going to beat us to the studio."

Molly stood frozen in front of her full length mirror. Yes she knew her hair was unruly, at best. She knew her padded bras were her best friends. She knew that the words beautiful, stunning, gorgeous were not generally used in conjunction with her name, but she couldn't help but wonder what it would feel like. If she were being honest she secretly wanted to know what it was to be admired by every guy in the room, but this was a risk that carried way too much weight. Sebastian, the Australian god, would never be seen with a girl like her. But, what if, what if by some magical chance, Kyle and his studio could transform her? She had seen before and afters of the stars but admitted they had a better blank slate to start with.

Bang, bang. Kyle pounded on the door before pushing it open. "What's the hold up?"

"I'm not sure about this."

"Have I ever steered you wrong? My boy Levon is the best. You will be sensational."

"I'm not putting myself down, you know. I'm smart, and kind of cute, right? I'm just a realist. I know my potential. I don't want to let Sebastian down, or Hunter for that matter."

"Let's make a deal. We go—we give my boy Levon a chance. If you're not happy, you don't have to go through with it."

"Thank you, Kyle," she said, throwing her arms around his neck.

The two headed to the studio. They entered through the back entrance just as Hunter came flying around the corner dress in hand. Levon, a tall, pencil thin man with deep mocha-colored skin sailed around the mirrors in the dressing room.

"Welcome all."

Kyle took the dress in one hand and with his best Vanna White flourish, showcased the green sequined stunner.

"On this side, I have a dress, on the other side I have a girl. I need you to marry them."

Levon first examined the exquisite dress, the detailing, the open back, front side slit. "Remarkable."

Then he turned to Molly, who at this point had cowered deeper into her hooded parka.

"I see a dress. I'm not convinced there is in fact a girl in that lump of, dare I say, 'nylon.'"

"Molly this is Levon, the best damn stylist ever to hit Hollywood," said Kyle.

Molly slowly eased out of her hood and extended her hand. "Pleased to meet you."

"Off with the coat," said Levon.

Molly hesitantly slid the coat off. Levon walked around her, eyeing her from head to toe.

"What am I to do with this?"

"You need to make her look completely different," said Kyle.

"Obviously, but how?"

Levon pointed to her gray tortoise glasses and asked, "What is this?"

"My glasses?" said Molly.

"Shh…a rhetorical question." Next, he pulled the sleeve of her sweater up, examining her skin. "You make a vampire look as if she just arrived home from the Caribbean. I'm used to working with skin and bones, but it's usually accompanied by height." Last he pulled the claw out of her hair. The spirals twisted and turned unleashing a mane three times the size of her head. He gasped, leaped backward and gnawed on his knuckles. "I am Levon. I am fabulous, but I'm not a miracle worker."

Molly's eyes teared up. "Hunter, I'm sorry. I can't do this."

"Red, you are the most fearless woman I know. You kicked ass in that pitch. You have it all, that fool just needs to be clobbered over the head to realize it, but man, when he does, you will have your prince charming," said Hunter. "Molly, you're my hero, win, lose or draw—enjoy this!"

*****

Levon, may I have a word with you in private?" asked Kyle.

Pulling Levon aside, Kyle put both hands firmly on his shoulders. "Levon, have you ever loved someone from afar, hoped desperately they would notice you even for a minute? Molly's career rests on this night being successful, but more than that, it is her chance to impress the man she has loved from afar for three years. He doesn't even know her name. For a few hours she gets to be that girl he can't take his eyes off of."

"Everett Randal, senior year. God, how I adored him. I did everything in my power to get him to notice me, but no. Every stupid jock in the school had his eye. For everyone who has an Everett, I will do it!" he said, his voice breaking, then bellowing with promise.

Levon ran back toward Molly. He called out to his staff, "I need Joss in hair, Fredrick in makeup, Charlene for a mani and pedi.

Snap to it people, chop, chop."

He walked over to Molly and took both of her hands. "Tonight, darling, you will live the fantasy for all of us."

Molly rushed off, hand-in-hand with Levon.

A spray tan turned her milky complexion a warm shade of bronze. Levon studied her face before deciding to toss the glasses.

"Eyes are the windows to your soul. Why do you hide those large emerald green beauties behind the unforgiving plastic bottles? They are meant to be seen, and I'm pretty sure under those caterpillar brows are arches like the Golden Gate Bridge." He held her chin in his hand, tilted her head to the left then the right. "Good bone structure. With a little waxing and dusting…"

"Waxing, uh, I'm not really into waxing," said Molly, rubbing her fingers across her caterpillar eyebrows.

"Not a question darling, just a statement. Don't argue with me. I like the fullness but for God's sake, woman, tame them."

"Joss, hair consult, now," he said, pulling wiry ringlets apart while wincing.

Joss, dressed in black head to toe immediately began parting, combing and wrestling with her mane. Next charts of hair color strands were laid on her head. Then like a stroke of lightning, Joss screamed with a revelation. "Yes, yes oh yes. I've got this. It is a bit risky, but we're going for it," said Joss, grabbing handfuls of platinum blonde extensions.

"Risky?" said Molly, grabbing two handfuls of curls.

"Let the genius work," said Levon. "This is Charlene. She'll be taking care of your mani-pedi."

"I'm actually wearing closed toed shoes, so I won't be needing the pedi."

"Darling, the pedi is for when he slips those stilettos off."

"I don't think they will be coming off."

"Let me spell this out. They come off when you move your dance party to the sheets."

Molly's eyes widened, and a crimson color washed over her face. "I'm just going to a dance with him. That's all. It's enough, more than enough."

"We shall see, girlfriend. You've never seen the work of Levon."

Three hours passed and the moment had finally come for the big reveal. Levon zipped her in and instructed her to bend over and shimmy her boobs together. "Hmm, we need more," he said, opening a drawer and returning with two silicone cutlets.

"These are for what Mama didn't give you. Put one inside each bra cup and voila! Now you can shake what Levon gave you."

"That's awkward," said Molly, shimmying, tucking and molding her breasts. "I'm not sure how I feel about all this," she said, reaching for her black pumps from her bag.

"*Eeeek*, what the hell are they? Do not tell me those shoes are going to try and invade my masterpiece."

"They are the only heels I own."

"Don't move."

Two minutes later he returned with a box. He pulled back the lid and revealed the most amazing shoes she had ever laid eyes on. Six inch stilettos completely encrusted in crystals.

"Oh my gosh, they are magnificent," said Molly, her eyes wide.

"You better believe it. They are a down payment on a car. Now here's the deal. The actors don't show up for hair and makeup until one o'clock. I need those shoes back here by midnight. Got it, Cinderella?"

Molly slipped the crystal delights on her feet. Her heart skipped a beat as she attempted to stand.

"Would you like to take a look at the new you?"

"No, can I show Hunter first?"

"Your wish is my command," he said as he escorted her to the stage door. Stepping on the stage, Levon said, "Gosh, this is like the Biggest Loser reveal."

Molly's eyes lowered. "No, I mean in a good way girl. You are hot. Just wait until they see their loved one. It is my pleasure to introduce Elizabeth James."

Kyle and Jeffery clapped wildly as she took the stage.

Hunter's eyebrows raised as his mouth dropped. "Oh My God," he stammered.

"Really?" asked Molly.

Hunter ran to her, took her hands and stared. "You, you, I…"

"He means to say, 'wow,'" said Kyle.

"Molly, I mean to say, you are the most gorgeous woman I've ever seen. He won't be able to resist you, and I'm pretty sure he won't be the only man drooling."

"I haven't looked yet."

"Why not?"

"My sisters are beautiful. My mother is beautiful. Me, well I'm plain."

"You are anything but plain," Hunter said, ushering her to the mirror. He lightly covered her eyes and then on three took them away.

Her hair now layered and straightened, fell to her elbows. The fiery red color was softened by baby icy white blonde extensions around her face. Her milky skin was now replaced with a bronzed glow. The row of freckles that danced across her nose had disappeared, replaced with a flawless complexion.

Levon placed his hands on Molly's shoulders and said, "Breathe, you're looking the color of sea glass. Do not ruin what Levon has tirelessly created."

"I, I just never imagined I could be pretty," she said, a tear welling up in her eye.

"No tears, my love. You carry the weight of all of us who never felt pretty enough. Tonight you will live out the dream of every invisible boy and girl. Hold your head up high. Go find your prince," said Levon, his voice now trailing into a whimper.

"I'll do my best," she said hugging him tightly.

Molly, Hunter and Kyle piled into Kyle's car and headed to the Tate and Price offices. Hunter went over the plan. "Don't get too personal, don't drool over Tate, hold it together, remember you're a confident desirable woman. Lastly you must be back to the car by eleven thirty. This will give us plenty of time to get back the shoes back. And most importantly, avoid the bitch at all costs. You okay Red?"

"No," she said, shaking.

"This is it Red. The night you've been waiting for, for three years.

Molly moved toward the doors of Price and Tate as she did five days a week, only this time she didn't feel invisible. She made her way to his office and waited for Hunter to make his way up there for reinforcement. Walking inside Sebastian's office, she caught a glimpse of herself in the large window. Barely recognizable, Levon was right, she would do this for every guy and girl who just wanted to be noticed. She heard footsteps, and somehow her new found confidence disappeared faster than icing on a cupcake. She should run, yes that was the plan, until the door opened and there he was. She tossed her glasses and drew in her breath.

He didn't seem to even look up at her as he browsed a packet of papers in his hands. But then when he lifted his eyes, he looked at her. Right at her. Sebastian looked her up and down and smiled. "*You're* my date?"

"Yes, that's me," she said quietly.

Molly bit her lip with the thought of her role in this crazy plan, but it all melted when she saw the excitement on his face. For the first time in her life, she felt beautiful. Sebastian left to call for the limo and Hunter snuck in.

"I can't do this," Molly said, scratching her neck.

Hunter didn't answer at first. He just stared at her.

"What, what's wrong? Why are you looking at me that way?

Am I wilting? Is it a hive?"

"No, sorry, you just look so, beautiful."

"Really?"

"You can do this, Red, and not for Sebastian, or me, or our jobs, for you."

Molly hobbled over to him and wrapped her arms around him.

"Okay, well, the walking part is questionable," he said, helping to steady her.

"I warned you I can't walk in these, and I need my glasses and…"

"Stop, look at me. He won't be able to take his eyes off of you. Just remember we need those shoes back by eleven thirty. Now go watch your campaign bring us to victory."

"Did you get rid of crazy Gina?"

"Yes, told her the restraining order was still in place. I let her know we would call when it was lifted. Close one, right? We got this Red. Now go, enjoy."

Molly stumbled downstairs where Sebastian was waiting for her. He held her hand and opened the doors for her. He sat close in the limo, allowing his woodsy scent to tease her.

"Well Elizabeth, this night is not going to be what I thought."

How after two and a half minutes and an introduction memo with her name on it did he remember her name? How could he not remember Molly?

"I don't know how my assistants wrangled you up on such short notice, but I am sure glad they did. I had another date." He paused. "We had been together for a while and suddenly she tells me we are over and that she is engaged to my biggest rival. My whole career rides on the success of this night, and I honestly believe she timed it so I would fail."

"Sounds like an awful person."

"She is, and I do believe she may have done me the biggest favor of my life. Now how about you? What do you do Elizabeth, besides escort?"

"I'm a writer. I'm actually writing about the male and female rituals in the single world of New Yorkers. So when Molly asked me to fill in it was a win, win."

"Really, it must be fate."

The limo driver parked in front of the gala and opened the door. Extending his hand to Molly, he gave her the once over and smiled.

This is what Maxie and Meggie feel like every day.

"Okay, I must warn you, the sadist is in here somewhere, and I'm pretty sure she will attempt to discredit you in some way. Ignore her. Stay by my side."

Stay by his side, *hmmm*, she sighed. Her heels hit the pavement and reality slapped her in the face as she teetered back and forth.

"You okay? Here hold on," he said, pulling her arm into his. She sighed at the touch.

Inside the crowd was thick and many of the faces were blurrily familiar to Molly as some of Marketing's greatest. She knew them all. She studied their work. Molly had a dream of her own that would someday require a great deal of marketing, ad work and pure genius. She learned from the best, but for tonight she would focus on trying to stay upright while maneuvering partially blind.

They put their things down at the Tate, Price table, and Molly made out what looked like Mr. Price coming over. She hadn't really thought about him recognizing her.

"Hello, who is this beautiful creature?"

"Hey Price, this is Elizabeth, she's a journalist."

"My pleasure, dear. We have a pretty exciting night ahead of us. Tate here put together an ad campaign that will knock it out of the park. We stand to gain a lucrative, game changer. You are in for a real treat."

She smiled slightly and thought it was actually her ad that was about to make history, but this night wasn't about her.

“I’m going to make a quick trip to the loo. Can I get you a drink on my way back?” asked Sebastian.

“Just a Diet Coke, please.”

Molly scanned the room and spotted Victoria. Damn, she was sexy in an all-white Vera Wang gown cut down to her ribcage, revealing more boob than four culets. Molly watched how she worked the room, confident she had ruined Tate. The fireworks were sure to be memorable.

Sebastian returned with two drinks, left again and started to mingle. Molly was fine just sitting alone and watching this gorgeous man in motion. Then she realized Waters had marked them. He summoned the blonde bitch and they were headed her way. Molly grabbed Sebastian’s drink and threw it back. Coughing, she wiped the tears from her eyes, swallowing hard the burning sting of straight whiskey. Stand yes, move no, panic had engulfed her. Just then Sebastian came from behind. Putting his hand on the small of her back, he spun her around. Looking dead into Victoria’s eyes he said, “May I have this dance with undoubtedly the most beautiful woman in the room?”

“Look at her eyes, they are wild with the notion that someone could be more beautiful and that I found someone on such short notice,” said Sebastian. He ushered Molly onto the dance floor, pulling her close. She was certain he could feel her heart beating wildly. His eyes twinkling, he said, “Is this okay?”

Half singing her response she said, “Thissss, this,” pointing her finger back and forth between him and herself.

He smiled. “Yes, this,” he said, pulling her in closer. Their lips grazed before she heard Victoria behind her, demanding Waters dance with her.

“How about this?” Sebastian said before pushing his lips hard on hers. Wondering if she should have had her head gear on to protect her teeth, she was so startled by the kiss she barely moved.

“May I have your attention,” said a white haired man on the

microphone. "Please take your seats as we prepare to show you the work of some of the world's finest minds. As you know, A.J. Manning has set out to find the best to represent his new line of high end sneakers. The only parameters set were to focus on a more wholesome ad, steering away from the current trend of being overtly sexual. After the final contestant is shown, a winner will be chosen to market the Winsor. Sit back and enjoy."

*****

Sebastian's eyes met Victoria's. He remembered how she pitched the spring breakers at the nudist camp. Full exposure, pushing the envelope, making tongues wag. She was out to destroy him from the start. This was all a set up. How did he not know this was the theme? She must have managed to mess with the Manning's paperwork. Then he said, "Molly," out loud.

"Yes," she answered. "Oh God, he figured it out," she said, closing her eyes tight, waiting for the explosion.

"What?" he said.

"What?" she said.

"I'm sorry, I just realized someone in my office saved my neck, and I owe her."

Molly smiled. They watched as Victoria waited for Tate and Price's ad to run first and revel in their humiliation. Her face contorted as they announced first up was Moore Marketing firm. As each ad dragged across the screen with boring, outdated or overused ideas, Manning looked uninterested. Next up the Waters' campaign. A beautiful woman wearing an evening gown slid up her dress revealing a pair of white and black Winsor's and said, "They go with everything."

Sebastian and Molly looked at each other. "That was the big campaign?" Sebastian laughed. "She wasn't what I thought she was at all. How could I have missed that when it was in plain sight?" he asked.

"Sometimes the best things in life are right in front of you. All you have to do is open your eyes and see," Molly said.

"I'm looking and what I see is divine intervention. If Victoria hadn't done what she did, I would never have had the chance to meet you."

During the intermission, they laughed and talked about marketing and dating in New York City. Fortunately for Molly, she knew everything there was to know about her boss right down to his shoe size. This part was easy, she would just love what he loved, agree with him on everything. She could be the perfect woman for one night. Finally, the last ad of the night was Tate and Price. The film rolled and the audience remained quiet at first. Then each one sat up and began to pay attention. As Molly scanned the room, she could read their excitement until she met eyes with Victoria, glaring at her with that "witch hunt" look in her eyes. The crowd roared. Sebastian hugged Molly and high-fived Price. The celebration only got better when the white-haired man called Manning to the stage.

"This year we tried something different. I'm not going to lie—I thought it would be a difficult choice with all the talent here. But to my delight, one ad caught my eye and heart. The nostalgic, family-oriented piece is exactly the message Winsor is looking for. Without further ado, I would like to announce Tate and Price as the newest creative team to join our Winsor family."

Sebastian jumped to his feet, pulling Molly up with him.

"No, you go. It's your night," she said. He leaned over and kissed her forehead.

Tate and Price took the stage, shaking Manning's hand. Sebastian took the microphone. "I think I speak for the whole team when I say, wow, what an honor. Just to be in the presence of such talented people as all of you humbles me. If I'm being honest, this campaign started out in a different direction entirely.

Thanks to two of my staff members, I switched the direction last minute. So although they are not here, I would like to thank Hunter Bentley and Molly McKenna for their tireless work on this campaign." The crowd roared. Sebastian turned to Elizabeth.

Molly looked up at him, it was the first time he ever said her name correctly. Her heart thumped with joy. Molly, who had taken her heels off to rub her sore feet, hadn't noticed the bitch coming for her.

"You, you had something to do with this."

Molly jumped up, grabbed her heels and ran toward the door. Victoria chased her. Sebastian followed, chasing both of them.

"You and that troll, Molly, are in on this. You think you can ruin me," Victoria yelled as she closed in on Molly, grabbing her arm.

Molly struggled to break free without making eye contact. She pushed Victoria, making her lose her balance but not before the witch grabbed a heel. Molly ran.

"Stop her," said Sebastian to the doormen.

Molly jumped in the waiting getaway car and yelled, "Go, go, go!"

"What's wrong?" asked Hunter, pulling her in.

"Victoria knows it's me or doesn't but knows I had something to do with all this. Either way she almost tackled me and blew my cover."

"Did we win?"

"Yes, and he gave us credit up there in front of everyone," she said, holding him tight. "He said my name."

"We make a great team," he said, kissing her forehead.

"Okay, let's get those shoes back Cinderella," said Kyle.

"Oh no, the shoes, I only have one. She must have grabbed one when I broke free," Molly said, now nearing full hyperventilation.

"No, this cannot be happening," said Kyle.

"I'll pay for them," she cried.

"Do you plan on robbing a bank?"

"I have a plan," said Kyle, pulling into the studio.

"Here is the other one," she said offering up the shoe.

"Keep it for a memory of your night as the princess of the underdogs," said Kyle.

Chapter Seven

Molly never found out what Kyle did about the lost shoe, but she kept the one on her dresser as a trophy. She had pulled it off—Molly, the beautiful girl. She spent one memorable night with the man of her dreams. It seemed like her feet hadn't touched the ground since the previous night. Somehow facing Silvia hadn't even crossed her mind.

"Our Christmas vacation officially begins," said Molly. "First we tell Santa what we want. Mine of course is simple, Sebastian Tate, done, now you Henry. What's that, a dog biscuit? Sending the memo to Santa."

Slipping into her Grinch p.j.s with Frosty slippers and her Victoria Secret Pink satin Santa hat she started mixing up eggnog. "Oh goody, *Elf* is on. We'll watch while we bake sugar cookies."

Three eggnogs later with Mariah Carey's Christmas CD blaring in the background, Molly heard a knock on the door.

"Hey girl, rocking it hard on a Saturday night," said Kyle. "Can I borrow some vodka?"

"Borrow, you mean 'have,' don't you?" she said as she skipped across the room, swaying a little.

"How much of the good stuff did you have, my little elf?"

"Three, four, who's counting?"

"Do you want to go out with me and the gang tonight? We are

hitting Rockefeller for some ice skating. Hunt is meeting us there after his date."

"No thanks, I'm putting on a concert for Henry. We're good."

"Okay, by all means, rock on!" said Kyle.

"I will, thanks," she answered as she swayed to "All I Want for Christmas." Standing on the coffee table with a coke bottle as her microphone, she sang her heart out. Pulling out her best dance moves, wiggling, shimming and even a kick, she serenaded Henry who was up on his hind legs wearing his Christmas red and green sweater and antlers. Her voice was sweet with the exception of that final note, an ear piercing, glass shattering, God-awful note. Bowing to Henry, she paused when she heard a faint clapping.

She turned to see Sebastian standing in her doorway. There he was, in the flesh, in her apartment, Sebastian Tate himself. "*Geez, Santa, you work fast*," she mumbled.

"That was undoubtedly the most disturbing display of holiday cheer I have ever experienced."

"Thank you," she said, staggering down from her stage.

"Yes, I did mean that as a compliment," Sebastian said. "The final note, wow, speechless. I don't have a word for it really."

"I tend to squeak a bit on high notes."

"I see. On a positive note, you certainly can bust a move. It looks a bit like a Chrissy volcano erupted in your flat," he said as he looked around at the sparkling winter wonderland she had created.

Chrissy. She never thought the word Christmas could get any better, yet somehow in Australian speak it was magical. My flat… he's in my flat. Gazing at his piercing blue eyes, she drifted into her fantasy of their torrid affair. Startled by Henry's rather loud snort, she looked at the Australian god in front of her. "I was um, just singing a few of my holiday favorites," she managed to say.

"Yes, I believe I know that one. Our version is a wee bit different.

Wow, it's been a while since I thought about that song."

She smiled dreamily at being sort of serenaded by her love. "Wait, what are you doing here, in my apartment?"

"I'm sorry, the door was open."

"Kyle, idiot."

"Excuse me?"

"Not you, sorry, but why are you here? Here in my home?" she asked, fixing her glasses.

"I need your help Ms. McKenna. It is McKenna right?"

Grinning ear to ear she sighed. "Yes, yes it is."

"First off, we won last night. I have you and Hunter to thank for it. I don't know how you knew, but your gut landed us our biggest ad campaign to date."

"I'm glad we could help," she said, dreamily staring into his pools of blue. "Is that why you came?"

"Not actually. The girl, Elizabeth, I need to find her. I can't eat, I can't sleep. I have never felt this way. I need you to help me find her. I'm going out of my mind. I have tried every agency in town. No one knows her."

"Maybe she doesn't want to be found," said Molly. "I mean sometimes the fantasy is better than the reality. Just let it be a great memory."

"What do you mean? Memory is past tense, implying I'll never have the chance to get to know her."

"What if you didn't like her when you got to know her?"

"Ms. McKenna, what aren't you telling me? Is she married or something? Is there a reason you are being so negative?"

"No um, Elizabeth is not actually an escort. She's an old..." she stuttered, "classmate. I ran into her the day of the gala. She was writing a piece on singles in New York. She agreed to do it."

"Then you know how to find her."

"Um, she's from Connecticut. We're not really friends, just acquaintances. I wouldn't know where to look for her."

"Ok, I get it, why would you help me? What do you want in return? I'll pay you time and a half."

"No, that's not it. I'm leaving for Connecticut tomorrow for the holidays. I don't know how much we could accomplish in one night."

"I'm desperate, please. Did you say Connecticut?"

"Yes, I did," she said, her mind spinning. "Maybe you…"

"What, I'll do it, anything."

"You could come with me to Connecticut, if you didn't have any holiday plans," she said, barely recognizing the words coming out of her mouth.

"I have no plans. Would that be awkward, you bringing your boss?"

"About that. Would you maybe be able to do a huge favor for me?"

"Name it."

"I sort of told my parents I had a boyfriend. They have been harassing me for a bit."

"That's perfect! I'll pretend to be your boyfriend. I mean, it's natural to bring your mate around for the holiday, right?"

Natural, she paused for a moment and thought "my mate." She could feel herself melting. Unbelievable that my lie could be a reality. Not really my boyfriend reality, but my fake boyfriend that I promised boyfriend reality. The positives, one, Mr. Tate will be with me for nearly a week, two, mother will explode with the fact that I'm not gay, and three, Mr. Tate will be with me for nearly week.

"Ok, we'll do this, but this does not come without a warning. McKenna family holidays are not for the faint of heart. They are a pretty tough bunch. If I'm being honest, Henry and I would be just as happy staying here, but you know, family."

"It can't be all that bad mate. We will have a splendid holiday while tracking down my dream girl."

"Hmm." She sighed, *dream girl? How would she get out of this one.*

"What time are we pushing off?"

"Around noon. Pack your cold weather gear!"

"Can't wait. I'll give you a tingle in the morning."

"A tingle, no need, I already have one. Did I say that out loud? Wait, what's a tingle?"

"A ring to make sure you don't need anything."

"Right, a tingle. You do know Henry is coming?" Molly said as Henry drooled a large amount of saliva on his shoe.

"Wouldn't have it any other way."

"And it's Christmas music the entire way."

"I'll have my bells on and ear plugs in."

"Very funny," she said.

Sebastian slid out the door as quickly as he had appeared. For a moment she wondered if it were a hallucination. Perhaps her fantasies were escalating to full blown psychosis. And then he popped back in. "Make a list of the things I should know about my gal."

Falling to the couch, she pinched herself hard. Squealing with pain, she jumped up and down on the sofa. Picking up the fleshy pooch, she kissed his slobbery face. "Henry, it's a Christmas Miracle."

Chapter Eight

Down the hall, Kyle poured rounds of vodka for Jeffery, Hunter and Rachel. Jeffery and Kyle canoodled in the corner while Rachel stared at herself in the mirror. She teased her over sprayed hair and applied a third coat of scarlet red lipstick to her silicone injected lips. Rachel, a Big Applehopeful, worked as a bartender at Chico's while patiently awaiting her call to fame. She and Hunter had been dating for three months, ever since he saw her over the bar that balmy September night. She was, by everyone's standards, a beauty. At five foot nine, she weighed not much more than the bottles of whiskey she twirled each night. Although obsessed with her looks, and pretty self-absorbed, there was something about her that Hunter found appealing. It might have been her never pushing the "serious" envelope. Rachel was content in seeing Hunter once a week, a five minute call a day sufficed, and marriage or moving in together a subject both avoided like the plague.

Never to be confused with a brain surgeon, Rachel's often missteps with the English language served as comedic banter for Hunter and Kyle. The four had plans to go out after a few rounds of spirits, but Hunter simply wasn't feeling it. It may have been her constant whining, insisting she was far prettier than the girl they picked for a small part in a film, or her need to constantly locate any item resembling a mirror to check herself out in, first the bathroom mirror, then the kitchen window and then at dinner, the knife. As Kyle and Jeffery talked about their plans for Christmas, they giggled like two high school girls. They had worked out their differences and were better than ever. They were perfectly in sync, sort of like him and Molly.

"Are we just going to sit here or are we going to the Rock? I mean I didn't put on a slip dress, which leaves little to the imagination, for two gay guys to gawk at. I look freakin' awesome and I need to share all this. You never know, tonight may be the night I'm discovered. I'm not wasting this on two fumigated guys," said Rachel.

And there it was—fumigated. "I think you mean 'intoxicated,'" said Hunter.

"You're so boring. This is enough for you, isn't it? Just sitting around drinking with friends in your two-by-four apartment?"

Hunter stopped and thought for a minute about the night he spent wrapping with Molly. It felt like enough, perfectly enough. He looked at Rachel and said, "It is enough for me. I don't think we're right for each other."

"Oh, hell no, you're not breaking up with me!"

This caught the attention of the canoodlers.

"Yes, yes, I believe that is exactly what I'm doing. Shall I call you a cab?"

"You will regret this, Hunter Bentley. One day when I am on the big screen, you are going say Caramel is a bitch."

"Yep, I'm pretty sure I'm not going say that," he said, chuckling at her massacre of the English language. He handed her, her clutch.

With one hand she snatched the purse while the other hand slapped his face, then she clunked out the door.

Kyle gasped at the slap and then placed both hands on Hunter's shoulders and looked him dead in the eye. "Are you drunk, man?"

"No, perfectly sober, and maybe for the first time in a while gaining some perspective."

"Philosophical Hunter is always fun."

"I'm serious. She is just not the girl for me."

"I'm sort of you know, not the best advice giver when it comes to picking out girls, but I know a hot one when I see one and that chick is Heat Miser hot."

"Yes, there is no denying she is hot. But I want a girl who is funny, smart, sweet, wholesome, a dreamer."

"I believe Mary Poppins is taken and that breed is not exactly falling off the trees in New York, my friend."

"I know, but she has to be someone I can have fun with, be myself with. I want to finish her sentences and she mine. I want to stay in and wrap presents with her and it be enough."

"Good Lord man, you're in love with Molly!"

Hunter stopped for a second and grabbed Kyle by the shoulders. "God damn, I am. She's the one. She's always been the one since she stumbled into the office three years ago. I've compared every woman since to her, and they've all come up short." He hugged Kyle and said, "I'm in love with Molly McKenna, crazy, silly, wonderful, quirky, perfect Molly McKenna."

He grabbed his coat and scarf, fixed his hair and then swiftly grabbed a small, wrapped gift from under the tree.

"Where are you going?"

"To tell her!"

"You do know she lives down the hall?"

"Yes, but I want to take her on a horse drawn sleigh ride to tell her."

"Crap, it must be love," said Kyle. Jeffery hopped up and down, clapping small taps with his fingertips.

"It's so romantic. I'm all tingly."

"Go man, before you lose your nerve."

"Not gonna happen. Nothing can stop me," he said beaming.

Like a school boy breaking free for Christmas vacation, he

sped down the hallway. Before he knocked, he straightened his tie and stood tall.

At first a gentle knock and then he opened the door to find Molly lying on the couch hugging a Frosty with her silly slippers slung on the back of the couch.

She popped up with the biggest grin he had ever seen. She skipped over to him, and then circled him singing, “It’s beginning to feel like the best Christmas of my life.”

Holding the gift in front of him, he wondered if maybe she felt it to. He said, “Molly, I have something to tell you!”

“Me too. Me first, pleasssse. I’m going burst if I don’t tell you the most amazing news in the free world.”

“Okay, you first.”

“He was here. Here in my apartment. In the flesh, the hot, steamy Australian flesh.”

“Sebastian? Sebastian was here in your apartment? Why?”

“The why, isn’t as important as the wow. He, the sexiest man alive, is going with me to Connecticut for the Christmas holiday. I’m the happiest girl alive.”

“What? Why? How?”

“He is going as my boyfriend. Just saying it makes my legs weak. He is all obsessed with finding Elizabeth. He wants me to help him track her down.”

“Okay, let me just get this straight. He is going with you, to help track down you?”

“Well, when you say it like that it sounds a little strange.”

“Strange? How in the hell do you think you’re going to pull this off?”

“Don’t get so huffy. We’ll come up with a plan. We always do.”

“Count me out. This is not a good idea. You’re going to get in deep and it won’t end pretty.”

“That’s why I have my bestie. You can help me woo him.”

“Did you say ‘woo’?”

"Yes, don't you watch the movies? Two people go away to meet the parents pretending to be engaged, etc. and in one simple week they fall madly in love and have a Christmas wedding."

"Yeah, that's very realistic."

"Mr. Negative Pants, what was your big news?"

"Never mind. I gotta go. Kyle and Jeffery are anxious to get going. Good luck, Molly. I hope you get what you've always dreamed of."

"Hey wait. Is that gift for me?" she said, reaching for the red and silver box wrapped with strands of silver ribbon.

Looking down at the present, he shook his head. She grabbed the gift and tore at the paper. Flipping the box open, inside she saw a note. *My wish for you this Christmas is to find the man of your dreams under your Mistletoe.* Inside the box, wrapped in layers of tissue, lay a porcelain Christmas ball shaped like Mistletoe with a red satin ribbon.

Pulling the ball out of the tissue, she held it over Hunter's head and gave him a kiss on the cheek. Jeffery and Kyle, who had snuck in the open door cheered. "Oh my god, I need a tissue," said a teary eyed Jeffery.

Hunter pulled away and said, "There they are. I told you they are impatient. Have a great trip, Red. We will exchange gifts when you get home."

"Wait, aren't you two…" asked Kyle.

"Aren't we two what?" said Molly.

"Molly has some amazing news, Kyle. She and Sebastian are going to be spending the holidays together. Isn't that great?" said Hunter.

Seeing the pain in his eyes, Kyle said, "Wow, okay, that's news. We really got to get rolling. Party's not going to wait forever. Merry Christmas, Molly."

"You too guys," she said, kissing them on the cheek.

"Love you, Bestie. I'll keep you posted," she said, throwing her arms around Hunter, giving him a bear hug.

Tears welled up in his eyes. Kyle grabbed him from her clutches and the three men headed to the door.

In the safety of the hallway, Kyle asked, "What happened? You didn't tell her, did you? What happened to nothing is going to stop me?"

"Sebastian, that's what. I can't compete with an Australian god. It's over. I'm too late. I want her to be happy and that man is her fairytale."

Kyle shook his head and then slapped Hunter across the face.

"Christ, that's twice in one night," said Hunter, rubbing the stinging skin on his cheek.

"First, pull yourself together."

"That would be easier if people stopped hitting me."

"You need some sense knocked into you. You are the best guy I know. Molly adores you. You need to throw your hat in the ring. Go fight for the girl. Don't you watch romance movies? The average Joe has to claw for his chance at the beauty."

"What is with the freakin' romance movies?"

"So good," sniffed Jeffery.

"Hunter, you are one of the most sincere, kindhearted men I've ever known. Molly knows it too. She just doesn't know you on a romantic level. Go to Connecticut as her pal and win her heart."

Wiping his eyes, Jeffery said, "God speed."

"What does that mean?"

"Don't worry, just start packing. You push off tomorrow," said Kyle.

"Why do I say I'm going?"

"Rachel has family there, wink, wink," said Kyle.

"We broke up?"

"Does Molly know that?"

"No."

"Okay, when you get there you tell Molly you had a terrible

break up. Can she suggest a place for you to stay until Jeffery and I get up there to pick you up?

“Christmas in Connecticut, I believe that’s a Christmas classic. Kyle, we must go,” said Jeffery.

“Focus Jeffery, we need to pick stylish outfits for the boy,” said Kyle as they headed back to the apartment.

“No, I’m not lying to Molly, she deserves better.”

“Hunter, you need her to at least hear you out before she and the Aussie set off into the sunset,” said Kyle.

“Face it, I’m no match for him,” said Hunter before slamming the bedroom door.

Chapter Nine

7 Days Until Christmas

Molly barely slept a wink that night. What to pack? What to wear? What to say to her family? The questions swirled in her head like sugar plums. Hunter most definitely was right. This had a very slim, actually, no chance of working. Lying always turned out disastrously for her. The outcome rarely promising, but this opportunity was simply too outstanding to pass up. Pouring herself a cup of high test coffee, she packed the last of her and Henry's things.

"Really, you're going to judge me?" she asked Henry whose big droopy eyes were fixed on her. "He is nice. You better be nice. He's my fantasy, I can't mess this up."

The dog lay down and groaned in disapproval. What did he know?

A knock at precisely twelve o'clock made her heart pound and a hive start to mount. This was it, game day.

"Hey Love. It is alright to call you that since we are dating, right?"

"Love." She sighed as she adjusted her glasses and said, "Of course."

"You need help with your bags?"

"Please. There is one by the door and just this carry on."

The two headed down the hall. She desperately wanted to bang on Hunter's door and giggle. If it wasn't for Hunter, this never would be happening. Note to self, *thank that man from the bottom of your heart.*

After stuffing the last of the bags into her small Honda, she instructed Henry to get in. He naturally hopped into the front passenger side.

"Not today, buddy," she said, pulling the dead weight to the back seat. He grunted and left a large pool of saliva in his wake.

"Oh gosh, I'm so sorry about that," Molly said, wiping the drool up with her extra blanket.

"No problem, the bloke has to get to know me."

"Speaking of which, here are some things you should know about me. I love Christmas. I have twenty pairs of glasses. I love to read. I'm a hopeless romantic and I'm allergic to garlic."

"Garlic, really?"

"Yes, very important."

"Got it. How about school, what degree do you hold?"

"You didn't read that on my resumé?"

"No love, you were in the right place at the right time."

"I have a Master's degree in Marketing from Wharton."

"You're joking?"

"No, really."

"Wow, why are you settling for a clerical assistant job? I know Hunter's deal. He likes overseeing the final art on the campaigns, but his real passion is architecture. He is just biding time until he gets that offer from the Cleary House."

"My Hunter?"

"Excuse me?"

"I mean Hunter from work Hunter? I never knew he wanted to leave."

"I had to write him a letter of recommendation for the program so he shared it with me. I get the impression he has been holding off for some reason other than the exam. I wish I could offer him more, he is very talented."

"That is crazy. I know why I stay, but I never knew that about him."

"Why do you stay?"

Silvia's new ringtone, the witch's theme from the Wizard of Oz, saved her from that question. No matter how dreadful the conversation would be with Silvia, it allowed her to avoid articulating her reasons for staying.

"Hello Mother, we're driving."

"Are you still bringing him?"

"If you mean Sebastian, yes. Why?"

"Thomas is stopping by with some poinsettias tonight and…"

"Mother, stop."

"Drive carefully. We will see you soon."

"Hmm, was that about me?"

"Sorry, my mother never quits. I sort of had this boyfriend, but that ended years ago. My mother is hell bent on reuniting us. That's where you come in. I just thought if I had a boyfriend she would let up."

"Perfect, I'll be your decoy, you find the girl."

Her eyes focused ahead on the thick rows of traffic and wondered how she thought she could pull this off. One lie to mother was bad enough, but how was she going to deliver Elizabeth? She needed Hunter at a time like this. The two studied the McKenna family tree as they rounded the last leg of the trip.

"Okay, two sisters, Megan oldest, Maxie middle child, you're the baby. Pretty good, eh?"

"Perfect. For your own good, say as little as possible, bearing in mind my mother will quiz you every chance she gets."

"Here goes," she said as she turned the car onto her street.

"Your house is lovely."

"It is from the outside."

The two barely unloaded their baggage onto the front porch before the door swung open and a flood of McKenna's bore down on them like a flock of wild geese.

"Welcome, let me grab those bags for you."

"Hi Daddy, this is Sebastian."

"Nice to meet you," he said, extending his hand.

"Pleasure," said Sebastian as Megan and Maxie sighed with glee at the sound of his accent.

"Megan, I'm Molly's favorite sister," she said, going in for a snuggle.

"Yes, I've heard lovely things about you. And you must be her other favorite sister," he said, pulling back a little.

"Handsome and smart," said Maxie, shaking his hand.

"She wasn't lying when she said you two were beauties."

Blushing, Maxie hugged Molly and said, "Thomas who?"

Princess Sophia eyed him up and down and said, "Welcome to my kingdom."

Olivia just giggled.

Chase, pecking at his phone seemed too distracted to care. Alex was cordial as usual and offered to take Sebastian's coat. Everything was going so smoothly, Molly forgot for a moment this whole boyfriend thing wasn't real, until Silvia pranced in.

"Come, don't let them freeze in the doorway," she said ushering them into the living room. The decorations were perfect as usual. Two fifteen foot trees flanked the entrance hallway framing either side of the staircase. In the living room was a tree so tall and full it seemed to be plucked right from a catalogue. The glorious glistening tree was decked entirely in silver. The fireplace was dressed with greens and white lights. The pillows tossed ever so perfectly, screamed "Don't come near me." Yes, it was like Christmas in the White House.

"You have an amazing home," said Sebastian with his eyes twinkling.

"You have amazing taste." Silvia smiled. "Have you two eaten? I had Larabee's on Main deliver some lobster and brie."

"I think we would like to settle in first, Mom."

"Okay, Dad and Alex took your things up to your bedroom if you want to freshen up before dinner."

"Where will you be putting Sebastian's things?"

"In your room, silly, now go, I can't wait to hear all about your special date."

"I, I well, it's just that maybe it would be better if he had the guest room."

"Why dear, we are all adults here. And besides, Princess Sophia turned that into the kingdom's headquarters. Unless your Sebastian wants to sleep in glitter and boas, I think he will be comfortable with you."

Molly's mind raced. This was a disaster. What was she thinking? There was no way she could sleep in the same bed as her fantasy. "Think, think," she mumbled to herself on the way up the stairs.

"Is there a problem?" asked Sebastian.

"It's just—I'm so sorry about all this."

"What?"

"Us sleeping together, not together, just us, you know, same room," she said, fumbling over her words.

"Relax love. Not a problem. I'm fine with it."

"Here it is, second door on the right. I have my own bathroom so if you want to clean up, go ahead."

"This is quite a room."

"Yes it is." He slipped into the bath. She sat at her vanity table and looked at her reddened cheeks. *Now what*? She imagined Operation Elizabeth would begin after dinner, so she might as well get this over with. The door to the bathroom opened and a very shirtless Sebastian appeared. Molly was so startled she fell off the edge of her seat. He rushed over and held out his hand.

"Are you alright?"

"Me, I, yes, I think I will head down now, if that's okay with you," she said, hoping he couldn't hear her heart pounding. Rushing out the door, she slammed right into Maxie.

"Holy crap Molly, are you okay? Your face is flushed. Do you have a fever?" she asked, pushing her lips to Molly's forehead.

"No I..."

Maxie threw her head back and with her raspy voice bellowed, "Shit, you just had a quickie."

"Good God, no! I mean we don't even..."

"Nothing to be ashamed of girl. You need that before what's waiting for you downstairs."

"What's waiting for me?"

"Let's go face the firing squad. It's nice having you around, takes the heat off of me."

"Glad to be of service."

Sebastian opened the bedroom door, wearing black pants and a black turtleneck. His cologne sailed through the hallway.

Who can look sexy in a turtleneck, thought Molly as the three headed down the stairs anxiously.

Silvia waited for her chance to grill Sebastian. Right on queue, the minute the two entered the room, Silvia patted the seat next to her and said, "Sebastian dear, I've saved a seat for you right here."

Molly held her breath for round one.

"So dear, let's hear how you two lovebirds decided you simply couldn't be without each other."

"It was sort of unexpected. One night we went to a work function. Elizabeth..."

Molly kicked him under the table.

Jumping, he cleared his throat. "I took one look at her and I just knew. She was perfect."

Molly's eyes glazed over dreamily, remembering that night.

"Really, my Molly? Was she wearing something other than

those dreadful sheep shoes?"

"Uggs, Mom."

"Actually, Uggs are made in Australia. I brought them back for her when I visited home."

Nice save. Molly smiled.

"We were delighted to hear you finally gave Molly the big promotion," said Silvia, eyeing her victim.

"Promotion?"

Sebastian was interrupted by the bell. Thomas' timing couldn't have been better. Silvia leapt to her feet as Thomas strutted into the room. Silvia linked arms with Thomas and ushered him toward Sebastian. "Take your coat off, Thomas. Allow me to introduce you to Molly's boss."

"Boyfriend, Mother."

"Sebastian, this is our family's dear friend Thomas. We have been friends with his family forever. He just recently became a physician. We are so proud of him."

Sebastian stood up and shook his hand.

"Congrats mate. Quite an accomplishment."

Mother hadn't intimidated him.

Thomas kissed Molly on the head then pulled up the chair on the other side of her.

"So Seb, you two are a couple? I ask because I am actually in the process of wooing her back."

Ballsy bastard, thought Molly.

"Good luck to you mate."

Molly met Maxie's eyes as they smiled with delight over Sebastian's cocky rebuttal.

"So nice of you to visit during Christmas. You must know how Molly feels about it?"

It's a trap. Molly panicked.

"Silly, everyone knows Molly is a Christmas freak. It's practically stamped on her forehead," said Maxie, winking at Molly.

God, I love her, thought Molly.

"How do you feel about the holiday? Any special traditions?" asked Silvia.

"Not really. My family doesn't really do too much around Christmas. It's a bit different in Australia. First off, the weather is warm."

Mayday, mayday. Molly's eyes twitched with panic.

"Now that you're with Molly, that will change. She is the closest thing I know to an elf," said Maxie.

Princess Sophia interrupted by standing on her chair and commanding her royal kingdom's attention. Never had Molly loved that over imaginative little thing more.

"Sophia, that's rude. We are talking," said Megan.

"I'm talking too and I'm the princess."

Megan excused herself and took Sophia into the kitchen. Molly followed, leaving Maxie and Alex on the interrogation block.

"Megan, are you okay?"

"Yes, I just can't reach Chase."

Molly hadn't even realized he slipped out some time during the interrogation. "Does he feel okay?"

"He just said he had to go to the office and now he's not answering. The girls need him here you know. Sophia acts out when she wants attention."

"I'm sure he'll call. I'll take Princess Sophia and Olivia up to bed," said Molly.

Shouting could be heard from the dining room. Maxie warned Silvia to stay out of her business.

Molly entered and asked Sebastian to help her with the girls. He politely declined, stating he was not much for kids. Her heart sank.

Thomas piped up. "I love the little buggers. I'll help."

"Since when? Last I recalled you said, 'If only children could be muzzled like dogs,'" said Molly as she took the girls' hands.

After tucking them safely in bed, she went down to find Thomas had left, but not before inviting her and Sebastian out to the club the next evening.

"Okay, I think I'll turn in, long day," said Molly. Maxie gave her the thumbs up. Swallowing hard, she made her way upstairs.

"You go first love. I'll be up in a minute," said Sebastian with a twinkle in those ocean blue eyes.

Once inside the bedroom, she dialed Hunter.

"Hey Red, how's it going?" said Hunter with Kyle leaning over his ear.

"Mayday! Operation Elizabeth is off course. I haven't actually brought her out yet, and he's sleeping with me tonight," she cried.

A large gasp followed "He's doing what?" huffed Kyle.

"What?" said Molly.

"Sorry, that was Kyle watching the Bachelor. Wait, what? You're having sex tonight?"

"Good God, not sex. What is it with all you people and sex?"

"Breathe and explain."

"My mom put us together in my room. My room, with one bed, that room. I can't breathe. This is a mistake. I'm out of my league here."

"Tell her now," shouted Kyle into the phone.

"Tell who what?" asked Molly.

"Kyle, please watch that in the other room. I've got this. Red, just ask him to sleep on the floor. You do know Elizabeth isn't actually coming, right?"

She hesitated. "Of course."

A knock on her door made her nearly jump out of her skin. "Gotta go, he's coming," she whispered.

"You decent?" Sebastian asked in his dreamy accent.

She had slipped into her red and black buffalo checked flannel p.j.s, fuzzy slippers and red fleece house coat. There were people in Alaska less decent.

"Yes, come in."

"Wow, expecting a storm?"

"No, I just get cold, that's all." The truth was the idea of being even remotely undressed in the same room made her blood run wild with anticipation. The fleece coat of armor protected her. *What was she doing? It was Elizabeth he wanted, not her. He hardly even noticed she was a girl.*

"I'm the opposite. Usually sleep in the raw, but I'll keep my skivvies on, being this is a little strange for us."

The raw, oh God she was sure she squeaked as she tried to bite her lip with the thought of that body in her room, naked. "Okay then, um here's a pillow and some blankets for the floor. Are you sure that's okay?"

"Yes fine. Any word on Elizabeth?"

"Um, yes, I think I may have found her on Facebook. I sent a friend request. We can check in the morning to see if she responded."

"I can't believe you are doing this for me. You really are amazing."

"Thanks," she said as she climbed into bed, robe and all. When she was sure he was asleep, she texted Hunter. *Operation Elizabeth just got ramped up. I need you to create a Facebook account for her. Pleaseeeee, pretty please.*

He read the text and growled. Why couldn't he refuse her? He had always been her go to guy, he couldn't let her down now. He pulled out his laptop and began creating the perfect girl.

"What are you doing?" asked Kyle, peeking over his shoulder.

"Helping."

"Helping who, man? Help yourself. You've got to go there soon. For God's sake, he's in her bed."

"Bedroom, it's not the same."

"Really? You're buying that. It's for your own good that I'm saying this. You're a wimp, chicken, pansy..."

"Okay got the point."

"Fight for her, or at the very least sabotage Elizabeth," snapped Kyle.

"I can't fight for someone who doesn't want me."

"How do you know that? She doesn't even know you're a contender. Throw your name in the hat. Let her choose the bachelor. But don't sit here sulking. It's Christmas, man, you know how that girl feels about the holidays. Buy some damn mistletoe and kiss her like your life depends on it."

Chapter Ten

6 Days Until Christmas

A lively Silvia pounded on the bedroom door. "Come on you two. Are you going to sleep all day?"

Molly, startled, rolled out of bed landing right on top of Sebastian. Still wearing her *Don't Disturb* eye mask she felt the warm sensation of his rock hard body. For a moment she thought it was a dream, then she removed the patch to realize she was eye to naked chest.

"Holy Thit," she managed to spill out. Unaware she was still wearing her nighttime retainers, she struggled to speak with a lisp.

"Hello," he said. Henry snuggled on top of Sebastian's designer shoes.

"I'm tho, thorry," she said as she rolled off and pushed her eye mask to the top of her head.

"Are you alright? You sound a little funny."

The door swung open and Maxie popped her head in. "Hey lovebird's, Mom said…" She paused. "Wow on the floor, kinky."

Molly jumped up. "Jeezth, Maxthie, knock firthst."

"Are you wearing?" she paused, "Do you have your mouthpiece in for real? Girl, we need to bring sexy back."

"Goodbye Maxthie."

"I'm going to get drethssed," Molly said, slinking quickly into the bathroom. She looked at her reflection, her hair standing like a cockatoo, her lips puffed out from her night guard. Her layers of clothing like that of a homeless women wearing every last article she owned. "Crap," she said. *What am I doing? If I want him to love me, not Elizabeth, I need to be, she paused, sexy. Maxie was right. Today starts operation "Molly Sex Goddess." Maybe start with "Sex Kitten,"* she sighed.

At breakfast Silvia continued her interrogation, Maxie studied the two, giving Molly the "I know you're up to something" stare. And Dad, he just sat quietly with his oxford sleeves half rolled like he was ready to go into battle if necessary, but preferred peace.

Silvia waited to go in for the kill. "Thomas has graciously offered to take Sebastian to the country club for the day. You know, meet some people, have a few drinks. Dad said he will catch up to them in a bit. Isn't that sweet of Thomas?"

"No, it's not, and I'm sure Sebastian does not want to go to the stuffy country club."

"I think it would be nice to meet your people."

"Oh, they are not my people," said Molly.

"Then it's settled, Thomas will pick you up around noon," said Silvia.

Molly worried about Thomas pressuring Sebastian to come clean, but it did give her time to work on Elizabeth. Thomas arrived promptly at noon dressed in a cardigan and khakis, his Burberry scarf and wool pea coat. He was a handsome bastard, she thought.

"I'm so happy you can join me today Seb. So did you give any thought to going out to the nightclub? There is a new one in town, *The Harbor*. I thought we could hit it up with Maxie and Alex and Megan and Chase. You know, whoever is sexy enough to hang with us. It's a week night, but given that it's Christmas week, it should still have a nice crowd."

"I'm in," said Sebastian.

"Really Thomas, what makes you think we, or anyone for that matter, wants to hang out with you?"

"Feisty! That's one of the things I love about her," said Thomas.

"I'll see if Alex can come," said Maxie.

The two men headed out, and Maxie suggested she and Molly handle the dishes. Silvia left for some last minute shopping and Dad headed up to the club.

"Okay, we're all alone. Spill! What's really going on between you two?"

Molly filled the sink with sudsy water and opened the dish washer. She hesitated before grabbing a few plates and dipping them in the warm suds. "Nothing, I don't know what you mean?"

"Really? Come on little sis, this is Maxie you're talking to. Something just doesn't seem kosher between you and this guy."

"Okay Maxie, I need your help. I think I need to be a bit," she paused, "sexier."

"You think? Oh Lord, if that's all, I got this."

Molly and Maxie went about filling the dishwasher and finishing the cleanup. Then the two headed to Maxie's room.

"Tonight is the perfect night to bring on sexy Molly," said Maxie as she flung open her closet and threw things on the bed.

"Now let's bring her out slowly. I'm not great in heels, so can we maybe find sexy pants?"

"Sister, feast your eyes on these," said Maxie holding up a pair of black leather pants. "They are way too small for my booty, but I think you will look hot as hell in them."

"Oh gee, I don't know about that."

"Nonsense," said Maxie as she continued putting together a killer ensemble.

Molly took the clothes back to her room and plopped on her bed. Henry opened one eye, and then stretched and made his way to the door.

"Traitor, you used to agree with me on everything," she said to the rotund dog as he waddled out in disapproval.

Maybe Henry was right, this felt like a mistake, but time was running out. Even Maxie had noticed something was up. It wouldn't be long before Silvia figured it out. She had to act quickly. She reached over and flipped open her laptop and logged into Facebook. As promised Elizabeth James popped up. Hunter had even managed to put a picture of a girl bundled on a snowy mountain with a set of skis. The face was too small to make out. Wait, she skis. She dialed Hunter.

"Did you survive last night?"

"Skiing really? You know I'm the least athletic person on two feet."

"Listen, Elizabeth needed a picture and I needed one without a visible face. Red, the real question is how long are you going to keep up this charade? It's going a bit too far."

"As long as it takes for him to give up his silly fascination with Elizabeth and finally see me as the woman he loves," she said with a dreamy sigh.

"So in other words, when they need parka's in hell?"

"Hell will not need to freeze for Sebastian to fall for me. You'll see, he just needs a few more days. I really feel him coming around."

Molly tried to convince herself that Sebastian was at least noticing her. She headed in to the bathroom and drew a hot bath. Allowing herself to soak in the fragrant bubbles, she imagined Sebastian's kiss under the mistletoe. It would be soft and gentle, like a whisper in the wind. His touch would send shivers down her spine. It would be the kiss that would prove to them both they were destined to be together. She toweled off and wrapped herself in a fuzzy robe. Now if only she could master the sexy. She spent what seemed like hours canvasing the internet for advice on how to bring your sexy out. She practiced how to walk sexy, talk sexy, even breathe sexy. Molly nearly jumped out of her skin at a small tap on the door. Quickly killing the "How to be sexy" page, she tried to appear calm.

The door opened and Sebastian walked in. "Hey, how was your day? I had a great time with Thomas. He's a lot of fun. Are you sure you don't want to give that guy another chance?"

Oh God, how she hated that man. He could charm a snake. He got to Sebastian. 'Getter.' Before she could answer he saw the computer screen.

"You found her," he said his eyes smiling like a kid.

"I, um, yes I did. She's online now." She texted Hunter, *Show time!*

"What do I say to her?" asked Sebastian.

"Hi, I wanted to thank you for the beautiful night we shared," she answered.

"Here, slide over," he said as he shimmied up next to her on the bed and started typing.

She held her breath, hoping Hunter was on the other side, ready to respond.

"You're welcome," was the return text.

Sebastian—"I see you ski."

Elizabeth—"Yes, avid skier, since I was a child."

Molly cringed, knowing her athletic ability rivaled a turtle.

Sebastian—"Do you like to travel?"

Elizabeth—"Love it. I have been to Paris, Italy, Japan and Russia."

Sebastian—"Do you speak any other languages?"

"No, please no languages," she whispered quietly with all fingers crossed.

Elizabeth—"Mandarin."

Sebastian—"That's sexy. Me too."

For the love of God Mandarin, who speaks Mandarin?

The conversations silenced. "Now what?" he asked.

"Ask her if she likes Christmas."

"Are you a big holiday person?" he typed.

Molly gushed with the thought of them enjoying her favorite holiday together.

Her eyes nearly bugged out of her head as she read the text on the computer.

"Nah, I usually work through it. All that commercialism crap."

Mandarin, Russia, hates Christmas. I'll kill him, thought Molly, beginning to sweat.

Sebastian—"I usually travel for Christmas. I like to change the scenery, get away from all the American traditional nonsense."

Molly's heart sank.

Elizabeth—"I agree. I'll be home this Christmas."

Sebastian—"Our mutual friend Molly told me home is Connecticut. I happen to be here for a few days. Perhaps we could get a drink."

Elizabeth—"Sure, let me check my schedule and get back to you when I get home."

Sebastian—"Perfect. Here's my number 719-663-8674. You can't possibly know how I'm looking forward, Elizabeth, to seeing you again."

He closed the laptop down and reached over and kissed Molly on the forehead. Stunned, she leaned in thinking another one was coming.

"You are a genius. I owe you Molly."

"I'm just glad you found her."

"She's the one. I know it," he said before falling back on the bed.

Alright, maybe he wasn't coming around quite as she had hoped but with Christmas and mistletoe anything was possible.

She looked at his beautiful profile, his bulging arms and tiny waist, his scent a woodsy, yet clean smell. He was perfect, she was not. She wasn't in his league, and she would never measure up to Elizabeth. This was a disaster. Thoughts of killing off Elizabeth or maybe having her admit she was married or pregnant ran through her brain.

"Knock, knock, I'm coming in, get dressed. Do you guys want to grab a bite at Shay's before the Harbor? Chase and Megan are meeting us later," said Maxie.

"Sounds good to me," said Sebastian.

"Okay," said Molly.

"Okay if I shower?" he asked.

"Alone?" asked Maxie pointing her finger back and forth between Sebastian and Molly.

"Maxie, go."

"Just saying—conserves water," Maxie said before closing the door.

When Sebastian slipped into the bathroom, Molly called Hunter.

"Are we done with this craziness?" he answered.

"What are you trying to do to me? Travel, ski, Mandarin—really? I'm already in enough trouble here, I don't need you making it worse."

"Wait, I'm making it worse. I just emailed a man as a woman. You are pretending to find fake you. You are lying to your family about Sebastian and I'm making things worse. Is that possible? And to make matters worse you don't even know Sebastian."

"Of course I know him."

"Really? Did you know he spoke Mandarin or that he skis? I picked Mandarin because it was on my computer screen advertisement. We don't know him, Red. You know some dreamed up version of him."

"He's perfect Hunter. You'll see, just wait until I get him under the mistletoe."

"Enlighten me again, how are you going to do that?"

"I'm working on it."

"Red, just tell him, enough already. I'm not going help you dig this hole any deeper."

"Fine then, I don't need you. You're messing it up anyway."

"Fine, you don't need me, good luck on your own." Click.

She didn't need Hunter. She could do this without him. She hung up the phone.

Sebastian came back in and asked, "You okay?"

"I will be," she answered.

"Molly, what is it you want, really want? If it's not Thomas?" Sebastian asked, shaking the water out of his tasseled hair.

She wanted to scream "You" but instead thought for a minute. She could redirect the question while allowing Sebastian into her world. She would open herself up to a part of her only her family knew. This undoubtedly would bring them closer. Molly walked to the closet and looked in at a mural inside. She paused then said, "Come here, I'll show you."

He walked over and then poked his head in the closet.

"This is what I've always wanted. A holiday village. Ever since I was a kid I started planning, sketching, envisioning. I drew this design before I moved to New York." She began explaining her vision of Candy Cane Lane, restaurants, shops and every charming event that guests could enjoy. She was so excited, she barely noticed he had stopped listening, his head in his cell phone reading work emails.

He barely looked up, pecking at his phone. Then a beep on the computer sent him leaping toward it, hoping to hear from Elizabeth. Turned out it was someone else messaging him on Facebook.

Molly choked back a tear, half embarrassed she was so uninteresting and half because the girl he wanted was not her. Noticing her silence, he asked, "Were you saying something about a Christmas sale?"

"No, it was nothing. I'm going to get ready for dinner."

She took her things into Maxie's room to begin the

transformation to sex kitten.

Maxie was dressed in a silver short mini with a cream and silver halter top. Molly sighed at how her glowing natural skin tone required no panty hose, no tanner. Her jet black hair, the color of coal, shined in a twisted ponytail with a silver hair band. She made sexy look easy, effortless. Molly slipped on the black sheer button up with small gold buttons. Her white bra flashed like a neon sign. *Too sexy*, she thought before she added a black tank underneath, then the pants. She wrestled them up over her legs like sausage casing. She tried on the black heels Maxie set out for her and glanced in the mirror.

"Ow, ow," purred Maxie.

"I look like the after school version of Olivia Newton John."

"Girl, sexy is in here," said Maxie, pointing to her head.

"I'm losing the heels."

"Okay, how about these?" said Maxie, offering a pair of black suede over-the-knee boots.

"At least they're flat." Molly sighed.

"Now the hair, how about we straighten it?"

"No," snapped Molly.

"Wow, you got something against straitening irons?"

"No, I'm sorry, this is enough sexy for my first night at it."

"Okay Sweet Potato, but you've got to buy into the sexy and he will too."

Molly pulled her bulging curls out of her bun. A loose ponytail was as far as she would go. Elizabeth had straight hair. *I'm not ready,* she thought. *Not yet. I'll know when the time is right to tell him. Not tonight.*

A final look through her leopard speckled glasses surprised her. From her neck down, dare she say, was a little sexy. Maybe he would fall for her and forget all about Elizabeth. Maybe they would kiss as Molly and Sebastian. She closed her eyes and giggled. She pulled out her phone and snapped a selfie to send to Hunter and then remembered their fight. She loved Hunter, but he was being difficult about this. She needed to focus on her mission.

Thomas, Sebastian, Maxie and Alex were all laughing in the living room when she entered. "Wow," said Thomas and Sebastian at the same time.

"Hello, sexy," said Maxie.

"I have to say Molly, this is a new look for you," said Thomas. "I, for one, like it."

"You look nice Molly," said Sebastian.

Nice, I look nice. Okay sexy comes from the mind. It's time to turn on the brain.

At dinner, she could feel both Thomas and Sebastian staring at her. Thomas made small talk about their relationship at its high point. "You know, we had a great time a few weeks ago at my party. Did she tell you about that?"

"No," said Sebastian, unsure of if he was supposed to know this or not.

"Nothing to tell," said Molly.

"Ah, nothing except we had a little too much to drink and Molls and I slept together."

"That's not true, well it's kinda true—we were in bed together but we didn't…"

"I trust her," said Sebastian confidently.

She could have kissed him right there.

"Hey, that club is calling our name," said Maxie, breaking the building tension.

They walked next door to Harbor. Once inside, Molly was reminded of what club goers' idea of sexy was, making her resemble a Sunday school teacher. Maxie headed to a table, waving both hands in the air like she owned the club. Megan and Chase were seated at a table in what appeared to be a heated moment.

"Hey Meggie," said Molly.

"Look at you baby sis. You look hot."

"Chase," said Molly.

"Hey, excuse me for a moment," he said, hurrying away from the table.

"Everything all right?" asked Maxie.

Megan rubbed her temples. "I just have a headache, that's all."

"Liquid courage," said Thomas, carrying a tray full of shots.

"Come on Molly, just one," said Sebastian.

"I don't really do shots."

"Loosen up. You'll be fine," he said, handing her a drink.

"Okay, one drink should be okay," she said, sipping the small glass.

"Molly love, you don't sip, you drink it in one shot. That's why it's called a 'shot,'" he said.

She grabbed the glass and threw back the drink. *That wasn't so bad*, she thought, with the exception of the burning in her esophagus.

Megan excused herself and went after Chase. Maxie stood up and proclaimed they were playing her song. "Come on Moll, let's show them how it's done," she said.

"Oh no, not me. I'm going sit this one out."

Alone at the table, Sebastian pulled his chair in closer. *Oh here it comes, he's going to kiss me.*

"Molly, can we talk?"

"Sure," she said, swallowing hard.

"I can't thank you enough for helping me find Elizabeth, but once we meet I think I can take it from there. I know I promised to be your date for Christmas, but I don't know how things will go for Elizabeth and me. I won't bail on you. A mate doesn't do that, but when are you planning on telling them?"

She waved her hand to the waitress carrying a tray of shots and grabbed one. Throwing it back she said, "Honestly, I hadn't given it much thought."

"Elizabeth isn't back in town yet so we have some time."

Yes time for you to fall in love with me. It was time to bring out her sex goddess. She closed her eyes for a second conjuring up every sexy thought she could then opened them to find Carey White right there in front of them. She hadn't changed a bit since that humiliating night, still gorgeous, slutty and a bitch.

"Hey Molly, long time girl since, you know, the falling into the orchestra thing. Who is this gorgeous specimen?"

"Yes, I did fall into the orchestra after I saw you pawing my boyfriend like a rabid dog." *Hmm, where did that come from? There is definitely something to be said for liquid courage.*

"Come now, that's old news. Thomas and I aren't a couple, so let's be grownups and put the past in the past. Besides, he has never gotten over you."

Extending her hand toward Sebastian, she leaned in, exposing an ample portion of breast and introduced herself. Sliding a chair from the next table she pulled up next to him.

No, no, no, this cannot be happening.

"So my name is Carly and you are?"

"Sebastian, Molly's boyfriend."

God, I love him even more, thought Molly.

"My, Tommy has his work cut out for him," said Carly, waiving a waitress over. "How about a round on me?"

Molly dropped her head to the table. *Why? Just why?* To make matters worse Thomas was heading their way. Megan had already left with Chase, and she saw no signs of Maxie.

"Molls, Doll, how about a dance for old time sake? I'm certain Seb won't mind, besides Carly will keep him amused."

"Nope."

"Really, that's it, 'nope?'"

"Yep, no old time sake happening."

"It's okay Molly, go ahead. I'll be fine here," said Sebastian.

"See that, wait what?" Sebastian was supposed to refuse to let her go. What choice did she have? One dance, how bad could it be? She slugged down whatever drink Carly had ordered her and slid out of the booth. Hmm, she didn't remember the floor feeling so uneven before. The lights blinded her as she stumbled to get her balance. The music pounded and before she knew it, Carly and Sebastian were next to them. Carly gyrated up and down, grinding against him. This was not Molly's strong point. She grabbed another shot as the waiter trolled the dance floor. Molly, bring your sexy back, as if it were ever here. Sexy is in your head. Tonight is sex goddess night, she coached herself. Willing her hips to thrust and bump she remembered dancing with Hunter at the club. She was wrong; she needed Hunter.

Chapter Eleven

Five Days Until Christmas

The buzzing of her vibrating phone made her head nearly explode. Molly, face down in a puddle of drool, struggled to figure out where she was. Reaching for her phone she looked around the room. It was somewhat familiar, yet she couldn't place it. "Hello," she moaned.

"Dancing Queen, so now you need me?" asked Hunter.

"Oh, yes Hunter, wait, but how did you know that?" she said, rubbing her temples.

"ESP and the four thousand texts you sent me last night begging me to forgive you."

"Oh God, Hunter, I'm so sorry. I was mean to you. I'm not me, I mean with all this lying about me being Elizabeth and Sebastian being my boyfriend, it's making me crazy."

"We'll go with that as the reason you're crazy, but I have a few other theories."

"It's true, you should have seen me last night. It was awful. I think, I can't actually remember it."

"Well lucky for you, I have the video of you winning a dance contest to *My Humps*. And might I say, those were some moves, tazer victims have got nothing on you."

"What video?"

"Hmm, I don't know, maybe the one you sent me around three

A.M. That came first, then the continuous texts telling me you needed me followed."

"Oh God, it's worse than I thought," she said, pulling herself to the mirror. "Is that a black eye? Wait, I think I have a tattoo on my hip. Where are you?"

"After my phone memory died, I caught the first train to Connecticut. The real question is, where are you? I'm with Silvia, who seems to be one step away from a strait jacket wondering where you are."

"You're here, really. Oh I love you so much. I'm coming just as soon as I figure out where I am."

The door opened and Thomas walked in carrying a piece of raw meat. "Morning sunshine. I figured you may need this."

"Oh no, I just figured out where I am. Don't move. I'm coming. And Hunter, in case I don't tell you enough, you're the best friend a girl could have." She hung up and attempted to stand.

"Where is Sebastian?" she asked, wondering why he was bringing her a raw piece of meat.

"I wasn't sure if you needed this after your fall from the bar. That looks like it hurts."

"Fall from the bar? No, no, no. Where is he?"

"He's here, on the couch with Carly."

She lunged at him.

"Slow down there Tiger. They didn't do anything. They are both passed out. How you feeling?"

"I hate you. Take me home. Now!"

"Ungrateful, really, after all I did for you. I'm the one who pulled you off the bar."

"I thought I fell off the bar?"

"That was the second time you decided to pull out your inner Coyote Ugly."

"No, no, no, what does Sebastian think? Elizabeth would never do that. What am I saying, I would never do that? What is happening? I feel like I'm having an out of body experience. I can't feel my hands."

"Who's Elizabeth? And you are so right girl, I didn't think you had it in you. At least you kept most of your clothes on."

Throwing her arms across her chest, she let out a scream that pierced the ozone. "My clothes, oh God I need to go underground. A new identity, perhaps I'll become a nun."

"That was too fun. You didn't take off your clothes but a guy can dream."

She threw a pillow at his head. "This is serious."

"Why, because your precious Sebastian doesn't know little old Molly is a homebody who can't hold her liquor? I know all about you love. When are you going to stop pretending you don't feel the same about me?" he said, leaning in for a kiss.

She turned her head. "The kiss at Thanksgiving was a mistake. I love Sebastian. Now stop holding me hostage."

"Now is that any way to thank me. I thought it best to bring you and Lover Boy here so Silvia wouldn't skewer you. You know appearances being so important and all. That has to count for some brownie points."

"Yes, thank you. But it's your fault in the first place, bringing Carly."

"I don't like Carly. I like you. Okay so maybe I'm not playing fair, but you aren't giving me much choice. Why won't you even consider that I may be in love with you?"

"I'm not having this conversation with you. I have to go."

Sebastian looked no worse for wear and barely seemed to even care about whatever Coyote Ugly she'd performed on the bar. She was pretty certain she didn't bring sexy back, and his mind was on another girl altogether. She did promise him an answer from Elizabeth today.

As soon as the car pulled up, she burst out of it, running to the door. Inside, she found Hunter seated in the grilling chair across from Silvia. She threw her arms around him then grabbed his arm and said, "Excuse us, Mother, we need to talk alone for a moment."

"Molly, what happened to you? Where is Sebastian? Why have you invited yet another man here? He said something about you forgetting some presents."

Molly pulled Hunter down the hall to the study. She closed the door and cried, "What am I doing? I've made such a mess out of everything. I'm so sorry I was mean to you. I, I have a black eye, apparently from falling off the bar and a, a…tattoo," she wailed.

"Good news, Silvia still doesn't like me. That should take some steam off of you. Next, I believe that black eye is the remnants of some very smudged makeup and let me see this tattoo. Hmm, a heart with Thomas in the center. Original," he said, rubbing it off with a baby wipe Megan had left in the diaper bag on the couch.

"Oh, it's fake. Oh thank God. What would I do without you?" she said, falling into his arms.

*****

He thought about what Kyle said about telling her, kissing her like his life depended on it. He took the first step, he was here in Connecticut. He would know when the time was right.

He held her tight then reassured her. "No need to worry about that. I'm here now and I'm going to see this through with you," he said, fixing the bent rim on her glasses, tucking her insane curls behind her ears and wiping the rest of the makeup off her face. "See that, good as new. And I thought you may need these," he said, handing her two Motrin and earplugs. "They will soften the blow when Silvia howls at you."

"You really are the best, you know that?"

"We'll figure out Elizabeth after breakfast, but for now you better go face the firing squad."

"You're staying, right? For Christmas, please, you have to."

"Are you sure? I mean with Sebastian and all."

"Never been more sure. It just hasn't felt like Christmas without you," she said, grabbing his hand and leading him to the kitchen.

They found Silvia and Sebastian waiting in silence.

"Thank heavens, I thought you had a black eye. You look like hell. This family has appearances to keep. We are important in this community. Our reputation is everything. Look at your sisters, both with upstanding men. I honestly don't have words."

"I think you just had plenty of words, Mother. And if you really want to know about last night, why don't you ask your precious Thomas. After all, he orchestrated the whole thing. I'm not hungry."

"Hunter, good to see you," said Sebastian.

"Mr. Tate."

"Call me 'Sebastian.'"

"*Molly*!" Silvia said sternly as Molly walked out of the room.

"Mrs. M, if I could just suggest giving her a little time to compose herself," said Hunter.

"It's 'Silvia,' and no you may not suggest anything when it comes to my family," she said as she huffed out of the room.

"Doesn't like me much. Never has."

"So you and Molly are pretty close?"

"Yeah, just friends, close friends."

"Doesn't matter to me. I'm here for Elizabeth. Molly said you know all about it."

"Yes, yes I do."

"Gentlemen," said Mr. McKenna. "Wait, I know you somehow," he said pointing to Hunter. "You're Molly's friend from New York. We met at her apartment a few years ago. Of course, Hunter, right? Molly speaks an awful lot about you, young man. You're a good friend. I know she sees you like family."

"Thank you Mr. M."

"Now what has Silvia in a rage this early? Let me guess, it's

Molly?"

The two men nodded. Sebastian excused himself and left to check on Molly.

Hunter and Mr. McKenna shared breakfast. They got along quite well. Talked mostly about Molly but also about their mutual need for the Giants to win a Super Bowl, Christmas and this season's Law and Order.

"You have a beautiful house," said Hunter.

"Thank you. That it is, but the house I love, that was over on Holly Lane, built in the twenties the detail was magnificent, arched doorways, window seats, and wide planked wood floors. That, my friend, is a home. I'll have to show you sometime."

*****

"Can I come in?" asked Sebastian, waiting outside the bedroom door.

Molly had showered and thrown on a velour track suit. "Sure, if you think it's safe to be around me," she said.

"Why would you say that?"

"I'm so sorry about last night. I don't drink really, and well, Carly just sort of sets me off and..."

"I drank pretty much myself and had a blast. Don't remember a whole lot. My mates back in Australia can throw back pretty well. We all act a little crazy when we're on the piss."

"I'm sure I don't know what that means, but again I'm sorry," she said as a buzz sounded on his Facebook page.

"Maybe it's Elizabeth," he said as he raced to the screen.

"Maybe," she said, wondering what to do next.

"I'm asking her when she's getting back. I can't wait."

Molly gave it a second and then decided they would meet or at least she would tell him the truth at the Christmas Pageant. There was always so much commotion mixed with holiday cheer, how could she go wrong? She texted Hunter to go ahead and answer. Time was running out until the pageant, it was go time. Then Christmas Eve, they would spend in each other's arms, perfect!

*****

"Good news, Molly asked me to stay."

"Stay, stay where? Does this look like a boarding home? All the hotels are probably booked due to the holiday, so perhaps you should cash in on that return train ticket," Silvia said before stomping out.

"Now seems to be a good time to show you that house. How about it?" Mr. McKenna said to Hunter.

"Let's do it."

Chapter Twelve

4 Days Until Christmas

The smell of bacon wrapped scallops, brie stuffed mushrooms and blue crab beignets wafted through the foyer as the delivery from Tony's made its way in large foil trays.

"Well, it's about time!" Silvia snapped at Tony.

"The order was for six and it's five fifty miss," said Tony.

Maxie, coming in right behind them, tried to steal one off the tray and said, "And besides, you have the owner himself delivering your order."

"I'm glad you're here. Tomorrow night's dinner needs to be perfect. I don't have to remind you some of the most important people in the community will be here. I need everything to go smoothly. Appearances are everything. You need to be here by six to have everything set up. I'm paying you handsomely so let your service reflect that. Now put those on the kitchen counter."

"Appearances are everything, do remember that," Maxie said, smirking at the chef.

"Speaking of which, I hope you have been practicing your talent for the competition. It's only a few days away," said Silvia, placing a plate on Maxie's head. "Posture for God's sake. You look like you're carrying a sack of potatoes in your rear end."

Maxie pushed her booty out and said, "Never had any complaints about this puppy."

Ignoring her sarcasm, Silvia replied, "You're avoiding the question. Your talent? If I didn't know better I'd think you don't even care about this pageant."

*****

Truth was Maxie didn't care about the pageant one bit, she had other things on her mind. As far as talent, Maxie's talent was her looks. She always got what she needed by batting those long black lashes and tossing her waving black locks over her ample breasts. She envied Molly who with her average looks, worked much harder to get the success she had and she earned every bit of it. Molly was talented. She had painstakingly practiced the piano five days a week as a child. Molly had talent but Silvia only saw Maxie's beauty, and like Megan, knew she would be a shoe in for this year's pageant. Still, this was a McKenna tradition that meant so much to Silvia, so somehow she would try and work on her hula dance.

*****

"Okay I'm not sure why you're still here, but the hors d'oeuvres are in here so you can leave," Silvia said to the young chef in the kitchen. "Now, where is Edward? We need to get ready for the Greens' party."

"Haven't seen him," said Maxie.

Molly and Sebastian came downstairs. "What is that amazing smell?" asked Molly.

"The food I ordered for the Greens' party. What are you doing tonight?" asked Silvia.

Maxie, grabbing another hors d'oeuvre said, "I have to run to the drugstore and then getting dinner with Megan. We have a skit to rehearse. Alex is having the guys over for poker night. Do you want to go Sebastian? It's probably an all-nighter."

"Sounds like a night I can't resist. Is it okay with you Molly?"

"Sure, go ahead. I've got a lot of wrapping to do. Megan asked if I would do the girls' presents."

"Where's Hunter? He can come to. You know Alex, the more the merrier," said Maxie.

"I haven't seen him," said Molly.

"I told him this isn't a boarding house, so he probably is heading back to the city. Besides, he took his bags," said Silvia.

"Mom, why would you do that?" said Molly, suddenly feeling a twinge of panic with the thought of Hunter not being by her side.

"For God's sake Molly, we don't need another man hanging around here. What will the guests think tomorrow night? You're a feminist Mormon bringing three dates."

"Right, because that is what is important," said Molly before the back door in the kitchen opened with Hunter and Edward breezing in all chatty with Cheshire cat grins.

"I don't want to know. Edward get dressed. We are going to be late. And Maxie, for heaven's sake, put down that scallop. What are you so hungry about? You're not going to fit into your gown. You look like you've gained a few pounds," said Silvia.

Dad winked at Molly and dutifully followed Silvia.

"Guys' night at Alex's. You in Hunter? You're just in time to catch the Maxie bus out," said Maxie.

Hunter looked at Molly. "No, I think I'll sit this one out. Molly mentioned something about a wrapping marathon, and I'm not gonna lie—I'm kind of a pro in that department."

Molly smiled. She felt a sense of relief that Sebastian was going and Hunter was staying. *Strange*, she thought, but she always felt nostalgic with Hunter at the holidays.

"Ok, let's move it Seb," said Maxie, kissing Molly goodbye and high fiving Hunter on the way out.

Molly turned to Hunter. "You could've gone."

"And miss a night of Molly/Hunter rapping. And I do mean rapping," he said as he started making beat box music with his hand.

Molly's eyes curled up on the ends. "This is why everyone needs a Hunter," she said, grabbing his hand and leading him to the family room. "I'm so sorry for my mother being rude. It's who she is. By the way, where is your stuff?"

"Your dad took me to see your house on Holly Lane."

"He did?" Her eyes widened.

"Why is that such the big surprise?"

"I don't know. I mean since we moved, it's sort of a bad word in this house. It represents our horribly embarrassing humble beginnings."

"First off not so humble, that's an amazing house. I can see why he loves it so and won't put it on the market."

"He loves it, really?"

"Yes and look at this," he said, holding a key above his head. "I'm staying there. Very generous and I think in a small way, his way of sticking it to Silvia."

"Oh my God, this is amazing. Let's go. I haven't been there in forever." Feeling like a high school student sneaking her boyfriend into the house when her parents weren't home, she giggled and grabbed her car keys.

They pulled up to the house and her heart thumped with excitement. "It's been so long."

"Why don't you come here more often?"

"I don't know, I guess my mother sort of views this as a black mark she wants to erase."

They opened the door and her eyes twinkled as she ran toward the living room. "Hunter, I wish you could see this place decorated for Christmas. It was simply magnificent. The fireplace had white lights and fresh greens. Our stockings hung right here. This is where we put the tree and under it the most perfect train set and village." Taking his hand she led him into the dining room. "Dad had this table made by an Amish man in Lancaster. It's recycled barn doors. The table seats fourteen. Mother always set it with a white cloth with iridescent snowflakes. She used white and silver china we bought from Shop and Go. A simple silver snowflake centered each plate. A whole ton of different sized white and silver candles lined the center of the table. It was magical."

"Where is all the stuff?"

"I'm not sure. I think it's in the basement. Let's go down and check."

The unfinished basement was littered with tall piles of labeled boxes. "Here look, this whole area is Christmas," she said as she rifled through them. "Look—Santa hats. One for you and one for me," she said, placing one on her head and one on his. Laughing and singing she pulled out glass blown balls, ornaments from years past and memories from the boxes. Then she stopped and looked down into the box. Reaching in, she gently pulled out a box labeled "Molly's Angel." Her hand moved quietly across the clear plastic window that revealed a beautiful porcelain angel.

"This would be the last ornament on the top of the tree each year. I always was the one to put it on. Dad would pick me up and I would gently place her on top. Then when we plugged it in she would light up, and Dad would belt out, "it's officially Christmas." The year my mother broke the news we were moving, Maxie was so heartbroken she wouldn't come down to decorate. She and Mom were screaming at the top of their lungs. Mom told her Antonio was like an old toy she would forget as soon as a new better one came along. Maxie ran down the steps and Mom ran after her. I was about to put the angel on and was startled by their yelling and dropped her. Her skirt and wings broke into a bunch of pieces. Maxie was yelling, I was crying and Silvia announced there would be no Christmas at this house this year or any other.

We left the next day and brought no decorations or memories to the new house."

"Red, I'm sorry. Let me see her."

"Mom wanted her to be thrown out. I never knew my Dad must have saved her."

He took her hands. "Can she be fixed?"

"No way, but I still think she's beautiful."

"What's this?" he asked, opening a large box.

A smile swallowed her face. "It's our Christmas village for under the tree. Let's go, I want to show you something."

The two headed back to the new house and Molly directed him to her bedroom.

"Is this my Christmas present? A beautiful girl brings me to her bedroom and wants to show me something, wink, wink?" he said.

"Hunter, focus."

"I'm honored."

She threw a pillow at his head. "Mind out of the gutter," she said as she opened the closet door. Inside she pointed to the large scale rough drawing of Holiday Village. "Here, come in. It's sort of a rough sketch of my dream. I'm not good in the art department."

Hunter's eyes lit from within. "What is this?"

"My dream."

"I don't understand? First off, I thought your dream was to run a Marketing firm."

"That's sort of Silvia's dream. Since I was eight, mine was to open a Holiday Village. I want to make every adult remember what Christmas felt like as a child. I want massive gates that have NP for North Pole and behind them a magical winter wonderland. With a train, Santa's workshop, dinner with Santa, a place where kids can shop for their parents and wrap too and a candy shop. A "Nice List" service center where kids who may need an extra boost to make it on the nice list can fill baskets for the needy, make cards for the seniors, etc., then after they have done something for others their name will flash across the nice list. A coffee house, bakery, restaurant and a hotel designed as a village with different color houses decorated with lights and greens. In the center of the whole village, a tree that would stand forty feet in the air. Here is where caroling will happen every night at eight with elves and Mr. and Mrs. Claus. What do you think?" she said literally without taking a breath.

His eyes brightened further. "I had no idea. How can I be your bestie and not know your dreams? This is unbelievable."

"In a good way?" she asked, squinting one eye and rolling her hands.

"In the best way. Red, you need to do this. I'm dead serious. This is a Christmas Disney World. What's the problem, woman?"

"It's a risk. You know there is no guarantee it will work. And Silvia would flip."

"All the more reason. Listen Red, there are no guarantees in life. Sometimes you just need to let your gut guide you. If we always listened to the logic in our head this would be a very boring world."

"Speaking of taking risks, why didn't you tell me about the Cleary House? I had no idea you wanted to leave. Why haven't you made your move?"

"Sebastian told you, huh? I don't know. I guess it's scary leaving, you know, and it would mean leaving you."

"Never! I live less than ten feet down the hall from you. You will never lose me."

Her phone rang. "Hello."

"Hey sis, I really owe you for this. I know I sort of went overboard with the gifts for the girls, but I so appreciate you offering to wrap them. I have a lot going on over here," said Megan.

"No problem. Hunter and I got this. We are a regular wrapping machine."

"Thanks, Maxie and I are almost finished the routine. Have you noticed anything going on with her? She seems sort of off. She says she's just tired and has a little stomach bug. I just don't think she's herself."

"I'll keep an eye on her. We can talk to her tomorrow at the biggest dinner of the year."

"Right, don't remind me," said Megan. "Thank Hunter for me. Love you."

"Love you," said Molly, hanging up the phone.

"Is everything alright?"

"I'm not sure. Megan is worried about Maxie. And we seemingly have fallen behind on our wrapping job. Here is your Santa hat. Let's go down stairs. You get the presents and the wrapping paper in the library. I'll get some eggnog," she said, putting on her Santa hat.

The two wrapped six-foot high towers of presents. After two hours they were a little punch drunk. Still wearing their hats, they held empty rolls of paper as microphones and sang with the radio a rousing duet of "Baby, It's Cold Outside."

They were so busy singing they hadn't heard Maxie walk in.

Hunter took one end of a new roll of paper and wrapped Molly once around.

Molly spun one more time into the wrap, bringing her closer to Hunter. She sang the wrong words but the best she could after several eggnogs.

Hunter wrapped her closer in the long sheet of wrapping paper. Molly sang, "*I don't think these are the words,*" her voice sank to an awkward low tone.

Hunter grabbed her hand and sang a bit softer. His face inches from hers.

Their eyes locked and without a thought their heads moved closer. Their lips were a mere inch from each other when Maxie accidently hit the end table, startling them both.

"I'm sorry, I didn't mean to…"

"No, you're fine," Molly said, her face flushed. "We were just wrapping."

"I can see that. So given you're all wrapped up, who is getting you as a gift this year?" Maxie asked, winking at Hunter.

"What? Sebastian, why would you even ask?" said Molly, trying to compose herself.

"No reason."

"I've got to take Henry out," said a flustered Molly. "Damn eggnog," she whispered.

"Do you need company Red?" asked Hunter.

"No, I just need some air," Molly said as she hurried Henry out the door.

*****

Left alone, Maxie and Hunter sat down on the sofa in the living room.

"So how long have you been in love with her?" she asked.

"What…er…no we're just friends," he said then bowed his head. "That's not true. I don't actually know, but when I figured it out I raced here to tell her."

"And have you? You know…told her?"

"I can't, it's complicated."

"You mean because there are already two men fighting for her?" she said with a husky giggle.

"There's that, and your mother would never approve."

Her eyes welled up.

"Sometimes we give up what we want for someone else's approval."

He leaned across the sofa and took her hand. "Are we still talking about me? Can I help?"

"No one can. I know the wrath of Silvia's disappointment, and I'm about to be her biggest one of all."

"It can't be all that bad. I find everyone needs to find their own happy. It isn't always the one scripted for you, but you owe it to yourself. Whatever you're feeling Maxie, I'm sure if you just told Silvia what is going on, she would come around," he said.

The door opened and Silvia and Edward made their way into the living room.

"Janet and Marcus really dropped the ball. The main course was cold. The dessert tasteless, and those tacky decorations made by their grandchildren…If I didn't know better, I would think she is having an all-out breakdown. Tomorrow night will be nothing like that debacle."

"And she checks her broom at the door and is here to boil someone," said Maxie.

"For heaven's sake, look at this living room."

"It's just wrapping paper Mom, relax."

Molly walked in with Henry in his little shearling sweater.

"Molly, I don't have to remind you this place needs to be immaculate for tomorrow."

"I'll clean it up, Mom."

"I'll help," said Maxie.

"That's perfect. Then you can go back to wherever it is you're staying," Silvia said, glaring at Hunter.

"Mom, stop being rude to my guest. I want him here," Molly retorted.

"No, it's fine Molly. I'll go. Can I borrow the car?"

"Sure," she said, half-relieved he was leaving so she could shake her head back on straight.

Edward and Silvia went to bed after ushering Hunter out. Maxie and Molly stayed to collect shreds of wrapping paper and tape.

"He's a good guy, Sweet Potato," said Maxie.

"Who?" said Molly, pretending she didn't know they were talking about Hunter.

"Hunter. Why have you two never, you know?"

"Oh no, never, we're just friends."

"It didn't look like that."

Molly, needing to get out of this uncomfortable territory, switched the tables and asked, "How are you feeling? You look a little pale."

"Just tired. Sweets, I won't push, but just one piece of advice. I know you have Mom pushing Thomas and a great guy in Sebastian, but there is no rush. Love is rare and wonderful and it shouldn't be rushed or entered into lightly. I'm going to bed, sis. I love you Sweet Potato," said Maxie, kissing her forehead.

Molly hid the stacks of presents back in the closet and headed to bed. In her room, she noticed the door ajar and saw a glimmer of her drawing. She remembered how she shared them with Sebastian and he barely looked at them. He was so preoccupied with finding Elizabeth he really hadn't noticed much about Molly. Her plan to get him to love her for her was not working. It was time to bring out Elizabeth. She decided to enlist her sisters. She would tell them the truth before dinner tomorrow and then they would figure out how they could spring Elizabeth on him. After all, the pageant was forty-eight hours away. Snuggling Henry, she whispered, "What have I gotten myself into?"

Chapter Thirteen

3 Days Until Christmas

Tonight the McKenna house would host some of the most influential families in Greenwich. For Silvia, it would be like winning a Grammy to have their seal of approval. Dr. and Mrs. Thomas Landon II, Alexander and Kate Jonathan Dolan whom she could undoubtedly celebrate her matchmaking skills with their son and Maxie, Kenneth and Gigi Green, Walt and Tandy Filmore. Last, William and Joanna Trundel, owners of the new chain of high end hotels being put up by the waterfront. Yes, this was a dream come true for Silvia, yet to those around her, an absolute night terror. Silvia started barking orders at seven that morning. Everyone had to be on board to make this the party for the ages.

"Knock, knock," said Hunter, coming in through the kitchen. "Whoa, what is going on in here? Presidential inauguration? Queen Elizabeth and Prince Charles visiting?"

"Worse, Silvia's crew," said Megan.

"Can I help?" asked Hunter.

"Mother has hired two cleaning women, a butler to answer the door, a valet to park the cars and two waiters to serve the food, each in black and white tuxedos, I might add. But if you don't mind, would you check on the girls? They are in the playroom. Mother has us all so busy we don't have a minute."

"Consider Hunter's babysitting services here to help."

"You're the best."

Megan was beautiful, just as Molly had described, but she couldn't hold a candle to Molly in his eyes. Molly McKenna was the most enticing woman he had ever known. The near kiss practically rendered him unconscious. He felt the very air in his lungs escape, leaving him light headed. While they had slept in the same bed, been wrapped in blankets for endless movie nights, last night was different. Her eyes were looking at him the way she had Sebastian for all these years. Maybe he did have a chance. There was only one way of knowing, now if only he had the guts to tell her. He headed down to the princess' lair and found Henry in a pink boa with a bedazzled dog bowl.

"Henry, good man, whatever are you doing at high tea?" he whispered into the fat Pug's ear. "We'll chase a squirrel or bury a bone later. Manly stuff, I promise."

"Hello Sir Hunt-a-lot. Would you like to join us?"

"Only if I get a boa," he answered, pulling up a spot at the tea table.

*****

Edward occupied Sebastian at the country club for most of the day. Silvia didn't need anyone in her way when she was on a mission. Molly, Megan and Maxie were all given hand written chore lists to complete, each with a specific time frame allotted. They fluffed garland, set gifts around as if Santa had arrived a bit early and arranged black and white photos of the family in each room. They lit every one of the thousands of tiny white lights that covered trees, mantles and stairwells. They checked and rechecked the silverware, seating arrangements and exact placement of the fifty white poinsettias delivered by the florist at noon. They were grateful for the hired staff so they might actually be able to relax and enjoy the night.

The three sisters worked for hours until the place beckoned for the cover of House Beautiful. They plopped on the couch and cringed at the thought of the next few hours.

"Is Hunter coming tonight?" asked Maxie.

"Oh, I haven't even talked to him today," said Molly.

"Crap, I left that poor man in the playroom this whole time," said Megan as she jumped up to check on him. She and Molly headed to the playroom.

Inside they found a sleeping Olivia in a pile of fluffy pink blankets and Hunter in a tiara and boa drawing a princess castle with Sophia.

"You are a gift from God," said Molly. Molly's heart couldn't help but respond with a twinkle of joy. There he sat amidst tea cups and frilly dolls just making this little girl beam with excitement. Not an easy chore when it came to Sophia. She had become extremely demanding as of late and few had patience to deal with her. But Hunter did.

"We have read every book in here," said Hunter.

"Hunter you are an angel," Megan said as her phone beeped. "I need to take this."

"Go on. We got this," said Hunter.

"Lucky for you Sophie, I'm a great story teller," said Molly. The little girl snuggled up to her as Molly began. "Once upon a time there was a princess who lived in a castle. She dreamed she would find her prince someday, but she wondered how she would know him. She worried she might meet a prince and think he was the one, but what if he wasn't the right one? So the princess went to a village where she met an old woman. The old woman gave her a little ball of greens wrapped with a red bow. The old woman told the princess it was a magic mistletoe. She told the princess to place the mistletoe above her head and when she kissed her prince, if he was the right one she'd know it. The old woman promised the mistletoe was never wrong. The first prince was handsome and the king and queen thought him to be the perfect man for the beautiful princess. After a lovely ball held at the castle in honor of their meeting, the princess pulled out the mistletoe and held it above them for a kiss. She kissed him gently but felt nothing. He was not the one. She told her parents and vowed to wait for the right one. Then one night she was out in the garden and a commoner passing by stopped to hand her a rose she had dropped. The man had kind eyes and made her laugh. They danced in the moonlight and then the princess pulled out her mistletoe. The man asked if he could kiss her. The princess said yes and like magic her whole body tingled throughout as he kissed her under the mistletoe. He was the one. She had found her true love. The two married and lived happily ever after," said Molly to the little girl who was now fast asleep in her lap.

"Hey, that was a beautiful story. Is that how it works in real life?" asked Hunter.

Megan and Maxie came in to gather up the two little ones. "What's going on in here? asked Megan.

"Two sleeping princesses," said Molly.

"Have I told you two how much I love you?" said Megan.

"Hey Hunter, you are coming tonight?" asked Maxie.

"What is it again? he asked.

"Three hours of hell with the most pretentious people alive," said Molly.

"With an invite like that, who could say no? Dress code?"

"I'm sure Edward will lend you a black suit and tie," said Maxie.

"Great, I'll go find him."

Megan had arranged for the nanny to pick up the girls as to not interfere with Silvia's night. Then Megan, Maxie and Molly retreated to Megan's room to get ready.

"Look what I brought," said Megan, pulling a bottle of wine and three glasses from her bag. Molly wasn't a drinker but she needed a bit of that liquid courage to tell her sisters. Maxie turned down the wine, saying she couldn't be held responsible for what came out of her mouth under the influence.

Maxie and Megan giggled like teenagers while Molly sat quietly wondering how much longer she could keep this a secret. Her sisters knew her too well and each had begun to see cracks in the armor of her boyfriend story. She watched as they drew thick black eye liner and red lips. They seemed so happy. Molly was the screw up sister who still after three years couldn't muster up a real boyfriend for the holiday. This particular problem never plagued her beautiful older sisters. Relationships were like melting butter on a warm biscuit, effortless to them. Megan zipped up Maxie's dress and dusted a bit of pink powder across Molly's freckles.

"This is great fun, all of us getting ready together," said Maxie, said fluffing Molly's curls.

"Moll, you okay?" asked Megan, "You look like you lost your puppy."

"No, no I'm not," she said as tears poured down her face. She wasn't sure where this meltdown came from, but it gained momentum and took off like a rolling snowball. "Sebastian doesn't love me, well not me, me. He loves Elizabeth," she balled louder, "who is me, but not the real me. He loves her, and I'm not her."

"Okay, slow down and stop speaking in riddles," said Maxie.

"He needed a date for a very important event. We couldn't find one. Price, our boss said if Hunter and I didn't find one we would be fired. So, Hunter convinced me to be Elizabeth, a date we hired. Hunter's roommate Kyle and his friend made me…" She paused and lowered her eyes. "Beautiful, unrecognizable. He thinks he's here to meet up with her. He has no idea it's me. I thought, I thought maybe he would fall in love with me instead. Now what am I going to do?"

"Jesus, Moll, I didn't see that coming," said Megan.

“We will figure this out, together. You will get your man. Have you met us? We do beautiful like it’s our job,” said Megan, wiping the tears from her eyes. “After the party we start planning the rebirth of Elizabeth. Okay?”

Molly nodded, wiping her tears.

The three hugged and then a bang on the door signaled Silvia’s impending breakdown.

“It’s show time,” said Maxie.

The three sisters made their way downstairs. Alex and Chase were already having a drink in the living room. Sebastian and Thomas were exchanging golf stories. Silvia paced, waiting for the food delivery. Edward and Hunter came in last, Edward fixing Hunter’s half-knotted tie.

Molly’s eyes lit up. She had never seen him in a suit. “Wow, you look great.”

“Who knew a monkey suit could change a guy?”

Silvia, now at a boiling point, marched directly toward them. Like a missile aimed at its target, she went in for the kill.

“What the hell is he doing here? Molly, it is bad enough we have bachelor number one and bachelor number two here, how do we explain this loafer? You are the only one of my daughters who has habitually not taken my advice and look where it got you. You have a nothing job, and you can’t see a good man when he is right in front of you. Thomas has done everything right. He is a physician, from a great family, the whole package. Look at your sisters – they’re happy. They understand the importance of appearances. And you,” she turned her rage to Hunter. “I’m not going to ask you so politely this time, leave this party now. It is not for your type. You don’t fit in. Go back to New York and get a life. Leave Molly alone to make up her mind. You are not, nor will you ever be good enough to be amongst these people.”

What Silvia didn’t realize was that during her rant the rest of the guests had arrived. Silence fell over the room. Molly’s eyes filled with tears. Before she could say anything, Megan screamed into her phone. Then with blood rage in her eyes, she turned to Chase.

"You lying bastard! You've been sleeping with that whore since September." She hauled off and slapped him across the face. All eyes now on them.

"She's not a whore. I'm going to marry her," he said in response to the slap. The group responded with a gasp. He turned and ran toward the kitchen. He slammed the swinging door open and revealed Maxie kissing the chef.

Silvia put the back of her hand across her forehead and leaned into Edward, her body temporarily turning to a boil.

Regaining her footing, she yelled, "Get your filthy hands off her," and headed toward the kitchen.

The couple came out hand in hand. "Mom, you remember Antonio from seventh grade. Yep, I never got over him. I love him and we're having a baby."

"You go girl," whispered Hunter to Maxie.

Attempting to do damage control, Silvia turned to Alex's parents. "Don't listen to her. He must be drugging her. I know she loves your Alex and would never embarrass your family in this way."

"Actually, Mom, Dad, Silvia, Edward, I'm gay," announced Alex. "You see, Max and I are great friends, but that's all it would ever be. I was honest with her early on, but we just felt like the charade was somehow easier for both of us. And Antonio is a great guy."

Antonio nodded to him with a smile.

"You have done enough damage to my family for one night," said Dr. Dolan, grabbing his wife and son and heading to the door.

The rest of the guests, still flabbergasted, followed suit.

"How could you ruin this night for me?" yelled Silvia to the three girls.

"*Enough*," Edward said with authority. He had never taken this tone with his wife before, but somehow he knew this had escalated beyond his usual quiet pleas.

"Molly, there are a group of young men here who are asking for your heart. I suggest you figure out which one you want once and for all. Megan, baby come here," he said as his oldest daughter ran to his arms and wailed. "The man is pond scum and you haven't been happy for a very long time. He set you free. It's going to be okay." Then he walked over to Antonio and stretched out his hand. "So you are the reason my Maxie giggles like a school girl on the phone. You make her very happy. I presume you are going to marry her?"

"I have loved her since the first day of seventh grade when she hit me with a softball. She is the light of my life, and I can hardly withhold my joy over the fact that we are able to share this with you all. Sir, my business is thriving and I can take care of them. With your blessing I would love nothing more than to make her my wife."

Molly and Megan ran to their sister and threw their arms around her. "You're having a baby," they gushed.

Hunter quietly made his way to the door, but Edward said, "I'm not finished. Hunter, I apologize for my wife's behavior. You are more than good enough to be here and are always welcome. You are a fine young man who I'm grateful has been so important in my Molly's life. Now Silvia, we need to speak in private," he said before ushering her upstairs.

Thomas raised his glass and said, "On that note, I think we all could use a drink," and he poured one for himself and Sebastian. "It'd be a shame to waste all that gourmet food. What do you say we get some in the kitchen?"

Sebastian agreed and the two made their way past the others.

"Meggie, I'm sorry about Chase," said Molly.

"I think I always knew, but when Bev called and said his

secretary was in and used his credit card to buy lingerie and said they were planning on going on vacation, it became real."

"Why did you stay?" asked Maxie.

"It's easier."

"Easier than what?" asked Molly.

"Being alone, letting Mom down, facing the truth that there may be another woman he wants more than me."

"Oh crap, speaking of letting Mom down, I can't be in the Winter Pageant. I don't think they let preggers in."

The two sisters looked at each other and at the same time said, "Molly."

"Molly what?" asked Molly.

"You have to do it. Yes, that is how we will bring Elizabeth to him," whispered Megan.

"Me, oh no, I can't. I could never. Look at me, I'm not beautiful."

"Yes you are and you play the piano brilliantly," said Hunter. "And they're right. When you walk out on stage as Elizabeth he won't be able to resist you."

"You know the whole Elizabeth thing?" asked Maxie.

"Yeah, I want to see her happy. So go for it, Red."

"You think?" she asked.

"I know," said Hunter with a quiet sadness.

"Okay, sorry guys, the party is over. Tomorrow is the pageant. We have much to do. We're going to plan our strategy," said Maxie.

Antonio grabbed her and kissed her, his hand resting on her stomach. "I love you, both."

"I love you, Tony."

"I need to get going myself. I have something to finish up. I'm sorry Molly, for ruining your mother's party."

"You ruining it? Ha, were you even here? I think Meggie and I took that award," said Maxie.

*****

Left alone in the kitchen, Thomas said to Sebastian, "Listen, I don't know your game but I know you don't love Molly. You don't look at her that way, hell, you rarely look at her at all. So what's the deal? Why are you standing in the way of my winning her back?"

"Mate, some part of what you say is true. I'm not sure it's love but in the last week I've become quite fond of Molly. There is something about her that gets to me. But if I'm being honest, I'm pretty sure I know someone who does look at her that way," Sebastian said, his eyes moving to Hunter as he walked out the door.

"Him? You've got to be kidding. After Silvia's roast over the hot coals of humiliation, he ought to go bury his head in the sand. He is no match for Molly."

"Can I ask why you want her back so bad? I don't necessarily see you looking at her that way either."

Thomas puffed out his chest and in his own arrogant style said, "I need a woman like Molly by my side. She's stable, not overtly sexy, not likely to cheat and someone the medical community would approve of."

"Wow, now that is a romantic proclamation if I've ever heard one," said Sebastian.

"There is plenty of romance between us. Don't kid yourself. You're all amateurs. You'll see when she comes to her senses she's going to pick me, especially after her sisters just ambushed Silvia. Molly will try and heal Silvia and that's all good for me. I know my girl Molly will do the right thing. So may the best man win," Thomas said, extending his hand.

"We shall see who is with her on Christmas Day," said Sebastian.

Chapter Fourteen

2 Days Until Christmas

The next day, Hunter hesitantly returned to the house. Silvia had made her feelings abundantly clear, but he didn't come all the way to Connecticut simply to be humiliated. No, he came to tell Molly how he felt. Now he just needed to figure out how. He knocked and was met by Princess Sophia who let him in. Last night had drained the life out of this family. The house was quiet. He made his way into the vast living room. Arranging himself on the sofa he began wringing his hands. His knees bobbed up and down with nervous energy. He needed to summon all the guts he possibly had to throw his name in the hat. Kyle, Kyle would know what to say. Pulling out his phone, he dialed.

"SOS, time is running out. Tonight Sebastian will win her heart. Man, I'm chickening out. I'm not sure I can do this."

"Three way call Jeffery, get on the other line. Hunter, you have waited long enough. It's now or never, man. This is your future. You love her," said Kyle, firm and without hesitation.

"Oh and what a Christmas if you two kiss under the mistletoe. I can't stand it, I'm weeping. Go get the girl," said Jeffery, sniffling.

"I do love her with all my heart. I have to at least try and tell her, but Silvia hates me."

"Battle axe, who cares about her? She'll find someone else to make miserable," said Kyle.

"I don't want to mess up things with Sebastian. He is the one she loves."

"It's Christmas, there is love in the air. You know her better than anyone, Hunter. You know she deserves to at least know the truth. She only thinks she loves him. Give her a chance to decide," said Kyle.

"Okay today, tonight I'll tell her I love her."

"Good luck," said Kyle.

"God speed," said Jeffery.

Hunter turned around to find Silvia standing behind him. "Hey, how long have you been standing there?"

"Not long. I owe you an apology for last night. I was completely out of line. While I still believe what I said is true, it was in poor taste to say it in front of the guests."

"Well, apology not really accepted. I mean no disrespect, but Molly means the world to me. I may not hail from the Landon or Dolan families but I have great parents. I grew up in a loving home where people respect each other. We build each other up instead of tearing each other down. In my world that makes good people, no money or titles required."

"I see. We agree to disagree. I assume you will be heading home now," she asked.

"Nope, then I would miss Molly in the pageant. I'd never do that to her. She's counting on me for support."

"You and Molly are quite close, but you know she doesn't think of you as anything other than a brotherly type."

"I'm kinda working on a surprise for her. I know how much Christmas means to her, so I have been putting this thing together for a few days. I plan on sharing it with her tomorrow."

"That's sweet, but I think she may be a bit too busy to be wasting time on a silly little holiday surprise. After all, I'm pretty sure Thomas is getting her a surprise. It's small but has many facets if you get my drift. You don't want to embarrass yourself dear."

"Hunter, I didn't know you were here," said Molly, flopping on the couch next to him, embracing him in a bear hug. "I can't do this without you."

"Do what? What could you possibly need his help with?" asked Silvia.

Molly bit her lip and managed to eek out, "Becoming Maxie's replacement in the pageant. Mom, I know this isn't what you want, so just let me know if you'd rather me not."

Silvia's steam for the pageant had dimmed. Molly knew her mother had little to no confidence she could pull this off but she did what Silvia would do, held her head high and pushed on. "You have much work to do and very little time if you're going to represent the McKennas in the pageant. We simply can't have Maxie drop out without any replacement. I suggest you say goodbye to Hunter and get working," Silvia said, heading to the kitchen.

"Can I pull this off? I mean pretending to be Elizabeth for Sebastian was hard enough, but I have to walk on stage as her, not me, in front of everyone I know."

"Red, how bad do you want Sebastian? I mean really, have you thought this through?"

"I have, Hunter. He is the man I've been waiting for my whole life. If things go right, all my dreams are finally going to come true."

"Nothing would make me happier than to see you get real happiness, whatever that means."

"What do you mean by that? Surely you're not moving to the dark side and rooting for Thomas."

Hunter took a step closer, reached out, grabbed both of her hands and swallowed hard. It was as good a time as ever to profess his undying love before it was too late. "Moll, you are the best thing that ever happened to me. You make me smile on the inside. I wake up wondering what you're doing. I go to sleep wondering if you're awake." He cleared his throat and said, "What I'm trying to say is..."

"Apparently you two did not hear the announcement that we are having an early bite to eat before we leave for the pageant. You weren't planning on staying, were you, Hunter? I didn't set a plate," said Silvia.

"Uh, no, I guess not, um..."

"Mother, don't be ridiculous, of course Hunter is staying."

"I thought you said you had some sort of surprise you were working on," said Silvia, grabbing his coat and tucking it in his arm.

"She's right Red, I have a lot to do before tonight, but thanks. Can I use your car?"

"Did you say a surprise? Is it for me?" said Molly, jumping up and down.

"Who else?"

"Please don't be late to the pageant. I'm not sure I can go through with it if you're not there. You give me the strength to believe I can do anything."

"You know you can count on me," Hunter said. As he walked toward the door, he wondered if it was too late.

Molly barely ate a morsel, her nerves were completely frazzled. She had practiced her piano number, practiced walking in heels, practiced saying, "Yes Sebastian, I love you too," and then practiced in heels again. She knew the importance of the night. First the pressure of not letting Silvia down brewed a hive that was building with the momentum of a giant snowball. And second, tonight she would reveal her true self to Sebastian. What she didn't know was how she was going to pull this off. Maxie and Megan packed the car with Molly's gowns and shoes. They kissed their baby sister and shuffled a pensive Molly into the car. Ready or not, it was go time.

They arrived at the pageant in plenty of time to pull off

Operation Elizabeth. Sebastian could barely contain himself over meeting Elizabeth, Molly could barely keep from bursting out the truth to Sebastian and Hunter could barely keep his secret another minute. Thomas, arrogant as usual, sat front row in the audience, telling anyone who would listen he and Molly were reuniting.

Molly performed in the opening act with the other contestants as herself. She would save Elizabeth for the talent portion. The thought of being beautiful again, of bringing Sebastian his wish consumed her. Her whole body shook with anxious energy just waiting to see Sebastian's face as she appeared as Elizabeth.

Megan and Maxie waited back stage for the moment they would transform her into the woman of Sebastian's dreams. The two sisters helped her put in daily contact lenses, painted on the foundation, then pressed powder and blush. They played up her green eyes with a bronze eyeliner and after dusting on glistening metallic eye shadow painstakingly put on a whole set of fake eyelashes. They took each strand of that jungle of hair of hers and straightened it. Her lily white skin was the perfect accessory to her shimmering satin silver gown.

"Holy shit Molly, Sebastian is going to lose it. You are a knockout, baby sis," said Maxie.

They had finally made it to the talent segment, and it was time to bring out Elizabeth. They were going to blow Sebastian Tate away.

"I'm so scared, what if he is disappointed it's me?"

"Sweet Potato, you have always been beautiful. Just know you don't need to be Elizabeth for a man to want you. The right man will love you for who you are," said Maxie.

"But God damn, you look hot," said Megan.

"Thank you, you are the best sisters in the world," Molly said, kissing them before making her way to the stage.

"Christ, look out there, you have three men here. I feel like we are in the finale of the Bachelorette," said Maxie.

"I know Thomas says he wants me, but deep in my heart I feel he's the same old Thomas. Now Sebastian, he really wants me, well not me, but Elizabeth me."

"Well, you certainly have the male population here in full support tonight, whoever you choose," said Maxie, fixing her gown.

"Speaking of support, where's Hunter? He said he would be here."

"Not sure, I'll go have a look," said Maxie.

Looking at herself in the backstage mirror, Molly's smile turned to worry. "I'm so nervous. What if he doesn't like the real me?"

"Not possible. He is just looking for Elizabeth because he doesn't know you are the one he wants. When he realizes you are her, all your fears will be gone," said Megan.

"Look who I found," said Maxie, giving him a tap on the behind. "Good luck," she whispered in Hunter's ear.

"Molly, can I have a minute alone?" Hunter asked.

Her sisters kissed her. "This is it, little sis! Go get the crown and your man."

Hunter stared at her for a moment. "Wow, you look amazing."

"Really? Maxie got me contacts. What do you think?"

"I think you are beautiful glasses or no glasses."

"You have to say that. You're my bestie."

"About that…I wanted you to open your birthday present before you go out."

Grabbing the present out of his hands, her eyes beaming like a five year old, she asked, "Can I open it now?"

He nodded. She tore through the paper to a gold box that had today's date engraved on it. Under the date an inscription read, *May you find the man you're destined to be with in the kiss you share under the mistletoe.*

Inside sat a giant glittering ball of mistletoe trimmed with holly and a red and black plaid bow. Hanging from the bottom, a crystal heart caught the light in its many facets.

Tears filled her eyes. "You remembered. I mean I loved the ornament but this is beyond fabulous. It's the real stuff, ya know the one that tells true loves kiss."

"Molly, I need to tell you something. I know this is really bad timing, but it's now or never."

"That's ominous. Should I be scared?"

"I sure am, but here goes. Molly, you have exactly twenty three freckles across the bridge of your nose. You snore when you sleep on your back. You sing adorably sweet from your shower. You dream big and love whole heartedly. You love Christmas so much you want to share it with the whole world in your village. Your favorite song is "White Christmas." You're kind, intelligent, sweet, funny and the most beautiful woman I have ever met."

"Am I dying?"

"Molly, you asked why I'm so picky about women. I realized it's because there is only one woman for me." He paused and wringing his hands he said, "That woman is you. Since the day you walked into that office, my life hasn't been the same. You are my best friend, confidant, my partner. You are the peanut butter to my jelly, the nut to my bolt, my better half. You finish my sentences, heck you start my sentences. You center me. You make me believe in happily ever after. You bring my soul to life and I can't think of anyone I would rather spend the rest of my life with than you. Molly, you are my home. I love you, Molly McKenna, with every part of me."

Sucking in a deep breath she leaned back on the makeup table, her face a mixture of shock, fear and an inability to move her lips to form words. Pulling herself up, she walked toward him and began what sounded like an apology.

"Hunter, I love you too, but not that way. You know how I feel about Sebastian. I've waited so long for the chance to be with him. I…I"

As if he hadn't heard her rejection, he clutched the mistletoe in his left hand, holding it above them. With the right hand he pulled her close to him.

Molly looked up at the mistletoe and panic quickly set in. Her eyes widening like saucers, she pushed off his chest with both hands. Her teeth clenched and her lips pursed as she straightened her back to distance herself.

Yet he ignored her body language and gently pulled her tighter until their lips met softly. He smelled like Burberry cologne, his skin soft, his lips softer. Her eyes, as if ignoring her every command closed as her lips gently opened, allowing him deeper into his kiss. The room went silent and black. Without warning her rigid spine arched comfortably forward, the muscles melted, pressing her chest in closer to his. Her arms slid slowly around his neck. Like the final piece of a puzzle, their bodies fit perfectly. Every neuron in her ignited as if she had awakened from a long uninterrupted sleep. Her skin tingled, warmly her face flushed. She was lost in what felt like a kiss she had known forever, like the mistletoe kiss that promised her true love.

"Molly, they are ready for you onstage in two," said Silvia abruptly, her eyes glued to Hunter.

Hunter pulled back at the sound of Silvia's voice, but Molly's eyes remained closed for a moment until Hunter released his grip. She opened them to see the mistletoe shimmering above them.

Flustered, she stammered, her legs weak, her breath spotty. She shook her head from left to right and instructed her arms and back to regain strength. *What just happened*? Every nerve in her body questioned the tingling sensation running through her veins. And why did she wish it hadn't ended?

"I…I have to go out there. I'm sorry Hunter. I just can't."

"Molly, I don't know what you want. And I'm pretty sure you don't either, but I want you to be happy, whatever that means. If it's him that gives you that happily ever after then I'm okay with that, but I bought you this mistletoe with the hope that the only girl I would ever kiss under mistletoe for the rest of my life would be you, Molly McKenna."

"Cue McKenna," said the stage hand.

He turned and walked out, leaving her a shaking pile of confusion.

Silvia walked in and put her hands squarely on Molly's shoulders. "Molly, you are here to win this thing. And by God I can't believe I'm saying it, but you've got this. You look truly beautiful tonight. There is a young man in that audience who is going to get the best Christmas gift he has ever received. Now clear your head with a few deep breaths. Find the man you choose in that sea of people and play that piano like the keys are one with your fingers and the melody is for him alone. Sebastian and Thomas are good men. Wealthy, from good families, established careers. Thomas, you know, is fighting the hardest dear, please keep that in mind. Now whatever just happened here means nothing. The holidays make people do crazy things. There is nothing to think about here. Hunter is your friend, nothing more. You're blushing. It's just nerves. You shared a kiss between friends, that's all. It meant nothing."

Silvia was probably right. It was just a kiss. After all, she hadn't actually kissed someone, really kissed someone, in a very long time. Any kiss was bound to stir something. She looked at her mother and saw that familiar look of fierce competitiveness in her eyes. For the first time in her life, Molly had the chance to gain her mother's acceptance. She could be the McKenna daughter her mother would brag about to the country club ladies. She could join the other sisters as one of the beautiful daughters of Silvia McKenna. Molly wished she could hug Silvia but knew better than to attempt that. She stood up tall and said, "I'll do my best Mom," and then headed to the stage.

The announcer said, "Now last, but certainly not least, we have Molly McKenna playing 'The Christmas Song.'"

Walking slowly to the center of the stage, she briefly looked out into the blinding white spotlights then headed to the piano. Her fingers found the keys like slipping into a favorite pair of gloves. Once the melody began she fell deeply into her music, and everything else slipped away. When she finished, she stood to bow and spotted Sebastian sitting between her sisters. His smile imploded with joy as he clapped his hands together feverishly.

"Thank you Ms. McKenna. Now please enjoy the children's choir as they perform carols to melt your heart. After a ten minute intermission we will conclude the evening by crowning this year's Ms. Winter."

The contestants were all given a minute to change back to their evening gowns. Molly slipped on her white halter evening gown encrusted in white sequins and crystal jewels. She opened her carry on and pulled out the Loubie, holding it close to her chest. She whispered, "Tonight we meet your other half. And all our dreams will come true."

Placing the shoe on her foot she released the gown down over her feet and then saw him standing in the doorway, his eyes even bluer than she remembered, his five o'clock shadow smoldering over those sexy dimples. His teeth glistening like fresh fallen snow.

"I think I have something that belongs to you," he said, pulling out the lone Loubie.

She lifted the hem of her gown to reveal the other one. Slipping it on, her sisters cheered silently, jumping up and down behind him. He pulled her up into his arms. Her legs felt weak as she attempted to steady herself in the skyscrapers.

"Why didn't you tell me it was you?"

"It's me, but not exactly. I don't ski or speak Mandarin. I wear glasses and I'm not actually a fan of the country club crowd. I'm just me, Molly, plain and simple. Elizabeth is much more cultured."

"You can learn to ski. I'll teach you Mandarin. And you're not wearing glasses now. You will love the country club, trust me. All that matters is that I found you," he said, his eyes pools of blue twinkling with excitement. She had been dreaming of this moment for three years, the day when he would hold her in his strong, muscular arms. They would kiss and their love would be sealed forever. As he moved closer, her breath became more rapid with each inch. His hand cupped the back of her head. It was finally here, the kiss, the kiss that would be her forever.

"Wait." She inhaled heavily as she wobbled over to the makeup table and snatched the mistletoe. Tiny, quick, awkward steps carried her back to his arms. Holding the mistletoe above them, she closed her eyes. He pulled her head in hard to his open mouth. His lips suctioned around her entire mouth like a vacuum head. The sexy scruff on his face abrasively removed more layers of skin than the Brazilian waxer. And then an unanticipated clump of drool slid like lava down her chin. Her eyes popped open. Gasping for air, she pulled back to catch the dribble of saliva as it hung from her chin threatening the very fabric of her evening gown. *Oh no, no, no, this can't be happening. This is the kiss. I'll know it. Try again* she instructed herself. Regaining her calm, she casually moved in closer, this time with the mistletoe directly overhead. Unfazed by the whole freak out, he again went in for the kill. This time suctioning her face like a Hoover mixed with the kiss of an English Sheep dog, he allowed saliva to escape between breaths. She felt nothing other than the need to find a lobster bib. No magic, no tingling, nothing like the mistletoe promised. How could this be? It must be a mistake. She was certain Sebastian's lips on hers under the mistletoe would be magical.

The ringing of her phone from her bag suddenly brought the oxygen back to her lungs. Grateful for the distraction, she stepped back and excused herself.

"Hello."

"Hey Molly, you okay? Sound a little winded," said Gus.

"Merry Christmas, Gus."

"Just wanted to let you know the kids opened all those amazing gifts. First time ever each kid got the gift they asked for. That Santa of yours is a one of kind. Tell him he gave some kids whose lives are otherwise very difficult the chance to believe in happiness and forget their troubles for one magical night. Molly, that is a Christmas gift I ask for every night."

"Hunter…" she said before the stagehand signaled the contestants to take their place on the stage.

"Thanks Gus. Tell everyone I love them and Merry Christmas."

"Go, go win this thing Elizabeth," said Sebastian.

"It's Molly."

"Sorry, it's going take some getting used to."

"What's my favorite song?"

He paused. "I don't know. Why does it matter?"

"What's my real dream? My dream, what's my dream?"

"I don't know what you mean?"

"The dream I showed you. In my closet. What was it?"

"A golf course?"

The music cued the contestants it was time.

"I have to go."

Walking onto the stage, her mind raced with a million thoughts. But the one thought that she couldn't stop swirling around her head was the kiss with Hunter. It felt like the soldier coming home from war kiss, the kiss that blended two people together seamlessly, the kiss that felt like home. *It was Hunter. Oh God, it's Hunter.*

"And the winner of this year's Ms. Winter Pageant is Molly McKenna."

The crowd squealed with delight. Molly was a beloved member of the town. Her kind heart and genuine sweetness made her the perfect girl to hold this title. The other contestants hugged her as Megan walked onto the stage to crown her with the sparkling tiara and fur sash.

"You did it, girl," Megan said, placing the tiara on her head.

Molly scanned the crowd, looking for one face, Hunter's. He had granted every child at the shelter their Christmas wish. He believed in her. He was the one who would be there for her, win or lose. He sacrificed his own happiness for hers. He was kind, funny, wonderful. He was simply the one.

"Oh God, I've made a terrible mistake," Molly said. "Thank you everyone, but I've got to go before it's too late," she said before rushing off the stage.

Sebastian stood at the edge of the stage. Extending his hand, he helped her down. She looked at him, his beautiful face, but he wasn't the face that would be her forever.

"Sebastian, I don't know how to say this. I'm not Elizabeth, she isn't real. I'm plain, simple, Molly, the same girl I've always been, sitting ten steps from your office door. I'm not the girl you want. I'm sorry I deceived you. I just thought you and I would be perfect together, but it turns out I was wrong. There is actually someone else for me."

"Hey, no apology necessary, you helped me get over the embarrassment of my public breakup. You offered an amazing distraction to my otherwise mangled life. I had a great time with your family, but you need to go find him. Hunter's a good guy."

"How did you know?"

"How did you not know? The way he looks at you. That guy would give his life for you. He said I won and I better take good care of the most amazing woman alive before he left. Now go," he said and gave her a hug.

She ran to the dressing room and slipped off the Loubies, then pulled on her Uggs. She ran for the exit, looking everywhere. She hurried to search the freezing parking lot. Scanning left to right, she ran into Maxie.

"He's gone," said Maxie.

"Gone?" Panic washed over her." Gone where?"

"He said he was heading to the train station. Last train out is at ten o'clock. He must have called a cab and it's a good thing, this parking lot is jammed. Father Stevens said we can head over for the live Nativity. It starts in fifteen. Face it Molly, you're boxed in."

"I have to catch him," said Molly, fishing for her keys.

"You'll freeze, for God's sake, you're in an evening gown and there is no way in hell you're getting your car out of the center of that grid locked lot. Call him later."

Tears welled up in her eyes. "You don't understand. I love him. I love Hunter. He's my one true love. The kiss under the mistletoe was right."

"Calm down Molly, you're not making any sense. You were so happy when Sebastian gave you the other shoe."

"I was wrong Maxie. I love him. I ruined everything."

Father Stevens walked up to Molly and Maxie and said, "Hi girls, heading over to the Nativity? Good heavens child, you are going to freeze. Mother said congrats are in order. What are these tears about?"

"Father Stevens, I have to get to the train station fast. It's an emergency and there is no way I can get out of here." She sobbed.

"Okay child, I have an idea. This is rash but under these circumstances I think it will be alright. Follow me."

Molly kissed Maxie and said, "Tell Mom I'm sorry I disappointed her."

"Go, Molly, find him. Don't be a fool like Megan and me. Trust your own heart. He loves you."

"You knew too?"

"Molly, everyone knew. The boy might as well wear a marquee on his head."

Father Stevens led them to an old shed behind the rectory. He pulled up the door, stepped in and pulled a string from the ceiling.

Inside he tugged a dusty blanket off an old moped. This is Sister Joan's bike, but she's a sucker for young love. She'll understand," he said, handing Molly a helmet.

Throwing her arms around his neck she squealed. "Thank you Father and thank Sister Joan. I only hope I'm not too late."

"Have faith Molly—if it's meant to be, you two will find each other."

Yanking her gown up to her knees, she gave the bike a quick dusting and jumped on. "Have you ever ridden one of these?" asked Father.

"Nope, but I've never been in love before, so it seems like a good time to try."

"Be careful, Moll," said Maxie.

"One more thing Molly, take my coat. It's freezing. You'll be frostbitten before you get to the station without it," said Father, handing her his long black wool coat.

Grateful, she slid into the large coat that nearly swallowed her whole. Wrenching the helmet on top of her crown she gave a thumbs up and turned the key in the engine. First a sputtering, then a gear grinding, gave way to a purr. The old moped still had some life in it. She steadied herself and released the brake. The deep snow mounds were tough to navigate, but many of the sidewalks were shoveled, allowing her to bypass stalled traffic. Unsteady at first, the thought of the kiss replayed in her mind, and she found herself pushing the moped to its limits. The cold air stung her face but she was determined to get to him.

How could she not have known? She had spent the last three years pining over a man who barely knew her, the real her, when the man she wanted was right there under her mistletoe. After what seemed like an eternity, she caught sight of the light of the train station ahead. Pushing hard on the gas, she raced to the entrance, not realizing she hadn't given much thought to stopping. Pulling hard on the brake, she attempted to slow to a stop but rather slammed into a snow mound, sending her face first into the icy snow. Hiking up her gown she climbed off the bike. Barely feeling the icicles as they formed on her face and ringlets, she darted into the station. Like the quiet after a tornado, the old station was still. No signs of life. She rushed into the station and saw a sign swinging across the ticket window that read, "Closed."

Inside, she saw the foot of a man behind the door. Banging hard on the glass she begged him to come to the window.

"Lady, can't you read? We're closed."

"A man. Did a man get on the train to New York?" she huffed.

"Now, let's see a man, hmm. No, never saw a man."

Sarcasm was about the last thing she could take. "Please, I'm desperate. When did the train to New York leave?"

"Left the station about ten minutes ago, and to answer your question, yeah, a bunch of men were on it."

"I'm too late." She sobbed. Reaching into her pocket, she pulled out her phone and dialed Maxie.

"Did you get him Sweet Potato?" asked Maxie.

"Noooooo, I ruined everything. He's gone. How could I have been so blind?"

"Listen sweetie, go home. We will figure something out. The traffic will be better after tomorrow. Call him later. You can go back to the city after Christmas."

"No, I lost him. You should have seen his eyes when I told him I didn't feel that way. I did, I just wouldn't let myself believe it. That kiss under the Mistletoe—it was my forever. I'm going to the house on Holly. I think I need to be alone. I can't bear mother's gloating tonight."

"Be careful Moll. We love you. We'll figure it out tomorrow."

She turned toward the exit and heard the man behind the glass open the ticket window. "Hey lady, Christmas has a funny way of making things work out like they're supposed to."

“Thank you, Merry Christmas,” she said as she slumped her way toward the door. Reluctantly straddling the dirt bike, one more time she headed down Main toward the house on Holly.

The roads were snarled at every pass. The lawns glistened with fresh powdery snow. Icicles dangled from rooftops. Plumes of smoke puffed from chimneys with hints of warm logs burning below. The lights on the houses twinkled with warmth and holiday promises of joy.

Riding alongside the piles of cars filled with families she watched as they merrily sang Christmas songs. Through windows she saw couples snuggling. She thought about all the nights she and Hunter had snuggled.

She bypassed the crowds by taking the sidewalks. A chill clenched her bones as the snowflakes began to thicken. The cold had begun to take its toll on her as she rounded the corner to Holly Lane. She nearly lost control of her moped when she spotted the house. She could hardly believe her eyes. Twinkling multi colored lights trimmed her childhood home. Each window had a candle and sprigs of fresh greens with holly all finished with a red bow. The door was dressed with a large wreath intertwined with colorful balls. Hunter had done this for her. Her heart racing, her eyes tear-filled she sped up to get there and lost traction as she pulled up the walkway. The back wheel slid out as she careened head first into a three foot mound of snow. Struggling to gain her footing, she grabbed a string of garland from the porch and pulled herself up.

Grabbing the banister, she climbed up the porch and reached for the door handle. She prayed with all her heart Hunter would be standing on the other side. Opening the door, her heart sank as her eyes panned the room. He wasn’t there, but he had decorated her home just as she remembered it as a child. He had thought of everything. The fireplace mantel blanketed in greens with white lights. Three red fur stockings, Meggie, Maxie and Molly hung, each filled with candy canes. The tree still bare, except for lights, had boxes next to it filled to the brim with balls in red, silver and green. Tinsel sparkled from the box on the floor, twinkling lights begging to be strung on the tree. He had left the tree for them to decorate together as they had the last three Christmases. The train and village were exactly as she had told him.

Next to the tree stood a four foot gift wrapped in red and white snowflakes. The tag read: "*To Molly, I believe in Santa Claus and I believe in you! All my love, Hunter.*"

Picking it up, her eyes welled as she looked at the strangely shaped package. It looked very much like a roll of wrapping paper. She pulled off the bow and pulled back the wrapping. Beneath a white glossy poster board, she unrolled the poster and caught her breath in her throat. It was the mock up logo for Holiday Village. He had captured it exactly as she had imagined it. Gold scrolled gates with the letters N and P slightly opened, revealing a twinkling Christmas village in the background. Under a snowy night, the warmth of the village seemed to invite with a promise of yesteryear. Like a Norman Rockwell painting, the images magically danced off the page.

She slid down to her knees and let the flood of emotion overtake her. He remembered what she showed him in her room that night. Not just remembered it but he had embraced it, every detail. He believed in her. He knew her dream. He knew everything about her. The most amazing man in the world loved her. She didn't see it. Even the mistletoe kiss told her, but she chose to ignore it. Now he was gone. Sebastian was a fantasy, but in reality he wasn't her forever. He was safe, someone to love from afar, never having to deal with real emotions. Silvia had drilled so deeply in her brain the characteristics she wanted for her, that Molly had forgotten what really mattered, someone who loved her for her, not some version of herself she didn't even recognize.

Through her sobbing, she thought she heard sleigh bells. She wiped her frozen cheeks and sat up. Again she heard jingling of bells, this time louder. She rose to her feet and went to the front door. The bells, even louder now, seemed as if they were heading straight for her house. She flung open the door to see a horse drawn sleigh racing down the street, driven by what looked like Santa Claus. The driver struggled to stop the horses and slid up onto the front lawn. The man jumped from the sleigh and ran toward her.

"Molly, you're here," yelled the Santa.

She knew that voice. "Hunter, is that you?" she cried.

He pulled down the beard and smiled.

She leapt off the porch into his arms. Hoisting her gown up around her thighs she wrapped her legs around him. "Wait, why are you here? How are you here? You got on the train. The roads are all deadlocked."

"First, you are the most beautiful thing I have ever seen." He smiled, pushing back the icicles she used to call hair.

She thought for a minute about what she actually looked like. She looked down at her oversized man's trench coat, tattered, nearly black dress and Uggs. She reached up and felt the tiara dangling sideways from beneath her helmet. "I, I had to stop you."

"You did? Why?"

"Because I love you madly and truly, like nothing I've known before. Can I have a redo?" she asked.

"Only if you can forgive me for running out before you were crowned? I promised to be there to support you. I just didn't want to get in the way of you and Sebastian."

"What changed your mind?"

"Not what…who?" He turned to the sleigh and waved to someone in the passenger side. Molly hadn't even noticed anyone there. The woman wrapped in a hood and scarf made her way to them.

Molly could hardly believe her eyes. “Mom?”

Silvia threw her arms around the two of them. “Oh Molly, can you forgive me for almost making you lose the love of your life?”

“Wait, what? I don’t understand? Why are you here? Where is Thomas?”

“Can we go inside before your little button nose freezes off?”

Hunter put her down and squeezed her tight. The three headed inside. Silvia stopped right inside the door. Her hand grasped her mouth as her eyes glassed up. She said nothing as she slowly walked around the small home, running her fingers across the vintage decorations, a Santa that held a light up candle swaying back and forth, three wise men facing a manger lit from within. Inside the small manger, straw flanked Mary and Joseph. She remembered how each year they put up the manger without baby Jesus until Christmas day. She moved to the tree and looked at the boxes of ornaments the family had collected over the years. A Raggedy Ann that had Molly painted on it, a softball bat with Maxie, and a pair of pink stilettos that said “Meggie.” She turned to Molly and said, “My God, what have I done?” before bursting into tears.

Molly wrapped her arms around her and said, “It’s okay.”

“No Molly, it really isn’t. You see, you’ve been right all along about everything. Look what I did to your sisters. Megan is about to begin an ugly divorce, and Maxie is having a baby with a man I refused to know. And you, poor sweet Molly, with your vision of Christmas.” She paused and looked around the room. “I was afraid to let those emotions back in because they meant life before, before this pretentious world I’ve built. This man standing before you is your true love. I saw your kiss under the mistletoe, but truth be told I knew it long before either of you. I knew when I met you in New York. You finished each other’s sentences. You took care of each other and the way he looked at you, Molly, like there was no other woman in the world. I was too selfish to admit it."

"So she grabbed a cab and followed me to the station. I was about to board when she called me. Molly, Silvia loves you, she just may not always show it the way you want. She knew you would go back to this house. We tried to catch a cab but the traffic was jammed. I had to get to you. Mr. Halley rented that sleigh for his granddaughter. Your mother here begged in the name of love to borrow it. Only catch—I had to be Santa for little Kendra first. So here we are, a tad late, due to the Santa thing and all. Can you forgive us?" said Hunter, grabbing Silvia's hand.

Her mother and Hunter holding hands in a Christmas-filled room was almost more than Molly could handle. "Oh my gosh, yes. I love you both."

Silvia pulled back, eyes beaming, "I know how to make this right, all of it. You two, can you get the sleigh back to Mr. Halley? Dad is on his way, we have so much to do. Tomorrow is Christmas Eve, family meeting at the house, nine o'clock sharp. I'll tell your sisters. I think you two might want to stay here tonight." She winked. "Get some rest—tomorrow is going to be a huge day."

Dad honked the horn out front. "That's me, I've got to go. And Molly, thank you, for showing me what really matters."

Molly followed Mom out the door and asked, "Mom, what about Thomas?"

Silvia put her hand on her daughters face. "After I saw you and Hunter kiss, I went to look for Thomas. I wanted to tell him he needed to up his game, that's when I saw him kissing Miranda Wiseman behind the curtain."

"That bastard," said Molly.

"After pouring the bucket of dirty water someone had left backstage on his head, I warned him to stay far away from you. Then I came back to see you with Sebastian. Your face was trying so hard to feel what you did with Hunter. I knew I had to find Hunter, but he had already left for the station. So I took off running."

"I love you Mom, and thank you."

"I love you, Molly, and thank you for getting this family back on track," Silvia said, hugging her daughter.

Chapter Fifteen

Christmas Eve

Silvia rang Molly's cell at eight o'clock that morning. "I need you two over here for a family meeting, remember nine o'clock sharp."

Molly rolled over and saw Hunter sleeping sweetly next to her. A smile so bright she was sure it would wake him washed over her face. She moved closer and snuggled in. It had been the most amazing night of her life. She wasn't sure if she should pinch herself to see if this was all a dream.

"Good morning, gorgeous," he said, giving her a groggy kiss.

She popped up and jumped on top of him. Straddling him she said, "Do you know what today is?"

"Way ahead of you, Red," he said reaching under the bed and pulling out a dozen red roses and a gift bag. "Happy Birthday to the sweetest girl I know."

"Yay," she said, grabbing the bag. She reached in and found a pair of pink Uggs. "You remembered," she said, slipping them on with her white tee shirt and undies. "I love them. You were busy. How did you get all these?"

"Ya know I have trained as Santa's helper. I stopped at Forever Spring Florist up on Church Street before the pageant. The Uggs, silly girl, they were ordered months ago. There's something else, but it's for tonight," he teased.

"We have an important family meeting at the house at nine and I sort of forgot about Henry. I need to check on him. Although I wish we could just stay in bed all day."

"That could be arranged," he said, pulling her close.

"Nope, it's Christmas Eve. We must seize the day, then we can resume tonight." She giggled.

The two grabbed coffee and bagels at The Bagel Hut and headed to Silvia's meeting. Henry greeted them with reindeer antlers and bells on his collar, Sophie and Olivia not far behind. Megan and Maxie, already seated in the living room, waited to hear what the big meeting was about.

Silvia took center stage in front of the large fireplace. "I know you're all wondering why I have called you here. While it will take time to mend some of the mistakes I've made with you girls, there is one mistake I can fix right now. Yes, today we will have an old-fashioned McKenna Christmas. Tree trimming, Molly, Hunter we need another tree for the house on Holly Lane. I want the girls to help us make popcorn and string cranberries. Cookies, yes, we will need to make lots of cookies. Tonight we will make homemade pizzas and salad. Maxie, call Tony, ask if he can deliver the food to Holly Lane uncooked tomorrow morning, and of course make sure he will join us. We will prepare the bird, make the fixings etc. Christmas outfits, please. We will be taking a family portrait at the house and caroling begins promptly at eight. We have a lot of work to do. Megan, you and the girls can help Dad and me get the rest of the boxes from the basement."

The room fell silent at first and then erupted into cheering, laughter and excitement. "What are you people waiting for?" Silvia asked. "Molly, Hunter can you stay behind?" she added.

The others ran to get dressed and start the fun-filled day. Silvia sat next to them. "Megan and the girls need this to fill the hole in their heart. Chase left for Florida today with his girlfriend. I don't know how I missed the pain she was in."

“You don’t know what this means to me, to us. We’ll get her through it. It’s going to be the best Christmas ever,” said Molly, jumping up and down.

Her phone rang. “Hello.” She was surprised to hear Sebastian’s voice on the other end.

“Hey Molly, I’m hoping you were able to catch Hunter.”

“Yes, I did,” she said happily.

“I’m glad. I’m calling to thank you two. When I got back there was a message on my machine from Marcy, a girl from my past that I had lost touch with. She’s back in the States and said you two left her a message about me. Long story short, we’re spending tomorrow together. Thank you.”

“I’m so happy to hear that,” she said.

“Happy Christmas to you and your family.”

“Merry Christmas, Sebastian.”

“Any regrets over letting him go?” asked Hunter.

“Not a one.”

“Thank God, I can let Kyle and Jeffery know they can uncross every part of their bodies.”

“They knew?”

“They forced me to tell you.”

“I love them.”

The day couldn’t have been more perfect. She and Maxie baked chocolate chips, peanut butter blossoms, sugar cookies, gingerbread men and raspberry thumbprints while Silvia and Megan strung popcorn with the girls. Dad and Hunter set up the tree. Everyone took part in the tree decorating, something Sophie and Olivia had never done. The second tree was just for the little ones filled with homemade ornaments. The family laughed and reminisced about past Christmases while they made homemade pizzas with a little help from Tony. After dinner, the group gathered around the piano while Molly played their favorite carols. Sophie and Olivia seemed not to notice the absence of

Chase, and for that matter, neither did Megan. Maxie and Tony snuggled in the corner by the fireplace with Henry nestled in with his reindeer ears on.

"If I could have your attention please," said Hunter after returning from the kitchen. Pulling out a birthday cake from behind his back, he said, "Lights please." He lit the candles and the group sang Happy Birthday to Molly.

Edward stood up and took the floor. "Molly, we are so proud of all you have accomplished, but your sister Maxie brought something to our attention after you left Thanksgiving. We all met in your closet for a reminder of the dream you hold. If I'm being honest, I for one had forgotten about it. I had forgotten all the detail you put into it. All the heart. Then a certain young man shared a drawing with me the day we spent some time together. He told me you have a business plan and a marketing plan already established. We had no idea how much this dream meant to you, so I did a little digging around at the club. Turns out Ken Mendelsohn has a piece of real estate for sale that piqued my interest. Do you remember Bell Mountain?"

Molly, looking confused, said, "Yes, the ski resort?"

"It's for sale, but the interesting thing is they want a developer who will make it a destination site. We checked it out. It has twenty trails, a lodge, and a restaurant. There is quite a bit of undeveloped land at the foot of the mountain, the perfect place for your holiday village."

"Oh my gosh, are you serious? You guys are on board with this? I mean, I thought you wanted me to be in the business world?"

"Molly, what better way to put your degree to work than opening your own business?" said Edward.

Putting her hand over her mouth, Molly broke down. Maxie and Megan gathered around her, hugging her. "It's really happening, baby sis, if you want it," said Maxie.

"If? It's all I've ever wanted."

"Then it's settled, we will meet Ken next week after the holidays and check it out."

The girls jumped up and down, crying, cheering and hugging.

"Happy birthday Molly," said Silvia. "We believe in you."

"Now let's keep this Christmas party going," said Edward. "Who wants hot cocoa?"

"Wait, one more gift to officially get this party started," said Hunter, taking Molly's hand and leading her to the tree. Underneath a large oblong box wrapped in silver paper sat with a tag reading, "To Molly, Love Hunter."

She pulled back the paper and stopped. Her eyes softened when she opened the box and saw the porcelain angel. Unbroken, perfect, exactly as Molly remembered her as a child.

"Hunter how? How did you manage to fix her?" she said, wiping her tears.

"Not fix, rather, find. Internet is a pretty handy tool. Seems you can take a picture and hunt one down on the net. I thought I would have to wait a few days but turns out the seller lived right here in Connecticut. He bought her probably around the same year as you."

Molly climbed up on a stool and placed the angel on the top of the tree.

Edward stood up and proclaimed, "It's officially Christmas." Everyone cheered, even Henry in his Santa sweater opened one eye and let out a small howl.

Hunter pulled Molly aside. Holding his hands she had to stop herself from crying. "This means more than you know. When the angel broke that Christmas, so did my family. Now it really feels like we are us again, the McKenna clan sharing the holidays the old fashioned way. You're my angel, Hunter Bentley."

"Follow me," he said, leading her outside to the front porch. "Close your eyes." Eyes closed, she stepped lightly as the wooden porch squeaked beneath her. "Okay, now you can open them."

Her eyes widened when she saw the porch had been strung with balls of mistletoe, and in the center hung a large ball suspended with frilly red ribbon. The street now blanketed in a glistening coat of white was aglow from the homes with twinkling lights. It was magical.

"I love you, Molly McKenna."

As the snow began softly falling, Hunter pointed up to the green ball filled with tiny white berries. She looked and then looked again. The crystal that dangled from the center was different than the one he had given her yesterday. This sparkling crystal was a diamond ring. She screamed, then looked back to Hunter, who was kneeling on one knee.

"Forever is exactly what I want Ms. McKenna. I want to have a dozen tiny elves with you. Will you laugh with me, dance with me, grow old with me? Will you do me the honor of being my princess for life?"

"Yes, yes, yes!" she cried as a flood of McKennas stormed the porch.

Sophie yelled, "Just like the fairytale!"

Henry howled. Kyle and Jeffery cheered from the phone in his pocket.

Molly's lips met Hunter's in the kiss she had dreamed of her whole life.

"Yes, Sophie, just like the mistletoe fairytale. It's true you know, the kiss under the mistletoe will show you your true love," Molly said, slipping the ring on. At midnight the church bells chimed ushering in Christmas day. Molly smiled as she looked around at the family she cherished, the man she loved and the old-fashioned Christmas she dreamed of.

If there was a Santa, he certainly gave Molly McKenna every wish on her list.

The End

Stay tuned for *Megan's Millionaire Kiss*, the second in the McKenna sisters' trilogy.

As Molly prepares for her Christmas wedding and adds the finishing touches to Holiday Village, a newly divorced Megan reluctantly reenters the dating pool upon her sisters' request. She quickly learns while dating when you're young and single is hard enough, dating when you're divorced with two meddling sisters and two young daughters is as easy as teaching a T-Rex to apply lipstick.

Author Bio

Suzanne lives with her husband Joe, three children and Shih Tzu in New Jersey. She is passionate about Christmas, has a mild addiction to fabulous shoes, and is a believer in happily ever after. When not writing, you can find her spending time at the beach with her family, redecorating her home or snuggled under a furry blanket with a good book.

Visit Suzanne at www.suzanneryleeridolfi.com

Thank you for reading Molly, Mistletoe & Mr. Right.
I'd love to hear if you enjoyed getting to know Molly!
Write to me at: suzanne@suzanneryleeridolfi.com

CPSIA information can be obtained at www.ICGtesting.com
Printed in the USA
LVOW06s2030211215

467401LV00017B/1061/P

9 780692 574669